CW00749875

A Forest Wi

Book One

JP Solanki-Davie

JP Solanki-Davie

Manor House

Library and Archives Canada
Cataloguing in Publication

Title: A forest without trees. Book one / J.P. Solanki-Davie.
Names: Solanki-Davie, J. P., author.
Identifiers: Canadiana 2022043557X |
ISBN 9781988058955 (hardcover) |
ISBN 9781988058948 (softcover)
Classification: LCC PS8637.O42225 F67 2022 |
DDC C813/.6—dc23

Notes: This novel is a work of fiction. Any resemblance to locations or persons alive or dead is purely coincidental.
Parts of this book may be triggering for some: *A Forest Without Trees* contains torture, implied sexual assault and rape.
www.nofi.ca

Edited by Aliya Mughal
Cover design & photography by Yote
Illustrations for cover from pixabay.com by Screenpainting and Clker-Free-Vector-Images

First Edition
Manor House Publishing Inc.
452 Cottingham Crescent, Ancaster, ON, L9G 3V6
www.manor-house-publishing.com   (905) 648-4797

To all seeking a deeper connection
beyond the concrete jungle.
Om Namah Shivayah

Acknowledgments

Donovan, my love, you supported me throughout this whole journey. You were present while sharing story ideas, supporting my writing process and helping me with random ideas that needed clarifying. You've held my hand through remembering how to use photo editing software and the ins and outs of publishing. And of course, raising our child, Juniper. I am forever grateful to be your partner.

A special thank you to my Fairy Godmother, Keira. It was you who first heard my story idea, which started from a dream that I shared with you. My gratitude for your support throughout the creative process cannot be explained in words. Love you bunches!

To my Didihood, because of you I have owned my identity to the fullest. Everyday is another day I am grateful to share with you. Thank you to Aliya for all your editing. Thank you Aditi, Channdika, Ekta, Jamie Priti, Jen, Sonia and Susanna for always being there.

Thank you Jenny Jay for your course that gave me the push I needed to start writing.

A big big thank you to my family for your love and support throughout this whole process: My parents, Vijay and Brenda. My siblings Jay, Raj and Ram. My extended family, Changafoi, Bhavna, Akhilesh, Pankaj, Deepti, Girish, Kirti, Shyam, Jyoti and Pranita, along with the rest of the Solanki family. My family by marriage, Mike, Philippa, Nana, Poppa, Sarah, Ryan, Siobhan, Jesse, TJ, Steve, Larissa, and the rest of the Davie family.

I also want to thank all of my friends who have shown their support in my process.

Table of Contents

Praise for *A Forest Without Trees*:

*"**A Forest Without Trees** takes you deep inside a disturbing reality pitting a small group of rebels against powerful sinister forces that take over the minds of others, intercepting thoughts and planting false memories as they exert terrifying, destructive control. It's an epic power struggle with the survival of humanity, the environment and the world itself at risk. This is science fiction-fantasy writing at its finest – a compelling must-read!"*
     - Michael B. Davie, author, ***The Late Man***, and, ***Great Advice! Your 7 Keys To a Better Life***

"The world that JP Solanki-Davie has imagined (or perhaps it's an alternative reality that she has the insight to foresee) is disarming and emboldening to anyone who wonders about the divisions that we humans create and suffer for. Her depth of understanding of what makes people fight for hope or impose and weave sinister order out of fear, necessarily arrests you as a reader, and makes you think – as all good writing should. Her work conjures ideas of dystopia and utopia but it goes way beyond that because beneath any contemporary narrative that might be inferred about the state of the planet as we know it, is a sense of optimism in the power and potential of the human spirit to be better. This is a must-read for anyone who cares for the complexity of ecosystems, who wonders how we might be, who desires an intelligent departure into another way of seeing. It's fiction that carries weight beyond its finely crafted words."
     - Aliya Mughal, author of an upcoming collection of essays, is a nonfiction writer whose work has been published in The Learned Pig, NERC's Planet Earth magazine, The Idler, the Partially Examined Life and the London Literary Review.

6

Prologue

Gather near, Auntie Stella has a story to share with you. It's important you pay attention, it's up to you to carry this story on so others know it. I was only a part of the end of the story, which is of course, just the beginning of the next. And like so many beginnings, we begin during a dark time in human history.

Hundreds of years ago, when the world was consumed by pandemics, socioeconomic collapse and a climate catastrophe, humanity was in a crux of survival.

The ignorance of our ancestors toppled the capitalist empire and caused divisions across society.

Earth contracted and humans across the globe struggled to adapt. The devastation and environmental impact have persisted for centuries. This was when the oceans filled with plastics, super storms began to ravage the land and global temperatures fluctuated between extremes.

This time is known as, the Great Unrest. Many wanted to buy into new products that would continue to bring convenience to their lives, the residual mindsets of the old-era were still heavily ingrained

It's important to remember that at this time in history, humanity was divided on a great number of issues.

Those who fled to the mountains shielded themselves from nature for centuries, while those who remained, adapted along with nature. They cultivated communities that we call home today.

Those who were indigenous to the land before colonization, had been reclaiming their culture before the Great Unrest. It was through their efforts that maintained the ancient wisdom that burns within each of us still today.

As the storms grew, so did the numbers of those who sought a life steeped in the sentience of all beings on Earth.

Integrating new technologies to assist in surviving the diseases that emerged as the waters rose, our people were adapting to the fluctuations in climate.

Over the centuries these groups remained connected and declared themselves the Roozistem, a diverse group of individual communities linked in a global network.

They devoted themselves to ensure that ancestral wisdom and knowledge was carried forward. As the waters calmed and the landscape changed, these groups developed cloaking technologies to hide their communities from detection from the rising power of the Federation, the governing structure from the mountain elite.

The Federation was blissfully ignorant to the growing network of the Roozistem.

When they left their mountain bunkers, they saw the landscape was available for them to expand their territory. They offered humanitarian aid to the climate refugees who they discovered lived in the hills. This created a hierarchy between those in the mountains and those below.

Kharis the Great, was the leader of the Federation that defined its borders and rules. He allocated land to different elite families, they were given the title of controller and had dominion of their division.

Everyone was guaranteed a safe place to live, protection from the wilderness, proper nourishment, healthcare, and free access to entertainment.

In exchange for these benefits, citizens fulfilled their positions unquestionably and supported the Federation through viewership of the games.

I share all this with you because so much has changed. You may not remember the stories of the Arcade games or the circuits our elders used to play. It's important to keep in mind that reality within the Federation was drastically different than here in Jyotpur. It's hard to imagine such a voyeuristic society, but that's where our story takes place.

Remember, I said the Federation was unaware of the existence of the Roozistem. It was their ignorance and narcissistic tendencies that blinded them to the potential of humans living in relationship with nature. As you know, we are nature. But within the perimeter shield, that was not the case.

The Roozistem, on the other hand, were fully aware of the Federation and kept a watchful eye on their borders as they do today.

Now, before I share the actual story, you must hear about the festival grounds. For a decade those who were fed up with the games in the Federation moved to the grounds and created an encampment.

Kharis' grandson, Kragen, was enacting new bonding laws as the new Main Operator of the Federation.

More and more citizens were seeking freedom to choose their mating partners and how they choose to live.

Families sought refuge and were learning to reconnect with nature. This was the spark that became the catalyst for the revolution. An awakening was underway. I was born the year of the fires. Some other time I'll share more on that.

The Federation was building towers for the perimeter shield at the same time. Their fear of nature had pushed them to such an extreme reaction they were blind to the impact the shield would cause.

The energy pulse the shield caused, altered the very atmosphere of the planet. This created a chain reaction that resulted in everyone on Earth developing extra cerebral abilities (eca).

The fear by which the Federation operated caused them to impose control over their citizens. They chipped them to inhibit their eca. Can you imagine living without your eca? I know what it's like. Growing up with your eca is different than learning to use it later in life. You know, eca is like a muscle, when you use it, it becomes stronger; if you don't use it, then it's weaker.

Now, our story begins about two decades after the fires. The star of our story was imprisoned in the Federation's Boost Academy along with so many of our other heroes. I'll start by telling you about the day everything changed...

Map of the Federation
2565-2640

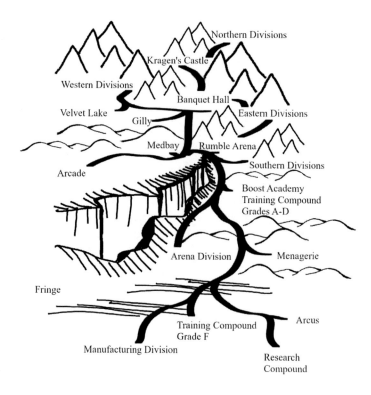

1

March 6th 2640, waning crescent moon

It was a quiet morning; the sun was low and an iridescent shimmer lay across the forested landscape. Tara was barefoot. A mossy earthen aroma filled her nostrils as she stepped lightly. A subtle breeze warmed her face as she gazed up at the rock that cut through the canopy of trees. Without concern, Tara began to climb the rock, ascending the slab and pulling her small frame over the top to rest on her back. The sky was clear and blue, a few fluffy clouds drifted by. She lay there for awhile enjoying the fresh breeze and bird song.

Tara was walking again, each step led her towards the river ahead. Tall trees surrounded her from three sides as she knelt by the water's edge. She sat in awe of nature, listening to the waves lapping against the river bank. There were some deer on the other side of the river, a mother and her babies, drinking from the flow.

A glint of light caught Tara's eye. She looked downstream at a row of lights. They were out of place, it confused her. Machines behind the headlights were revealed as they continued to travel up stream. Tara was frozen in place as the lights grew. A strange smog slowly blocked out the light. Stumbling to her feet, dread building in her chest, she ran through the forest, feeling the threat of people chasing her.

The trees disappeared, replaced by tents and the remains of old era buildings covered in light powdered snow. A sharp noise filled the air followed by a rush of wind and explosions.

Chaos broke out. Armoured vehicles blocked every route. People rushed passed frantically. The scent of blood was in the air. There was so much screaming. A voice over a loudspeaker demanded immediate cooperation.

Tara's mind was filled with the hush of her mother's voice. Her reassuring familiar words and her gentle melodic voice reminding Tara to restrain her abilities and to trust in her love. Rough hands grabbed her and a suppression collar clicked around her neck. It ripped away the mental connection with her mother. Tara was pushed into a security transport. After the door slammed shut, all that remained were the whimpers and cries from everyone around her. Tara's teary eyes caught sight of Vi, hir expression was hard and serious.

"You're from the wild? You're here to meet my dad?" Vi's words were hushed and quick. Tara was shocked but nodded several times. Ze continued, "Be my shadow and we'll get by. Feel no way, we'll slip out and get back to my fam. I'm Vi. What's your name?"

"Tara." she whispered.

The alarm rang through Tara's ears pulling her from her dream.

Reluctantly, she opened her eyes to the grey walls around her. Her cot was set up next to row upon row of others. She watched as one by one the others rose from their beds to line up for the morning head count. She followed quietly, pulling her long dark hair into a hasty braid. Her friend Vi knotted back hir matted locs and they exchanged a short nod as they lined up.

Caretaker Bridget entered with a security team. She scanned the trainees with her brown beady eyes as she toyed with the switch in her hands. Her black hemp uniform was adorned with a copper broach on the lapel and she had her dark hair slicked back in a tight bun that pulled her olive-skinned face taught.

Today's the day! If I can pull this off we can all get out. Tara thought hopefully as she stared at the back of the person in front of her.

An enforcer walked down the line, counting everyone. He wore the sharp black hemp uniform demarcating his position in the security sector.

"Today is the day many of you have been anticipating. We are giving you one chance to prove that you have what it takes to be a player." Bridget announced. Her critical stare surveyed the group as she walked down the line. She focused on Tara, Vi and some of the other older trainees.

"Most of you have failed to show the necessary qualities to be a player in the Federation games, that is why you remained here in grade F. Controller Pierce has expressed his disappointment in your lack of self-betterment. He had higher hopes for you feebler runts. If you had applied yourself to the training we provide here at the Boost Academy you could have levelled up by now, to grade C or D at the very least."

She turned on her heel and paced back up the line as she went on, "It seems some of you refuse to accept your position. Either that or it's your lack of potential. Either way, we will test each of you without birth records to determine who is mature and therefore eligible to be collected for the games. Those who are not mature but show potential, have the opportunity to level up to grade D. Anyone over the age of 18, who fails the obstacle course, will have the opportunity to serve in the Manufacturing Division. The rest of you will stay here with me."

She gazed upon the group with disdain, "Our Sovereign Kragen has issued a command to allow you this opportunity to run an obstacle course and prove your worth within the Federation. I want you all to give it your best. There are elite controllers from the mountains who have come down to assess those who show potential. Rook, Bishop and Knight Division controllers with top ranking are here to consider the lucky few to level up their position. It could be you who is collected by a noteworthy controller."

She focused her extra cerebral ability and radiated a wave of anxiety through the group. Her stare challenged someone to speak out of turn before she marched down the hallway.

The line shuffled forward, as everyone bathed and dressed in their polyester trainee jumpsuits, pale green with black trim. The group moved to the mess hall, the anticipation in the room was palpable. There was a quiet murmur as everyone ate their bowls of mush: a blend of food scraps processed into a slurry injected with all the needed nutrients for survival.

Tara slurped the grey bland sludge from her bowl and ran through the plan in her mind again: *Run the race. Meet in the holding room. Vi draws attention, I unlock doors until I get out of the compound. Deactivate every obstacle. Dash for the perimeter.* She spooned more sludge, swallowed quickly to not taste it, *Ain't a good plan, but we're out of time. So many of us have reached the age of maturity. Vi's slated to be collected and become a player. So many of us will end up in the work camps. I'll never get home. No! This is my one chance to make a break for it. Without my abilities it would be impossible, but with them, and Vi's distraction. No, it'll still be a fluke. I can't shut down the chip with my abilities before I know what could happen. I've gotta get to the Cullis first. Mama's alive and safe. I know she is. My dreams have shown me she'll be waiting for me. I trust in that. She'll know how to get the chip out.* Tara clung to hope, *When I escape I'll find her.*

She glanced up at Vi, across the table. Their eyes met. Vi pressed hir lips together in a tight smile.

"You could come." Tara whispered.

Vi's dark eyes opened wide and ze whispered back almost inaudibly, "You need a frenzy." Vi glanced at their other friends and added quietly, "You're the only one of us who can do it."

Tara looked over at Hami and Hori. They had crossed the perimeter shield with her and had also been apprehended by security at the Seds fringe encampment. *They need to get home to their mom too.* She looked past the twins to Brill who pleaded with her big brown eyes for Tara to agree. Tara nodded reassuringly to everyone and bit her lip, *I can't fail. Everyone is counting on me.*

They deposited their empty bowls in a large basin at the end of the table. A brawny scrapper with grey-stubble chewed a pick while he waited for all the trainees to shuffle through. The glint of his dangling earring caught the light as he lifted the heavy load of dishes away.

They were divided in two groups, those with birth records and those without. Those with records were led to an arena under a large dome, and would form the first heats. Tara filed in behind the others without records at the clinician station. She kept her head down as she waited her turn to be tested. The clinicians wore crisp white hemp jumpsuits with a circular grey and white striped patch on the shoulder to mark status in the domiciliary sector.

A clinician loaded a clean nasal swab into a narrow cylindrical device and approached Tara. The swab was inserted up her nose and pulled out a second later. The device ticked as it processed. Once it finished, the clinician read the screen out loud, "Trainee Tara, born April 5th 2621. Age 18." Tara was shuffled along with the others who were above the age of 18 to wait in a holding room.

A big screen was on the wall, it showed the elaborate course they were challenged with. Tall towers with ropes and netting, a swinging pendulum that swooped over a large pool, several tall walls with a rope to climb and many other obstacles were coloured bright, yellow, red and orange. At the far end of the course were ten figures stepping into their starting rings.

Bridget was standing by the screen surveying the group. Waves of anxiety were radiating off her, increasing everyone's tension.

Tara was focusing on her breathing trying to calm herself. *Inhale, one, two, three, four. Exhale, one, two, three, four.*

"Remember," Bridget said looking down her nose at the screen, "It's not just about finishing the course, it's about putting on a good show." She turned her eyes from the screen and directed them at Tara before she added, "Your worth is in your capacity to perform and impress. Those who succeed will be rewarded. You want to be rewarded, don't you?"

Tara focused her eyes on the screen and tried to ignore Bridget's glare.

The first heat ran the course, followed shortly by the next. Tara waited nervously with her friends. They were the last ones left in the holding room. Bridget gestured for them to rise and marched them down the long hall. They entered a brightly lit room where two clinicians waited for them. One by one the trainees approached the clinicians and were injected with a blue eca serum.

Tara dreaded this moment. She had to keep her true extra cerebral ability a secret for fear of what the Federation would do if they knew. The surge of energy moved up her arm as the serum spread through her bloodstream. It was the biggest dose she'd ever been given. She closed her eyes and took a deep breath to steady herself. She sensed the chip at the back of her neck; it had been implanted after she was apprehended six years ago. Every electronic device in the room hummed inside her, the devices held by the clinicians, the ambilights and the security recorders.

A cool breeze travelled around her neck and the familiar scent of filtered air filled her nostrils as they walked the tunnel to the arena dome. One by one they stepped up to the playing grounds. As Tara was about to step out, she felt a hand on her shoulder. Startled, she looked back to see Caretaker Bridget's arrogant expression.

"Let's see you try and stay on your feet this time." Bridget said and shoved Tara forward.

Tara tripped over her feet and stumbled onto all fours beside Hami and Hori.

'Ça va?' Tara heard Hori speak in her mind as he helped her to her feet.

She gave a grateful nod.

A loudspeaker signalled the course would begin, the horn blew and they sprinted towards the first obstacle. They climbed the tall wall, balanced along a beam, leaped over small boxes and swung from a rope to a platform. Tara saw her friends Desma and Pin running through the course with ease, throwing their bodies from each obstacle to the next. It was like watching an acrobatic dance. They were agile, graceful and exhibited incredible strength and speed. Their abilities were well suited for the games and they were destined for a controller's collection. They were like Vi, possessing increased strength ability. Vi was close behind them. Tara knew ze was holding back hir ability for fear of collection. Tara was always amazed at how Vi could seemingly do anything with hir body.

Teetering on the ledge over the pool, Tara was waiting until the pendulum swung within reach again. She jumped, clung to the rope as it swung the other way and let her body fly. She landed roughly on the other side. Looking around she saw her friend Lino falling from a high beam. He landed hard on the ground. He lay there immobile, his lean frame at awkward angles, clearly hurt. She watched him move slowly, gather himself and throw himself back into the course. *I wonder if the audience is entertained,* she thought sarcastically.

Tara turned her attention to the next obstacle, it was the projectile run. She focused her eca on the mechanical device responsible for the projectiles and hung back. She could see the pattern in her mind and waited until the sequence restarted, then she ran. It was a long sprint, where large rubber balls shot from the sides and would often take out a player. Tara managed to get to the end untouched. She watched as Brill and Khalil dodged the last two rubber balls and threw themselves beside her. Their anxious expressions reflected how she felt.

Glancing up at a camera rigged to the high domed ceiling, she quietened her eca and stepped into the next obstacle. Intentionally, she stumbled down a long ramp after she missed the rope ladder. She scurried up the opposite side to get out of the pit.

Tara spotted Vi bent over hir knees catching hir breath at the end of the course. Tara kept an eye on the others to make sure she didn't finish before anyone. As she pulled herself up the last wall, adrenaline surged through her body. *This is it! The course is over and now Vi can make hir move.*

The group was escorted to another holding room with the rest of the trainees. Tara's heart leaped into her throat as the anticipated moment had arrived. She focused her eca and spoke to Vi's mind, 'I'll come for you when I can.'

'I know. You got this, Tara. Be easy.' Vi replied telepathically. Their eyes met and Vi gave Tara one last reassuring nod before moving into the crowd of trainees with Raha and Twitch beside hir.

Tara caught Hami and Hori's attention, she focused her eca so they both would hear her in their minds, 'Be no way. I'll bring the Cullis back with me.'

'We know. Good luck.' She heard them reply in unison in her mind. She side stepped towards a door on the opposite wall and waited.

Vi walked into the middle of the room, the others stepped back to create a small circle around hir. Ze closed hir eyes and squeezed hir hands into fists. Tara held her breath and waited for Vi to move. She had to unlock the door with her eca at the same moment as Vi's distraction to confuse the eca detection sensors in the room. Vi took a deep breath and focused hir eca, ze squatted low before ze leapt from the ground.

Tara watched Vi soar through the air, as though in slow motion. She quickly unlocked the door with her eca and ran through before the security alarms rang out. To sneak by the surveillance recorders undetected, she focused her eca to cause a static disruption. Holding the map of the compound in her mind and dashing through the halls, she used her eca to track the locations of the guardians, clinicians and enforcers through their communications devices.

Vi's body flew into the air as ze did a back flip, flew down to the ground and hir fist pounded into the floor. The floor shattered underneath hir strength, cracks radiated outward from the centre of hir fist. Chaos broke out as the other trainees were using their eca, taking advantage of the opportunity to riot and adding to the destruction. Alarms rang out as the detected eca usage levels surged beyond allowed limits, triggering the security protocols. Several trainees were struck by electric shocks, falling limp to the ground. A sharp noise filled the room as anti-eca currents blew from the ceiling depleting everyone's eca levels and blowing people over. Enforcers rushed into the room and blasted their neutralizing pulserods.

Vi stood in the middle of the chaos and destruction making no attempt to resist. Hir eyes were closed tight as ze held onto the faith that Tara would make it. The enforcers neutralized hir and ze collapsed to the ground.

Tara rounded a corner and sprinted down an empty hall until she came to a dark grey door. There was only one main entrance in and out of the Training compound, however there were a couple of windows which Tara knew she could slip through and one was behind this door.

She unlocked the door with her eca and entered the dingy room. It was quiet with a singular window near the corner, the afternoon light dimly filled the dusty room. She dashed for the window and climbed the wall just as fast. She gripped tight to a pipe and held up her other hand. As Tara focused her telekinetic ability, the window slowly trembled until it exploded outwardly. She quickly pulled herself through.

The crisp spring air made her skin tingle. She inhaled deeply as she stared at the blanket of grey clouds that covered the sun. She stood completely still. In front of her was an electrified fence, behind which were towers with automated motion sensor blasters. Further beyond was a vast field that seemed to stretch on to the horizon. She had to get to the other side of that field and into the forest.

Tara focused her eca and tuned into the compound mainframe. She read that Vi had caused a huge disturbance and had been placed in an isolation chamber. Enforcers were restricting the rest of the trainees and performing a headcount.

Whatever happens to them is my fault. Tara's heart lurched. She focused her eca and deactivated the motion sensor blasters, then the section of fence in front of her.

Tara swiftly slipped between two of the rails and scanned the field of grass. She saw the nanoKbot detonators that burrowed their tunnels under the field. With a thought she deactivated them all, the field would now be safe to cross. She peered into the distance, set her feet and gave a tremendous push. While sprinting she was keeping part of her attention on the compound mainframe and the rest of her attention on the horizon.

The cool air against her skin felt amazing. She inhaled the damp earth and grass as her feet hit the soft ground. Each step was the most exhilarating experience of running that her legs had felt in all those years. Her chest was throbbing and her lungs were burning, but she kept pushing her legs to go faster.

Then she saw it: a flicker of tall green trees. A surge of hope pushed her forward. She was almost at the expanse of forest when she saw the alarm in her mind.

No! I'm almost there!

In the next moment, sirens were ringing around her and she felt the presence of drones hovering close. She pressed a hand to the stitch at her side as her breath hitched.

Tara turned her eyes up to the drones, saw them in her mind as they took aim. Without a second thought she deactivated the drones and they fell from the sky with a sudden drop. Turning her attention back to the trees, she kept running.

She saw in her mind the anti-eca canon charging to fire when all of a sudden she heard static and felt her connection break.

No! The serum ran out! There was a sharp noise as the current rushed into her and blew her forward to her knees.

A drone flew in and fired a net that pinned her to the ground. Before she had a chance to react, the neutralizing pulse hit her body. Everything went blurry. She was consumed by darkness.

2

March 7th 2640, waning crescent moon

Tara inhaled sharply, her eyes wide with fright. Immediately, she squeezed them shut from the bright ambilights of the room. Strong hands held her down and she felt a needle pulled from her arm.

She'd been given a stimulant serum to reverse the neutralizing pulse. Two enforcers yanked her up to her unsteady feet as the clinician stepped back. She blinked a few times and took in her surroundings. The enforcers let her go, making space for Caretaker Bridget, who was holding a cup on a tray. Tara's eyes focused and she realized she was in an isolation chamber. Instinctively she brought her hands up to find an eca suppression collar around her neck. Her heart pounded as a ball formed in the pit of her stomach.

"You gave us quite the scare." Bridget said too sweetly, "Once again you've disappointed me with another one of your selfish actions. What would possess you to try and flee into the woods? From what you demonstrated on the course you wouldn't survive an hour alone outside of these walls. Not from lack of effort, we tried to train you and the rest of the feebler runts. We were tasked with reforming you, but you have persisted in resisting our methods. We have tried to inoculate your rebellious tendencies, Tara. Tried and failed."

Bridget's eyes narrowed as she went on, "To learn, that all these years you've been playing down your skill and your extra cerebral ability." She curled up her lip, clucked her tongue and continued, "To learn that you have been lying to us since the day you arrived and that you are more powerful than you have revealed, was a shock for me. I admit. But you think you're so smart for hiding your ability all these years? Don't you realize the whole world has now seen your stunt with those drones?"

She let her words linger in the air as Tara tried to follow. Bridget extended the tray forward. Tara's stomach growled as she took the cup shakily. Bridget pulled out a small tablet and held it in her palm. A holovid lit up of Tara running in the field and a ring of drones gaining on her. The projection showed: Tara glance over her shoulder then the drones power-down falling from the sky with a crash.

Bridget returned the tablet to her pocket and said, "That clip has been viewed over six million times since news broke of your 'attempted escape.' It has been quite sensational! We've been reviewing your training course footage and you have been playing us this whole time. Haven't you? You used your ability to shut down our security defences, including the subterranean nanoKbot detonators. And you did this without tripping any alarms. As impressed as I am with your performance, I'm afraid you will not be staying with us much longer." She leaned forward to get even closer to Tara and whispered, "You will be shipped off tomorrow."

Tara's mouth went dry as she stared up at Bridget in shock.

"Now drink up, you'll need your strength." Bridget smiled.

Tara drank the thin grainy liquid and coughed as she finished. Bridget snatched the cup from Tara's hands and left without another word.

The enforcers grabbed Tara again and held her still. The clinician approached her with an empty vial. Her sleeve was yanked up and her arm stretched out by the enforcer. She felt the pinch of the needle and watched the vial fill with her blood.

When the clinician stepped back, Tara noticed a tall controller with cream-coloured skin standing in the doorway. His dark hair neatly combed, his platinum grey suit unwrinkled, and shiny grey shoes that sparkled in the bright ambilights of the chamber. There was something about his face that seemed familiar, but Tara couldn't place it. She had never seen this man before. His curious look burned through her. As he approached, the enforcers tightened their grip. Dread built in her gut as he stepped within arm's distance.

His piercing blue eyes locked with her dark brown ones and she felt him press into her mind, 'Who is your mother?'

Before she could even process the question, she was thinking of her mother. Her comforting arms, the smell of her woolly shawl, the last time they were together at the encampment. Tara could feel her mind being peeled open as images of her mother flooded her vision. Her heart pounded as she struggled to breathe.

Blood drained from the controller's face as he watched the images of Tara's mother in his vision. He closed his eyes to break the telepathic link. With his hand over his mouth he looked back at her with new eyes. He was searching her whole body as though trying to read more from her without invading her mind again.

"Wachu want with me!?" She blurted out.

The enforcers immediately tightened their grip and pulled her back. Stunned at her outburst the controller eyed her more cautiously. She glared back at him through her tears.

"We'll see." He replied softly.

He left the room. The enforcers released their grip and followed.

Tara was left to crumble to the floor. The sound of the lock echoed through the bright chamber. There was nothing in it except pale grey walls and a floor toilet in the corner. The ceiling glowed brightly. Tara shifted into a corner and pulled her knees to her chest. Her body shook from the reality she struggled to process.

I failed to escape. Fek! Who was that? How did he know Mama? Was it true what Bridget said? Do they know about my eca? Is that controller collecting me? Where am I going? What about Vi? Ze's in an isolation chamber too. What'll happen to hir? Tara closed her eyes and tried to block out the light. She couldn't settle her mind and could only find more questions.

~~~

Tristan replayed what he had just seen in Tara's mind as he walked through Training compound, *She is Sheena's offspring.* He recalled the festival grounds and those humid summer nights spent under the canopy of colourful tents. His heart ached in a way that unsettled him.

There was that one night we coupled in my tent. I was lost in her soft brown skin and the floral scent of her hair. We had spent hours together with that one glorious night of pleasure. That was the night we made Tara. The realization that the young woman in the isolation chamber was his offspring made his skin chill and he quickened his pace.

How did she end up here? I didn't even know there was a grade F Training compound until a few days ago. Tara's been here for six years. Six years! I never even knew she existed. I have to make this right. She belongs with me.

Tristan set his mind on what needed to be done. He knocked and entered Caretaker Bridget's office. Bridget was at her desk listening to a slender woman with straight black hair sitting across from her.

"Ah, Controller Tristan!" Bridget called, "I was just discussing with Investigator Ada your predicament with Trainee Tara. Operator Stone sent her directly to handle this case. I have no doubt that you two will have an illuminating conversation."

Ada walked up to Tristan and motioned toward the door. Tristan followed her down the hall to another room. It was small, but had several black sofas, a large tapestry on one wall and a small bar in the corner.

Tristan didn't wait for her to sit down before stating, "Your reputation precedes you, Investigator Ada. It's a pleasure to finally meet you in person."

She flashed a pearly-white smile as she settled into one of the sofas, "Thank you, Controller Tristan." Tristan smiled politely as he sat. Ada's smile dropped and she said, "Operator Stone wants to know how it is that you, a Platinum Knight Division Ruby ranking controller, has any connection with a trainee from this compound."

Tristan straightened up and replied calmly, "I met Tara's mother, Sheena, at the festival grounds. As you know, in those days bonding wasn't yet mandatory for coupling. To put it simply, we had a relationship that was brief and I was unaware that she had become pregnant."

"You were at the festival grounds?" Ada surveyed Tristan's spotless suit, "What were you doing there?"

Tristan cleared his throat, "Our Sovereign Kragen had me stationed at the festival grounds to convert it into the Arcade. I also supervised the nearby construction of the towers for the perimeter shield. I reported directly to Operator Stone."

Ada pulled a tablet out, tapped the screen a few times then read, "According to security records, you visited that region on more than one occasion over several years."

"Yes, my position for the shield had me visit the grounds over the years. I had also visited a few friends." Tristan said carefully.

Ada tilted her head to one side, "Allow me into your mind, Controller Tristan. Show me."

Tristan regarded Ada's bright smile with reluctance but slowly nodded his consent. Instantly, he felt the presence of Ada pop into his mind and he focused on the memories from two decades ago at the festival grounds. He poured open his memories:

Our Sovereign Kragen sent me to the festival grounds to integrate within the community while the perimeter shield towers were built. At the same time, he wanted to establish new games for the future Arcade that he envisioned at that location. Zedrik's infamous rage quit from the 2nd Quarter Circuit 2614 had influenced people to leave the parks. Our Sovereign Kragen wanted to entice Zedrik to rejoin as a player so his following would return to the games. Rumour was Zedrik was living on the grounds. I had confirmed this when I visited my friend Controller Yoshiro the summer before.

"Controller Yoshiro?" Ada interrupted, "He stayed at the festival grounds? Hmm. I was under the impression the grounds were full of free-spirited parties with people claiming we could live safely with the untamed wild."

Tristan shifted in his seat and adjusted his suit jacket. He spoke quickly, "Yes, many were pushing back against the perimeter shield construction and held the ridiculous notion we could live in symbiosis with nature. Controller Yoshiro would vacation there, but was not aligned with those feeblers."

Ada nodded to encourage Tristan to continue sharing his memories.

Tristan closed his eyes as the memories of that time flowed through his mind. *Rumour had it, Zedrik was living there with Noble Remi. We had all been in the same player cohort, and Our Sovereign Kragen wanted me to use our friendship to reconnect with Zedrik and ultimately, Noble Remi. She had cut off communication with Our Sovereign Kragen for seven years. He wanted to link up with his sister again and sent me among the feeblers for her protection.*

I dressed the part and blended in. But what I wasn't expecting was for Zedrik to welcome me into his tent with open arms. He introduced me to his friends and embraced me as a brother. That first night was one wild party. The next day he got me set up near him and that's where I camped all summer.

There were loads of people of all ages, collaborating on projects and caring for a group of babies and little kids. It was there where I found Noble Remi, reading stories and singing songs to the young ones.

As we had suspected, Zedrik had bonded illegally with Noble Remi and they had been living on the grounds. Neither of them wanted to play any Federation games and avoided the conversation.

It was a night in July, when Sheena arrived. I had been talking up the new games with Zedrik when a young man ran in. He whispered into Zedrik's ear.

Tristan felt Ada hold his memories and heard her in his mind, 'What was the young man's name?'

Tristan concentrated harder, *Chester, I think. Yes, Chester.*

Tristan focused back to his memory and let it play out,

A handful of people were welcomed into Zedrik's tent. Sheena was among them, her thick dark hair was tied up with a yellow scarf. We were quickly introduced. Her dark lined brown eyes were mesmerizing and I spent most of my time trying to get closer to her. Eventually, I won her over.

Tristan smiled at himself. Ada was impassive as she listened.

One day, Our Sovereign Kragen came to meet with me and Noble Rawlyn at the grounds to look over the towers for the perimeter shield himself. Sheena saw us and realized my aims. She confronted me and mentioned the benefits of the wilderness. I got mad at her and she left the grounds that night.

I waited like a fool for her to come back, but she never did. This was what was wrong with all those feebler people in the festival grounds, they had this fantasy about the wilderness and thought they could never get killed in a storm or worse, get mauled by a beast.

Sheena was just like Zedrik, they didn't listen to anything I tried to tell them.

Tristan let out a sharp exhale as Ada left his mind.

"Her name is Sheena." Ada re-stated. "She is part of a group associating with the Seds. Yes, at the time of the festival grounds, the Seds were not officially formed, but it was Zedrik who instigated the acts of sedition against the Federation at that time. His death was declared after the fires but we have no evidence this is true. His death was heralded by the Seds to rally support and his name continues to carry weight among feeblers." She scanned the document, "Sheena was detained during the raid on the feebler encampment six years ago, same as Tara. The arresting enforcers did not keep proper records though and there seems to be no background data on her in the Federation system. That's peculiar." She turned her attention back to Tristan, "I will accompany you back to your residence and remain there to assist in monitoring Trainee Tara. These are my orders from Operator Stone."

She pulled out another tablet and handed it to Tristan. He read it, "Yes, of course," and handed it back.

"Good. I'm going to cut to the chase, Controller Tristan," Ada explained, "Trainee Tara is a security risk. This whole situation is unprecedented. I have been reviewing her previous training courses with Caretaker Bridget and I suspect she is hiding her true extra cerebral ability and has been eluding our tests since she came to the Boost Academy."

"It would be in hers and your best interests" Ada continued, "to be forthcoming about her extra cerebral ability. Out of respect, I will grant you the time to obtain this from her in trust and will only use my eca if she does not cooperate. Her new position of player has been granted."

"Her integration into the games will not be an easy one considering her record," Ada added.

"Her training will be within your control, as is your right, but Our Sovereign Kragen has made it clear to me that she will run the courses of his choosing. She will remain here until tomorrow, after the blood work is finalized, then she will be transported to your residence."

Tristan cleared his throat, "Of course."

3

March 8th 2640, waning crescent moon

When the door eventually opened, Tara's eyes were bloodshot and puffy.

A guardian was carrying a tray with a cup and a bundle under her arm. She wore the distinctively plain blue uniform made of hemp that all guardians wore, her hair covered in a wrap. She didn't say a word but placed the tray on the floor near Tara then stepped toward the corner with the floor toilet. Tara crawled over to the cup and drank the thin grainy liquid. The guardian placed her hand on the wall, some panels clicked open and a shower-head appeared with a small ledge. She placed a towel and a folded jumpsuit, then turned to Tara, "You'll shower, now."

Tara blinked at the demand, finished the last of her disgusting drink and stood up shakily. The guardian averted her eyes as Tara went to the shower and began to undress. She dropped her dirty green jumpsuit on the floor, stepped under the shower-head and icy cold water began to pour out. The shock jolted her awake. She washed quickly, towelled off, put on the fresh beige jumpsuit laid out for her and the flat shoes she only just noticed. Tara ran her hands over the soft material of her new clothes as she moved back toward the other corner of the room. The guardian remained silent, picked up the towel and green jumpsuit, pressed her hand against the wall so the shower would retreat back. She left Tara alone again.

Time passed painfully slow as Tara wondered, *How long will I be kept in this dreaded place? What are these clothes made from? Why wasn't I given another green jumpsuit? Ugh! This collar is heavy! I wonder what happened to Vi. Who was that controller?*

What felt like hours later, two enforcers entered holding restraints. Tara's stomach flipped over knowing she would soon have some answers. Her wrists were restrained in front and the enforcers gripped tightly around her upper arms as they ushered her out. Tara's eyes were having a hard time adjusting to the light, she kept seeing spots and couldn't follow where she was being taken.

Her heart leaped into her throat as she recognized the big door that led outside. *It's true, I'm leaving!* The fresh air rushed into Tara's lungs and she smiled to herself at the pleasure of non-recycled air. The sun was high in the spring sky without a single cloud in the blue expanse, but everything looked over exposed from the hours in the isolation chamber.

The enforcers led Tara to a security transport and lifted her into the back. Patton, an enforcer with grey eyes, smirked at her as he took hold of her arm. *Oh, Source fend! It's him!* She gasped as he tightly strapped her into a seat with a restraining harness over her shoulders and around her waist. Her ankles were fastened to the floor with a cable and her hands remained restrained in front of her. Patton tightened the last strap and stepped back. His eyes trailed slowly over Tara's body.

Tara struggled a little before she glared back and said with more courage than she felt, "Is all this needed?"

He paused. His eyes grew colder as he leaned his weight forward. Tara tried to ignore his domineering presence but trembled as he leaned so close she could feel his breath on her face.

"I volunteered for this assignment. Just had to see you off. Shame we won't get to spend more time together. Gotta make sure the controller's new package arrives in one piece." Patton said and yanked on the straps to secure them more tightly. Tara winced as they dug into her shoulders. The last thing she saw was his dark hooded eyes before he stepped out and closed the door.

Tara was left in darkness and again her eyes struggled to adapt. She felt the vibration of the transport powering up then pulling out. She was overcome with fear for what would happen when they got wherever they were going. She focused on her breathing like her mother had taught her to calm herself. *Inhale, one, two, three, four. Exhale, one, two, three, four.*

The drive was long and bumpy, there were several stops where she heard muffled voices then they'd be off again.

When the transport finally stopped and powered down, Tara heard voices outside as the enforcers exited the driving cab.

Her heart was thumping so loudly she was afraid it would burst out of her chest. When the door opened there was a rush of cold air. She squeezed her eyes closed as light flooded in. Rough hands removed her restraints, then lifted her out of the transport.

When her feet hit the ground, Tara pulled her free hand to cover her eyes from the bright light. Patton steered her to take a few steps around the transport where she saw a large house.

She struggled to focus her vision as she peered under her hand. The controller from the isolation chamber was standing at the base of the steps leading up to a large house with big windows. He was accompanied by several other people, there to greet her.

The other enforcer walked up to the controller and handed him a tablet. They exchanged brief words and the controller handed the tablet to a tall thin woman with shoulder length black hair who stood beside him. She took it, then walked back toward Tara with the other enforcer.

She stood in front of Tara casting a shadow over her. Tara felt a wave of reassurance wash over her and relaxed. She lowered her hand to see the kind expression on the woman's face.

"Let her go. I will take over from here." She ordered.

"Yes ma'am." Patton released Tara's arm and unlocked her collar, then left.

Tara immediately wrapped one hand around her arm where his hand had squeezed and the other to the sensitive skin of her throat, relieved to be free of both.

"My name is Investigator Ada." Ada wrapped an arm around Tara's shoulder and steered her towards the house.

I'm in the mountains! Tara realized as her eyes adjusted to the wondrous view. It was late, it was cold and the fading light was glowing off the mountain peaks on the horizon with a subtle sheen from the perimeter shield.

"Salutations Tara, I am Controller Tristan." The sound of his voice pulled Tara's attention back. Another wave of reassurance washed over her and she felt her body involuntarily relax.

Tara eyed Ada suspiciously as she realized, *Ada is using her eca to calm me down.* She was accustomed to Bridget's anxious radiations; Ada's reassurance radiations made her feel anything but.

"Why did you bring me here?" Tara asked nervously.

A smile broke across Tristan's face, "I brought you here because this is your home. I am your father."

~~~

Stepping into the large house Tara was struck by the smell of old wood and the incredibly high ceilings. Old era paintings and photographs covered the walls and there were statues of marble displayed in several alcoves.

She was guided by Ada into a dining room where there was a large ambihearth that glowed beside a table covered in all kinds of food the likes of which Tara had never seen. After six years of eating bland, colourless foods, the sights and aromas from the table were overwhelming.

"Come, sit down. Eat." Tristan gestured for Tara to sit down.

She gaped at him, unable to speak. A chair was pulled out and Ada guided her down, then sat next to her. Two others were at the table; a woman with shoulder length blond hair and a pinched nose, and a younger man who had short wavy brown hair. They both looked at Tara with curiosity. Tara kept her attention on the food in front of her.

"Eat now and I will tell you everything you want to know." Tristan helped himself to a bite of salad as he watched Tara carefully.

Tara took a slow breath and closed her eyes, *I give thanks for this food.* Opening her eyes and picking up her fork she chose some fish, taking a bite. The taste exploded on her tongue and she pulled her hand up to cover her mouth. The last time she had tasted fish was from before she entered the Federation. The flavours flooded her mind with memories of lakes surrounded by tall trees and the adults who worked with nets in the water. Tara glanced at Ada who watched her with a glint in her eye. Tara swallowed the fish and shut down her mind to her memories. *Be on guard. Remember, she's an investigator.* She continued to take small bites of fish, some of the salad greens and rice until her stomach began to stretch. When she finished she put her fork down and glanced up at Tristan who keenly watched her but now with a contented look on his face.

"Good." He said. Leaning back in his chair and tenting his fingers, he told his story, "I met your mother, Sheena, twenty years ago. We were young and spontaneous. This was before the energy pulse. Things were different then. We met at the festival grounds during the peak of those free-spirited encampments. I had been working with Operator Stone on the Federation's project to develop the perimeter shield. I had also been positioned in the festival grounds as a controller to supervise the transition of the grounds into the new Arcade. Sheena and I spent a summer socializing and of course, coupled. Things didn't work out as we realized our differences and we went our separate ways. This was before the bonding laws. I never knew she was pregnant. Never."

Tristan emphasized the last word again. He peered into the artificial flame of the ambihearth as he continued, "The energy pulse was a result of energizing the perimeter shield. The unforeseeable side effect consumed my life. The world changed with our newly formed extra cerebral abilities. I bonded with my mate Claudia and we had Gerrit shortly after."

He gestured at the blond woman and the young man who sat beside him. He took a deep breath and explained, "When I saw your image among the trainees eligible to be collected, I was struck by your resemblance to Sheena. I honestly had not thought of her since that summer."

Tara gaped at him, *You never thought about her? After you coupled?*

Tristan wrung his hands in his lap at her reaction and stammered, "Your likeness. Truly, uncanny." He collected himself, "Something was pushing me to suspect that you could be mine. I was curious. So, I came to the compound to view your race in person. Your stunt after the race was much more intriguing. A better representation of your potential, I am certain. But I knew your fate after your true display of your skills and needed to know if you were mine. Your date of birth lined up with my memory. So, I pressed Caretaker Bridget to allow me to question you personally and explained you were my offspring. Of course, after you told me with your mind that Sheena is in fact your mother, I knew I had to bring you home. The blood work was only a formality after that."

This man is my father? My father. This is surreal. Tara was stunned. She looked at Claudia, at Gerrit, then peered out the big window to the last glimpses of light that shimmered over the mountains.

She cycled through his story, then to her childhood memories searching for any instances where her mother talked about her father. *Mama barely talked about my father. She didn't even tell me his name. Mama said, he was in the Federation but she didn't know if he was alive. The festival grounds had been devastated by fires when the shield went up. It wasn't until I was old enough to understand, that Mama even told me about the Federation. Our family was at Sundarvan in the Sanctum. Mama said that my uncles Vishal and Akshay were just as much my bapuji, that I could always depend on Bricker or Jahnu; them and Nani and Nana. Why didn't Mama tell me more about Tristan? Did she even know who he was?*

She glanced back at Tristan, whose face expressed patience but his eyes were telling of a secret he hadn't shared. She chewed her lips and averted her eyes. *It was something that I wondered about with Hami and Hori. They'd lost their father in those fires too. Except, turns out my father's not dead. Would*

Mama know he's alive? I never thought I'd actually meet my biological father. Yet, here he is. And here I am in his house. He came to see if I was his offspring, and saved me from a worse fate. What's worse than that compound? Filled with worry, she thought more about his story. *He's responsible for the perimeter shield going up! That's what Bricker said was disrupting wildlife and pacifying the population within. Tristan's the cause of it? Did Mama know that!?* A ball in her gut formed and she knew there was something missing.

"What do you want with me?" Timidly, she repeated the question she had asked him in the isolation chamber. The hairs on her neck raised at the sight of his portrayal of kindness.

"I want to provide you with all the opportunities afforded to one of my offspring." Tristan said. "You will live here, with access to all the privileges that come with being a player in my Platinum Knight Division. There are many styles of courses to play and I am sure, given the choice, you will find one you will enjoy. Gerrit has played hundreds of courses successfully and I am certain you would also draw a large viewership."

Gerrit nodded at his father's words and pressed his lips together in a half smile as he looked at Tara.

"You want me to play games?" Tara was confused.

Tristan's smile spread wider and he nodded.

"What if I say, no?" She asked flatly.

His smile faded as his brow furrowed in confusion. He shifted in his seat and glanced briefly at Ada before he answered, "You want to say, no? My dear, you will find that playing the games are much more sensible, than not. Given your talents, it is in your best interest to play the part while you have a choice. The Federation is built on the Eight Pinnacles, the first is to strive for excellence. It is your duty to level up, my dear. This is the recreation sector, you have free will, but know that your choices will have consequences and you would be wise to cooperate."

"Level up?" Tara's face twisted with distaste.

A reassuring wave washed over her again. Her body softened immediately. She turned her attention toward Ada who sat quietly beside her. The ball in her gut continued to clench but her head felt fuzzy. She closed her eyes and tried to focus but a pressure behind her eyes consumed her.

A soft voice came into her mind, 'Yes. Yes, I will stay here. Yes.' The cadence of Ada's song-like voice was hypnotizing.

Tara opened her mouth, "Yes. I – I will," she felt each word being pulled from her, "I will stay, I will be a player in the games." Her eyes widened in shock as she heard herself speak.

Tristan crossed his arms across his chest with a satisfied grin. He glanced at Ada and gave her a small nod. "Excellent! Now let's show you to your room so you can get settled. You must be tired after such a long day."

He gestured for Tara to stand and they left the room. Claudia, Gerrit and Ada following behind. Tara was led up a grand staircase and down a long hall filled with art from the old era. *Tristan has quite the collection.*

Her head spun with the realization of her position, but she was exhausted and that large meal sat heavy in her stomach, she needed to rest.

They came to a door with a wistful painting of dancers in tutus hanging beside it.

Tristan waved opened the door and stood back to let Tara go in first. Tara was overwhelmed at the sight of a huge bedroom with a large four post bed, an ambihearth on the side wall glowing warmly, a tapestry on one wall, some lounge chairs, a desk by a large window and a private bathroom.

A guardian was standing by the window waiting with a nightgown in her hands. Tara stared, openly in shock.

"All this for me?" She asked no one in particular.

"Yes." Tristan chuckled from the doorway. "Now, get some rest and we can talk more in the morning." He gave her a reassuring look before turning to leave, pulling Claudia and Ada with him.

Gerrit stayed behind and lingered in the doorway.

Tara eyed him curiously, "You're Gerrit?"

He nodded and stepped into the room. He had his hands in

his pants' pockets and let his shoulders roll forward as he chewed the inside of his cheek.

The guardian handed Tara the nightgown, gave a small bow and left.

"Do you know where your mother is?" Gerrit asked quietly once they were alone.

She gasped at his unexpected question, "No."

He peered at her quizzically and asked, "Do you want me to help you find her?"

Tara eyed him cautiously and stepped closer, "Why?"

"Because I'm curious if she's alive and where she is." He shrugged.

Confused by his answer she asked, "Why do you care?"

Gerrit pulled his hands out of his pockets and straightened up, Tara's head only met his chest. She looked up at him determined to understand his motive.

"I care," he said softening his eyes, "because things are not at all what they seem. The truths we're meant to swallow are lies. But that footage of you with the drones is raw truth. You're divergent. You're my half-sibling. You're family. I care."

Tara blinked, *That's not what I was expecting him to say. I know Mama is safe, I can feel it in my heart. But I don't have proof.* She studied his facial expression, *He seems sincere.*

"I don't know where she is. Last time I saw Mama was at the fringe encampment when it was raided. She was taken in a different transport, I was with the rest of the saplings. I've no guess where she was taken."

Gerrit nodded, "Alright. That's where I'll start looking." He turned to leave but at the doorway turned back. "You know, I look forward to getting to know you better. Based on that footage of you and those drones I'd love to see you use your eca in person." He said then left, closing the door behind him.

Tara's mind kept spinning with distrust. Looking down at the nightgown, feeling the soft fabric in her hands, she let out a slow exhale. "I don't know if I can trust them, but what choice do I have?" She whispered.

4

March 9th 2640, new moon

Tara was running. She could feel someone chasing her. Her feet pounded the earth. Running in a young forest with slender trees, feeling lost. There was a hiss in her ear and she spun around expecting to see his grey eyes. But instead, the darkness pressed in and the tree trunks formed a cage that surrounded her. Sirens rang out. There was a flash from her left.

The scene changed, she walked through an encampment with brightly coloured tents. She passed people singing and dancing. Still filled with a sense that she was being chased, Tara moved away from the people and music. It was snowing and she left footprints behind her as she wandered, lost in the maze of tents. Then she saw her mother standing in front of her. Her long dark hair was loose, she wore a green tunic and a yellow shawl. Tara's heart jumped into her throat and she ran. There was a sharp noise and a gust of wind blew into her face. She fell backwards.

Tara looked down at her body strapped to a medical table. She stiffened. A clinician hovered over her and attached something to an IV in her arm. When the clinician stepped away, Tara saw a bone-thin grey-haired man at the foot of the table. The man's hazel eyes started to glow brighter until the whole room was filled with light. She opened her mouth to scream but no noise came out.

Tara woke with a start, sitting up in bed gasping for air, eyes like saucers darting around the unfamiliar room. Her breath slowed as she rubbed her dream from her eyes. Startled by her surroundings, it took her a minute before she recalled where she was. Light streamed in from the large window and drew her attention. She glanced out to the view of the snow-capped mountains and it took her breath away. *Wow! It feels surreal to be here and to wake up to this beauty.*

She noticed a dresser by the bathroom, inside were various garments made from soft fabrics that she caressed with her fingers hemp, linen, cotton, silk. *Guess they don't make trainee jumpsuits from these lovely fabrics,* she thought choosing a light grey shirt and some blue slacks.

The bathroom was another elaborately decorated room with a large shell-shaped sink, claw-footed tub by a window, and a standing shower beside it. The walls were covered in a white and black mosaic with gold flecks. She found a single toothbrush and cleaned out her mouth. There was a large mirror that stood from floor to ceiling that she avoided as she made her way to the toilet to relieve her bladder and bowels. Under the spray from the shower, the hot water beat down on her shoulders and neck as she leaned her hands against the wall. She sighed with pleasure as the water washed away the last remnants of the Training compound.

Tara pulled on her clothes. Filling a cup of water, she drank it in one go. She found a brush and gazed at her reflection; her small frame surrounded by waist length dark brown hair. Slowly, she worked through her tangled thick hair and made one braid. *I don't remember the last time I could look in a mirror like this. I hardly recognize myself.*

She slipped on some flat shoes and headed out to find the others. While retracing the path they had taken the night before, she couldn't stop gawking at the lavish surroundings.

Quietly entering the dining room, she saw Tristan sitting at the head of the long dark wood table sipping from a steaming mug. He wore another freshly pressed platinum suit with ruby pins on the lapel. He didn't have a single hair out of place on his head. He was watching a holovid on the table. Beside him was Claudia, her attention absorbed by a Mochipet, a tiny electronic toy that fit into the palm of a hand. Gerrit sat a few chairs down from them, dressed in a black jumpsuit with ruby trim. He was eating fruit, his brown hair falling over his downcast eyes. Standing by the window, Ada was reading something on her tablet. She wore a slim cut black suit jacket with an emerald broach adorning her chest and a knee length pencil skirt. Tara looked back at Tristan and the holovid. It showed her running away from the Training compound. She watched herself take down the drones then the image cut to two people behind a white desk.

"Good morning, Tara." Ada's sing-song voice cut through the room.

Surprised, Tristan immediately shut down his tablet and plastered a jubilant grin on his face. Claudia glanced at her from behind glassy eyes then went back to her play. Gerrit looked at her with a small sideways grin.

Are they for real? Tara hesitated in the doorway.

Ada was immediately by her side, encouraging her to sit down at the table. A plate of food was placed in front of her by a quiet guardian, whom she only just noticed was there. Tara gaped at the plate of fruit, eggs, beans and toast. *There's so much food here! I can't eat all this.*

"Did you sleep well?" Tristan asked.

Tara nodded and bit her lips nervously.

Gerrit took one last sip from his mug and stood up. He tucked in his chair and said, "I'm sorry I can't stay. Tara, I hope you'll watch my game. I'm heading out now to the Arena Division." He bowed at his parents then turned back to Tara and winked, "See you later, Sis." With that he left.

So, this is my father and that was my half-brother. This place is like a strange dream. This house is huge, I've seen nothing like it. Are all these paintings from the old-era? Look at all this food! Who's eating all this glut? Not the trainees in grade F. Tristan must have a lot of power. I wonder if Mama knew that when she met him? Is he really gonna make me play those games? They'll call me Player Tara. Is that better than Trainee Tara? Is this place really any different than that compound? Ada's words easily permeated my mind last night. She influenced me to agree to Tristan's terms. It was as though she spoke through me. She's unlike any investigator I've ever met. Tara glanced over as Ada pulled out a vial and needlegun. She injected a blue serum into her own forearm. Tara was unable to avert her eyes and a worry line creased her forehead.

"I know you're having a hard time trusting me," Ada said as she put away the needlegun, "I don't blame you. In time you will. Until then I will prove it to you by helping you whenever I can."

Without thinking Tara said, "You gonna help me by invading my mind and planting servile thoughts?"

Ada smiled down at her and replied, "Yes."

Appalled, Tara looked towards Tristan for support but he just watched her thoughtfully. *He's just gonna let her manipulate my mind!?* Tara bit her tongue.

"Finish up your breakfast, my dear. I would like to show you something I found while going through my old belongings." said Tristan.

Tara dropped her eyes to her plate with rounded shoulders; Ada's presence a constant reminder she was under guard. She took a small breath, closed her eyes and thought, *I give thanks for this food.* She forked a piece of melon to start. The flavour exploded on her taste buds, making it impossible to hide her pleasure in eating real food again.

5

March 9th 2640, new moon

They entered Tristan's den, another lavishly decorated room. Tristan strode over to the desk and pulled open the top drawer. He retrieved a small box and placed it on a table beside some high-backed chairs. He gestured for Tara to sit. Ada stood behind the chair and radiated a wave of reassurance. Tara sank down and eyed the box curiously.

"I would like to know more about what Sheena was doing at the feebler encampment and any other information you could share. You have no idea how it pains me to know that you grew up in such terrible conditions. Now that I have you here, I know you're safe." Tristan watched her reaction closely.

He lifted the lid, carefully picked up a small tablet that looked like a relic and placed it on the table. A picture lit up of Sheena smiling sweetly. Tara had not expected to be face to face with her mother's image. Her heart cracked as hot tears pooled in her eyes. Her mother looked so young. It was almost as though she was looking at her reflection in the mirror. Her lungs heaved as she covered her tear-streaked face with her hands. Tristan switched off the tablet. His sympathetic expression creased his eyes as he bent forward to lower his face in line with Tara's.

"This is for you." He held the tablet out to her.

Wiping away her tears and calming down her breathing she said, "Thank you" tightening her fingers around the tablet.

Tristan stayed bowed over, "Why were you at that feebler encampment with your mother? What were you doing there?"

Tara met his eyes. The lie slipped off her tongue with confidence, "I dunno. She'd taken me to the market to trade herbal tinctures."

Tristan pressed his lips together in disappointment and straightened up. Ada circled around until she stood in front of

Tara. Tara felt the pressure build against her eyes, she looked down to the floor and tried to shut Ada out. There was a strong push and Ada was in her mind. She saw Tara's mother, her yellow headscarf sprinkled with snow, she was hopeful as she led Tara through the encampment to the rendezvous point with the Seds.

"She's lying." Ada said in her melodious manner. She focused her eca, "I will tell you who my mother was meeting at the Seds' encampment."

Tara heard herself say, "I will tell you who my mother was meeting the Seds' encampment." Her heart sank and she spoke, "Mama was meeting with Zedrik."

Ada glared at Tristan angrily then focused back on Tara, "I will tell you about my mother linking up with Zedrik."

The words were pulled from Tara's mouth, "I will tell you about my mother linking up with Zedrik." She tried to stop herself but Ada was too strong. She rolled her shoulders forward as tears streamed down her cheeks and said, "We didn't link up, the raid happened so quick and we were torn apart. I met Vi in the transport and ze told me to stay close, that we'd get out and back to hir family."

Tara's body trembled. She could still feel Ada in her mind as she knelt down to look her in the eyes, "I will tell you about Vi's family and our plan to break out of the Training compound. "Vi's my friend. Hir dad is Zedrik. All I know is Vi trusted hir family would come for us. Our plan was: I'd use my eca to get out of the compound, get past the field into the forest, link up with Zedrik and go back for hir and the others after."

"Zedrik is alive and Vi is his offspring." Ada stated. She focused her eca to pry further into Tara's mind, 'I will tell you about how I was going to connect with Zedrik.'

Tara closed her eyes and shook her head, but her mouth opened and she spoke, "I will tell you how I was going connect with Zedrik." her voice hitched as she continued, "The key was to find my way to the perimeter where we'd link up. Vi said, hir family and the Seds'll be waiting for us."

Ada leaned in again, her voice filled Tara's mind, 'I will

tell you where the Seds are. Where is Zedrik?' When Tara's mouth opened but nothing came out, Ada released her mind. Tara exhaled forcefully. Ada stood up and addressed Tristan, "She doesn't know."

Tara snapped her head up and glared at them. Bile rose in her throat, her breath ragged as she asked, "You gonna tell me what happened to Vi?"

Tristan raised an eyebrow surprised by her tenacity. Ada tilted her head to the side as she considered Tara's question.

Pulling her shoulders back Tara set her jaw speaking again, "What happened to Vi!? Ze was in an isolation chamber too. If you're gonna invade my mind and pluck info for your own gains, least gimme something. Is Vi alright?" Tara's lip quivered but she held her ground.

Ada smiled softly and nodded, "Yes. Thank you for your cooperation. Let me investigate Vi and I will get that information to you." She walked over to a high-backed chair by the window and sat down with her tablet. Tara glared at her with her jaw clenched tightly.

Tristan walked back towards the desk by the large window, then brought one hand to his mouth considering his words, "That footage of you gained a lot of attention. People are demanding to know more about the young woman who took out those drones. It is imperative that you are properly prepared."

Tara turned her glare towards him as he went on, "You never told me where your mother raised you before coming to the feebler encampment. I want you to tell me and not need Investigator Ada to pry it from you." He paused and glanced hesitantly toward Ada. She was seemingly not paying attention. Tristan turned back to Tara and watched her carefully, "There's no record of your mother in any Federation databases. There's no record of your birth. How could this be possible?"

Her heart rang in her ears as she flushed. She blinked slowly and tried to keep her face expressionless.

"When I met your mother, we were at the festival grounds. She was unlike any woman I knew. Only now am I realizing how little I knew about her. She too was quiet and evasive." he lifted an eyebrow at how similar Tara was as he spoke, "At the time I didn't really care because I was young and easily distracted. Now, I want to know. Where did your mother raise you?"

Tara wiped her sweating palms on her pants. *What can I tell them? I better speak quick so Ada stays over there.*

"In the fringe, near the perimeter." She lied and lowered her eyes. Her words hung in the air between them.

Tristan shook his head and said, "In the fringe? I need more than that, Tara."

She shivered as he said her name, "Um, deep in the forest."

"Deep in the forest? Where? Outside the Federation?" He demanded.

A tear ran down her cheek as she whispered, "Yes."

Tristan focused his stare on Tara, "That doesn't make sense! No one has been able to survive those super storms for generations. How could your mother raise you in the wild alone?"

Tara wanted to defend her mother's capacity to survive in the wild but bit her tongue. *No one can know of the Roozistem or the Sanctum the Cullis protects. I need to say something quick.*

"We weren't alone, we were in community. In forests." she spoke quickly glossing over the details, "Mom allied with Zedrik who wanted to thrive independently."

Tristan's expression hardened and he leaned his hands on his desk. He repeated her words back as a question, "Sheena was allying with Zedrik to build a community that would thrive outside the Federation?"

Panic rose in her chest. *I said too much. Sodz!* She noticed Ada had stopped her work on her tablet.

"That feebler has a community living outside of Federation territory?" His question was posed to himself. He focused back on Tara, "If this is true. How have these communities gone undetected by security drones?"

Tara shrugged, and lied, "I don't know. I was a sapling

when I was apprehended. I can't remember much before that."

Tristan lowered his head with shame. Pushing himself away from his desk he stood up, staring through her, his mind working over her words. Ada had placed her tablet in her lap and watched them both with interest. Tara waited nervously.

"I'm sorry." He finally said, "I'm sorry I didn't find you sooner and that you had to spend so long in that compound. You should have been here, with me."

Tara shivered, lowering her eyes to hide her fear.

His face dropped at her reaction but he pulled it back up. His angular features hardened once again, "How did your mother survive after the energy pulse with you, without a chip, for so long? Those early days were so tragic, all those deaths. I was busy analyzing samples to determine how to control the neural adaptations. I was developing a vaccine with Operator Stone. Everyone was chipped. There was resistance, but I never imagined Sheena would have been among them."

She shrugged her shoulders biting her tongue. *I can't tell them where I grew up no one has a chip. Mama wasn't even in the Federation when the energy pulse happened.*

Tristan inhaled sharply through his nostrils, straightened up to his full height and asked, "Is that why you have such elegant control of your extra cerebral ability? Did you grow up using it?"

Tara gaped at Tristan speechlessly.

"I'll take that as a, yes." He raked his hand through his neatly combed hair, exasperated. He leaned onto his desk and demanded, "Where are these communities in the wild?"

Her heart drummed in her ears and she started to count her breaths to calm herself. *Inhale, one, two, three, four. Exhale, one, two, three, four.* She couldn't bring herself to speak and just shook her head.

"You may not want to tell me the truth, but the truth will be known." He warned.

Tara felt the familiar wave of reassurance that made her body soften. Her fear amplified when Ada walked back towards her. *No, don't make me!*

Ada's tuneful voice invaded her mind, 'I will explain about these mysterious communities in the wild and how I evaded being chipped.'

She trembled as tears pooled in her eyes again, "I will explain about these mysterious communities in the wild and how I evaded being chipped." The words were pulled from her, "I grew up outside Federation territory with my family. We lived in wilderness, in community with others. No one there has a chip. Our homes are protected by camouflage."

Ada's voice came into her mind again, 'I will tell you where these communities are.'

Tara heard herself say, "I will tell you where these communities are. Beyond the expanse and the great river to the west." She whimpered quietly, "Please don't make me say more."

"That's enough for now. But Tara, this discussion is not over." Tristan said.

Tara trembled and wiped away tears as Ada left her mind.

"Whatever free-spirited commune you were raised in has skewed your perceptions." Tristan went on, softening his eyes. "Your fear is misplaced, my dear. The trauma you experienced in your youth has clearly ingrained your rebellious habits. You don't need to flee to the woods. You're safe with me. What's important now is to integrate you properly into society. We don't have much time; we will be attending a party later this evening. I will be showing you off as the newest player in my collection. I am certain Our Sovereign Kragen will want to appraise you himself."

Tara's gut clenched tightly at his words.

"Before then, we need to understand your extra cerebral ability. I want you to open up. It is clear that you have a unique ability and you've managed to expertly hide the extent of your eca for this long. If you continue to refuse to speak, I worry that your eca will be extracted from you by force in a way that is less than pleasing." He paused for her to volunteer the information.

She paled, panicking at the idea her ability could be taken by force. She glanced at Ada in trepidation. *What choice do I have?* She spoke quickly, "My eca connects me with electronics."

Tristan's grin extended from ear to ear as he gazed at her intensely. "Your eca allows you to connect with electronics." He repeated, his fingers forming a tent shape, "Like the drones from the Training compound. Did you connect with those?"

Tara nodded unable to speak.

Tristan lifted his chin and inhaled sharply through his nostrils, "Thank you for trusting me, Tara. This will be helpful in how I will manage the attention you will receive when we attend the party later."

Ada cleared her throat and took charge of the conversation, "Considering all that you've been through it's understandable to be hesitant to make choices. From what you have told us today, you have never been given the proper monitoring to apply your extra cerebral ability in a productive way. Our ecas are things that need to be controlled and monitored. This is why the chips were invented. Without them we would have no way to ensure the safety of our way of life."

Ada's expression softened, "The existence of encampments outside of the Federation is alarming. You do not seem to grasp the enormity of that risk. So, I want to share with you a part of my personal history." She took a sharp intake of breath before she continued, "I was coming into my pubescent years when the energy pulse altered the atmosphere. The effects were sudden for the elder population. My grandmother was among the early losses of the elder population that couldn't adapt and perished. It was devastating. Soon after we discovered the abilities, which quickly caused even more problems as many didn't know how to control them. My neighbour was one of those who lost control."

Ada paused and Tara noticed her slump slightly, "My parents had sent me out to play with a friend, while they had some alone time at home to sort through my grandmother's possessions. When I came back, there was nothing left. The neighbour lost control of their kinetic ability. The explosion took out half the apartment. The clinicians said that nobody within the blast radius would have felt any pain."

Tara stared at Ada horror-struck by what she had just revealed and said, "I'm sorry. That's awful."

Ada's expression shifted as she plastered on a sweet smile again, "You have confirmed what I already suspected about your electromagnetic extra cerebral ability." Her eyes glowed with excitement as she spoke. "What I would like to know is, how exactly do you connect with electronics? Do you possess any emotive radiation? Does your ability extend to kinetic projection or telepathic persuasion? But these are tests that will need to wait until you commence training. We'll begin first thing tomorrow."

Tara darted her eyes between Ada and Tristan as the weight of her reality crashed down on her. *Oh, Source fend! What have I gotten into? I told them about my ability and how to find the Sanctum past the expanse! How will I ever get home now?* As another wave of reassurance washed over her, she slumped helplessly back into the chair.

Tristan interrupted her thoughts, "For tonight, I need you to understand a few things. You will be popular with all the other guests wanting to meet you. It's important that you say nothing to them. Let me handle it, but try to keep a pleasant expression no matter the comment."

Tara frowned, overcome with her task ahead.

"A buzz has grown around you. The video of you and you being my long-lost daughter. The scandal is avoided because it was before the bonding laws. But you're attracting a lot of attention. You need to keep your eca and past a mystery," he smiled knowingly at Tara, "I know you can do that very well. Just be careful of anyone offering you any narcotics. They can cloud your judgment. These have become popular among the youth but unless properly dosed could be dangerous. I don't want you tweaking out and needing to visit the Medbay. Understand?"

What? Does he think I'm going to party hard? I don't want to go at all. I just want to go home. She swallowed her worry and nodded.

"Good." He said.

6

March 9th 2640, new moon

It was later that morning and Tristan had just outlined Tara's position as a player in the Federation. He explained the different types of games in the parks, the arenas, the Arcade, and the courses built in the ruins of old era cities. Tristan explained the importance of viewership but emphasized he wasn't worried about Tara attracting views. She was told that Ada would be monitoring her eca throughout her training and that Gerrit was going to train alongside her to help her transition as a player.

Tristan looked completely at ease as he sat back with his fingers interlaced on his lap, "There you have it. Do you have any questions?"

Tara closed her mouth. She was dreading this new position thrust upon her. *I don't care about those dank games. I wonder if he'll let me ask about anything. I'm far more curious about the energy pulse that caused everyone on Earth to have extra cerebral abilities. As far as I know, no one from the Roozistem knows the truth. Ada said the pulse devastated the elder population. That explains why the Roozistem renewed the elder circle. Growing up, everyone around me had such strong eca. Mine developed along with theirs as I grew. Once I reached puberty it was clear no one else had my ability. My eca was always unique. Even at the Training compound I was the only one. But I know there are a myriad of abilities one could grow, if they weren't restricted.*

Curiosity pushed her to ask, "You caused the energy pulse, right? Can you tell me how the altered atmosphere causes our extra cerebral ability? And why we have different abilities?"

Tristan blinked, startled by her question. He shifted uncomfortably in his seat and spoke slowly, "The atmosphere was altered by the energy pulse caused by the initiation of the perimeter shield; I was a part of that project, true. There were two side effects: the free energy we all have access to, and our extra cerebral abilities." His demeanour shifted as he presented himself with an intellectual air. "When the atmosphere changed, the water supply and our nervous systems were affected. This altered the neuroplasticity of our brains resulting in an increased brain capacity. Basically, our brains are able to process more and we have unlocked areas of the brain never utilized by humans before. The result was telekinesis and telepathy, which are level 1 eca. Everyone possesses this ability but some also have kinetic energy or enhanced sensory-motor abilities, which are considered a level 2 eca. Linguistic or optic abilities are level 3, and are rare. Most of the population are level 1 eca. Those that are level 2 or 3 have various combinations of eca that always include telepathy and telekinesis, interestingly enough. Some possess special abilities that let them persuade others through energy projections or emotive radiations."

"Your eca would be classified level 3 or possibly even level 4, which I'm guessing is why you've evaded detection for so long." The sound of Ada's voice was like a chime ringing in the room. The skin on Tara's arm tingled at the sound. Ada went on, "Most people with level 3 eca end up in the security sector. Your position as a player can be changed if your eca proves to be of more use for security purposes."

Tara's mouth went dry, fear clutching her gut again. She compulsively bowed her head and hunched her shoulders forward.

Ada smiled, "I found the information you asked for." Tara timidly looked up as Ada changed the topic, "Detainee Vi was relocated to the Research compound late last night. I have been corresponding with Operator Stone, who informed me that Vi will be there until ze's deemed safe to play games. Vi will be under Our Sovereign Kragen's net and relocated to the castle."

Tara's wasn't surprised by what she heard and her gut remained unsettled, but she took in a slow breath and quietly said, "Thank you."

Ada smiled her saccharine smile and stood up. She turned to Tristan and stated, "My duty calls. I will return tomorrow morning to begin monitoring Tara's training."

Tristan bowed his head towards Ada as she walked out the door. Once she was gone, he held up his finger for Tara to remain silent as he listened for sounds in the hallway. Slowly, he turned his attention back to Tara and said, "It was wise of you to finally open up. I need you to know that I will do everything in my power to keep you in the safety of my net. Do you have any questions, now that we are alone?"

Tara raised her eyebrows surprised by his change in tone. *What's his deal? I wonder if this is what he did to Mama? Showing her only one of his faces.* She chewed her lip as she pondered what she could ask him, *I wish Mama had told me more about him. Did she even know he caused the energy pulse? Does he even realize the harm the shield has caused? Would he know about the radiation? Would he care? Before we first crossed the perimeter shield Dib explained we needed to gather data about the shield from the inside. Something about radiation disrupting his devices and only from inside would his tools work. I didn't get it then and I don't get it now. But I remember Bricker emphasizing the dangers of staying too long under the shield. Then we got trapped here. Nothing went to plan.* Tara eyed Tristan's cleanly pressed suit, his ruby pins glinted in the light. His expression was patient but his eyes were heavy with remorse. She played with the hem of her shirt nervously, *It's because I'm trapped that I met my father. Although, I'm not sure if that's a good thing. He offered to answer any of my questions now that Ada's not here. I wonder if he'd tell me if I just ask?*

"You said, free energy and our eca were unexpected side effects of the energy pulse that was caused from the initiation of the perimeter shield. What other side effects does the shield cause?" She asked.

Tristan tilted his head to the side in confusion at her question and replied, "Other side effects? There are none, as far as I'm aware. Why would you ask that?"

Tara's shoulders tightened and she dropped her eyes to the floor worried she asked too much. Tristan watched her closely as she stammered, "Um. Since the shield caused the pulse, um. Wouldn't that still generate some radiation? It's different here, I dunno."

Tristan's expression softened, "My dear, the shield protects us from the harsh weather of the wilderness. If it sets your mind at ease, I'll explain more on how the shield works." He straightened up and folded his hands in his lap, "The perimeter shield was designed off the existing domes already within the Federation. For generations these shields have protected our ancestors from the harsh changes of the climate. It is used for hover technology, transportation and to contain players on courses. Operator Stone had spearheaded the project to erect a shield around the whole of the Federation. The shield towers contain ventilation turbines that purify the air we breathe. Through the towers, the rain or snow that fall on the shield are collected and redistributed within the shield. This is how we still have precipitation but not the harsh storms that rage in the wild. The dome of the shield is a barrier that nothing can penetrate."

"So, nothing can come in or get out." Tara said quietly.

"Exactly." Tristan smiled one of his manufactured grins, "Any other questions?"

Well, he won't tell me about the radiation. Would he tell me about the chips? She steadied herself and asked, "You pushed the chips to restrict eca?"

Tristan nodded.

Tara's stomach tightened as she prepared to ask her next question, "Why do we have chips but give eca serums to some? Why not let everyone be free to use their eca?"

Tristan pressed his lips together sympathetically, "My dear, some people's eca are too dangerous and need to be monitored. Just as Investigator Ada shared, some people cannot control their eca and in the worst cases have killed. I don't expect you to understand because you weren't born until after the pulse had already happened, but the chaos that erupted before the chips were mandated was devastating. The serums given to players before games or for security purposes are safe and properly tested. Small doses of one's eca enables us to benefit from our gifts as well as upholding the safety of the public."

Tara nodded, but was confused. As a child she witnessed communities of people that thrived with their eca. She had been one of them until they voyaged to the Federation and she ended up in the grade F.

Tristan watched her carefully and added, "If these communities exist in the wild, and there are others that are not chipped, then they and anyone they associate with are a threat to the Federation. You need to get your allegiance straight, my dear. Investigator Ada will be briefing Operator Stone on everything you've shared today. I expect there will be further investigation into these encampments outside of the Federation."

Tara's stomach dropped to her feet.

"Tell me." He said firmly, "You can connect to electronics. Do you sense your chip?"

The question lingered in the air as Tara hesitated to answer. She played with the hem of her shirt debating if she should lie. Tristan's eyed her suspiciously as he waited. She finally nodded biting her lips nervously.

"I suspect you've considered deactivating your chip the way you shut down those drones?" he asked.

"Yah. But I'm afraid what could happen. I mean, it's in my neck." She blurted out.

"That is wise of you, my dear. The chips are implanted near the spinal cord between the seventh cervical and first thoracic vertebrae. You will refrain from testing this idea further."

Tara's brow furrowed but she nodded her agreement. Another question popped into her mind and she meekly asked, "May I ask another question?"

"Yes. Of course." Tristan said gently.

"How do the serums work?" She asked.

Tristan pondered his response before he said, "To put it simply, the serum saturates your nervous system, allowing you to draw on that energy to use for your extra cerebral ability. The more you use your eca the quicker it gets used up. Depending on the dosage, of course." Tristan glanced at the device on his wrist and stood up, "Come, we will watch Gerrit's course. Let him show you how to embrace one's eca."

He moved towards a tapestry on the wall and waved his hand over it. A screen appeared in its place. A myriad of colours flashed across the screen and music filled the room. An announcer's voice excitedly shared the next event. Gerrit was to be trapped in a building. His task was to seek out several cards and escape the building before time ran out.

Tara watched as the screen switched to a shot of Gerrit. He was rolling his neck and hopping on the spot in his black and grey jumpsuit with ruby trim. Tristan grin spread across his face as he sat down in the chair next to Tara. She tried to ignore him and focused in on the screen.

7

March 9th 2640, new moon

The view cut to a drone view of a ruined city, one of the old era cities that had been destroyed by the great floods. An announcer was explaining the course, the building preparations and the dangers awaiting our hero inside. Tristan tapped the device on his wrist and the announcer went mute.

"The building has been reinforced with modern technology, rigged with holograms to make it more interesting." Tristan's excitement was palpable, "These escape courses are some of Gerrit's most viewed, growing his large viewership. He's made me proud as his father and as his controller."

Tara glanced at Tristan who was grinning ridiculously. She turned the corners of her mouth up politely. He tapped the device and the screen grew into a holovid that surrounded them. Tara gasped as the room transformed and they were transported to the course.

Gerrit sat in a chair with his back to a window with a singular stream of light in the dark room. Everything looked like a skeleton of a building but somehow held together at the seams with wall paper and paint. Gerrit was restrained in the chair with several thick metal chains, his face was calm and expressionless. The sound of a buzzer went off and a timer appeared overhead that started counting down. Gerrit struggled for a moment before he closed his eyes, concentrating hard. The chains that held him started to glow as they heated up.

Tara's eyes widened in amazement as the chains became red hot. With one big movement Gerrit threw the chains off and stood up. He dashed to the door and put his ear to it, listening carefully.

Gerrit tested the door handle. It was locked. Again, he closed his eyes in concentration, placed his hand to the handle and glowed red hot. He stepped back and kicked hard to break open the door.

The projection cut to another angle from the hallway making Tara feel as though she was whirling in the room.

Gerrit made his way dodging a couple projectiles. He jumped over a hole in the floor and made it to another room that had a large red X painted on the door. He pulled the door open and the view changed to the point within the room looking out at Gerrit standing in the doorway.

Gerrit walked up to a small box sitting on a tall table, the only objects in the room. He waved his hand over the top of the box for a moment before touching it. Carefully, he lifted the lid open and pulled out a small card.

He slipped the card into his jumpsuit pocket and turned to leave. As he did a metal cage fell from the ceiling trapping him inside.

A smile crept across the corner of his mouth. Grabbing one of the bars with both his hands he closed his eyes to focus. The metal heated up and he bent it to the side. He let go and repeated the process on the next bar creating an opening large enough for his thick build to get through.

Tara watched in awe as he continued back down the hall, working his way through a stairwell that was mostly rubble, he found three more boxes with cards inside, adding them to his pocket.

There were booby traps at every turn, some of them seemed impossible for Gerrit to manage. But his kinetic manipulation was strong and he was adept at focusing his eca.

Gerrit found all the cards needed to make his way out of the maze of rubble. The timer continued to count down.

Tara realized she was sitting on the edge of her seat, *How much further until Gerrit can escape?*

Gerrit rounded the last corner to the main entrance. The footage showed the light pour in through an open doorway, and he sprinted at the sight. Suddenly, he dropped out of view as the floor beneath him fell away. He crashed down several levels, his fall softened only by the rebound netting designed to prevent fatal injuries. He bounced off it several times before finally landing on the hard ground.

Tara was stunned. The holovid made her feel as though she was standing on the top floor looking down at Gerrit laying at the bottom of a pile of debris. She couldn't imagine how he was going to get out now. The clock was still counting down and he wasn't moving.

Clearly in pain, Gerrit pushed himself to standing. He looked around to asses his predicament and spotted a cable that hung from the uppermost floor. He placed his hand against a support beam just beneath it, with his other hand he grasped the cable, closed his eyes and concentrated.

The cement began to vibrate and crumble. As a large piece broke off, the cable was pulled with it. Gerrit flew up several stories until he landed on his feet on the top floor beside the door that led outside.

He sprinted out and down the front steps to the small box mounted on a post. He collected the cards from his pocket, placing them in the mounted box one at a time. When the last one got sucked in a trumpet sounded and holoconfetti erupted from above.

Tristan tapped the device and switched off the holovid. Tara looked around the room as the tapestry returned on the wall and she remembered where she was. Tristan leaned his chin on his hand and his elbow on the armrest as if asking for her critique of the show.

Tara stumbled over her words, "Um. What? Me do that?"

Tristan guffawed, "My dear, no! I don't expect you to run a course like that until you've been properly trained." He eyed her sideways, "Would you like to run a course like this?"

"Um. I," Tara looked down at her hands, "I do not."

He laughed again and said, "Come, it would be good for you to have some fresh air." He stood up and motioned for Tara to follow.

They left the room and walked back down the hallway, this time going past the dining hall and into the kitchen.

Tara saw several guardians busy chopping vegetables as she and Tristan made their way outside onto the lawn heading down to a small meadow.

Tristan stopped under the shade of a few trees. He placed his hands behind his back looking around at the view.

Tara reached out and touched the bark of a tree, gazing up through the leaves to the blue sky. Her mind flooded with memories of being in the deep woods as a child. Her heart swelled. She turned her eyes to the earth and knelt down to put her hands in the grass, it felt prickly after being cut recently.

Tara took a slow, long breath in then exhaled just as deeply. *I am grateful to be here with you mountain friends. I don't wanna be a player, but I don't have a choice. At least I am free of that horrendous compound.*

8

March 9th 2640, new moon

Operator Stone was in his office at the Research compound, he had just finished messaging with Investigator Ada, who shared:

Zedrik survived the fires of the festival grounds. Vi is Zedrik's offspring and is suspected to have more family. There is a risk of encampments outside of Federation territory with a population not chipped. It is confirmed that Tara has an electromagnetic eca.

Zedrik is alive. He survived with his offspring. So, Zedrik did couple with Remi. I suspected as much, but now we know for certain. Kragen needs to be informed. This changes everything. He typed a message and sent it to Kragen. Then he alerted the enforcers, clinicians and Investigator Duncan, to meet him in cell block B.

The knowledge that Vi was the offspring of Zedrik and Remi was sobering. He had already planned to investigate hir personally. The destruction caused at the Training compound was most impressive. Now, Stone was determined to use Vi to hunt down Zedrik.

He marched to the monitoring station where he paused to view the security screens. The detainee in the cell sat with hir arms resting on hir bent knees, hir long ropy hair covering most of hir face and shoulders.

Stone looked up from the screen and nodded to the three enforcers and the clinician, who entered the cell. Stone turned his hazel eyes back to the screen as the enforcers approached Vi.

Ze jumped to hir feet and moved hir back up against the wall.

After a brief scuffle ze had hir arms restrained behind hir back and was forced to hir knees, an enforcer on each side and one behind.

The clinician stepped in with a needlegun loaded with a pink serum and quickly injected Vi in the arm then left the room. The enforcers laid Vi on hir stomach, attached restraints to hir ankles and held hir there pinned to the ground. One of the enforcers produced a black cloth bag and promptly placed it over Vi's head. They lifted Vi and carried hir out of the cell.

The sound of Vi's grunts filled the corridor as the three enforcers carried hir out and proceeded down the corridor to the interrogation room. Stone switched the channel on the screen, he looked into a small room with no windows and two chairs separated by a single table with a solitary hanging ambilight overhead. The enforcers carried Vi to the chair, which had built in restraints and faced away from the door. Once secured, the enforcers stepped back but did not leave.

The clinician who was reading another screen with Vi's vital statistics said, "Hir heart-rate is elevated, but stable."

Stone gestured towards Duncan to come forward. As he did, Stone focused his eca and spoke telepathically to him.

After he outlined his instructions, Stone entered the interrogation room and signalled for the enforcers to step out. Without a word he stood behind Vi and focused his eca. He slipped easily into hir mind and mentally steered hir to think of Tara. Stone held onto the image of Tara in Vi's mind, her rich brown skin, big brown eyes and long dark hair.

He pulled the cloth bag off Vi's head and waited for hir to adjust to the light. Then he focused his eca and the room became hazy. A crooked grin crept across his face as he pulled back the image of Tara in Vi's mind.

Blinking hir eyes trying to make the haze dissipate, Vi saw Tara walk from hir left and around the table to sit in the chair opposite. Vi blinked again as Tara looked back at hir.

"What!? How? Tara! What. Wachu doin' here?!" Vi stammered, hir mouth dry and coarse.

Stone spoke as Tara to Vi's mind, 'I made it. I got to the woods and to the Seds. There was nothing there. Only the remnants of a camp.'

"What? Wait. You found the Seds? But Tara you're here!? Wachu mean Dad wasn't there?" Vi shook hir head in confusion.

Stone spoke again into Vi's mind, 'The Seds are gone. I returned to the Federation because I realized I was wrong to try and leave. You need to trust them. Tell them whatever they need and we can both be free.'

Vi furrowed hir brow in confusion. "What are you talkin' about!? Tara, we can't trust them!" Ze shook hir head and began to pull on the restraints.

Stone stood up and walked out of Vi's line of sight. He released Vi's mind as the door opened and Duncan walked in. Vi blinked as the haze dissipated, shaking hir head in disbelief that Tara had been there. Ze focused hir attention on the muscular man who now sat in the opposite chair. Stone stood silently behind hir.

Duncan watched Vi impassively and the room fell silent, after a long time he finally spoke, "You caused a great deal of destruction at the grade F Training compound. Points have already been deducted from your score, and you should know that you are now in debt to Our Sovereign Kragen."

He paused for dramatic effect letting Vi stew in the information before he added, "Oh and you will be under his net once you leave this compound. Until that time, you will be monitored by us and your primary goal is to tell us everything you know about the Seds."

Vi set hir jaw remaining silent.

Duncan grinned focusing his eca speaking into hir mind, 'We know who you are, Vi. We know you are feebler filth like your father, Zedrik. Just tell us what we want to know. Where can we find them?'

Vi glared back at him and tried to ignore his presence in hir mind.

"I'm not talkin'." Vi spoke through gritted teeth.

Duncan shrugged his shoulders as he released Vi's mind. As soon as hir mind was cleared Stone focused his eca and the room became hazy again.

Vi felt a shudder run through hir as the image of hir father came to mind.

"No." Vi said in almost a whisper.

Duncan stood up and moved to the side of the room as Stone stepped around back into Vi's line of sight. Vi paled with shock and disbelief as ze watched Stone's hallucination of Zedrik step around the table.

"Dad? How?" Vi whispered as hir eyes pooled with tears.

Stone spoke as Zedrik into Vi's mind, 'Yes. Vi, it's me. It's time to tell the truth. It's over, the Seds are gone. Tell them what they need to know. Where are the Seds' encampments?'

Vi winced at his words and yelled, "I don't know! Get out of my head! You're not my dad! Noooo!! Get out!"

Vi struggled violently against the restraints and Stone moved back out of hir line of sight but did not let go of Vi's mind. He observed the rush of hir thoughts and felt the emotional waves as memories surfaced and passed.

Stone thought to himself, *Just maybe.* Then he focused his eca again and brought to mind Vi's mother, Remi.

Vi's body stiffened as Stone focused on Remi in hir mind, her long dark hair and thin frame. He walked around into hir line of sight again. Vi's eyes widened in horror as ze traced hir mother walk around the table.

'Vi,' Stone spoke in Vi's mind as Remi, 'Don't be afraid. I want to help you. Zedrik took you to the fringe, but with who else?'

Vi's eyes watered as hir sibling came to mind.

"Xain." Vi said barely audibly.

Stone continued to speak into Vi's mind, 'Yes. Xain. That's right. Tell me about Xain.'

"He's my siblin'." Vi whispered.

'Yes. You and Xain are my offspring.' Stone spoke as Remi, 'Xain and Zedrik are dangerous and need be stopped.

Where are the Seds encampments? How are they penetrating the perimeter shield?'

Vi's eyes filled with fire finally able to see past the hallucination as ze spat, "You're not my mom!! I don't know anythin'! Nothin' will make me talk!"

Stone stood up and the haze cleared. Vi blinked away tears as ze saw a bone-thin grey-haired man standing where hir mother had been. His cold presence filled the room and Vi found it harder to breathe.

He leaned his bony hands on the table and glared down at Vi forming his words very slowly, "We have ways to make someone talk."

He tightened his hands into fists and pounded on the table three times. An icy ripple moved through hir with each impact from his fists on the table. Then it was like a heavy boulder was crushing hir chest. Hir breath became ragged and ze let out a guttural cry that echoed in the small room.

~~~

There was a quiet murmur in the dining hall as the trainees ate their evening meal. Everyone was quietly gossiping about the course from the day before. Tara and Vi's friends were among them, left in limbo after her attempted escape.

Brill whispered, "If you're not goin' to be collected then maybe we won't be sent to the work camps."

Pin glanced hopefully at Desma with his sharp green eyes. She chewed her lip and shrugged with uncertainty. They both looked to Khalil, who had also been chosen for collection.

Khalil lightly ran his fingers over the bumpy burn scar on his cheek, "No. Bridget didn't say we weren't bein' collected. She said, our processin' had been put on hold. It's just a matter of time."

Brill dropped her eyes to her bowl of mush, "Oh."

Hami tenderly placed her warm hand on Brill's, "It's not over. Hold hope."

"Do you think Tara got out?" Twitch asked quietly.

Khalil pressed his lips together tightly and shook his head. The weight of their grief surrounded them.

With no access to the public channels, they knew nothing of what was happening to their friends after the destruction in the holding room.

They only had the information Bridget shared, and they knew that wasn't to be trusted.

"Our plan was always flawed, but Tara was a fast runner. Not as fast as me, but I couldn't sneak past those kbots. I think she made it." Lino said hopefully.

Ritu glanced nervously at the other trainees at the table and noticed Nebba dart her eyes away. She furrowed her brow with worry as she quietly said, "Tara was probably collected."

"What about Vi? I bet ze's been collected too." Vipin said.

"You think they were collected?" Hori asked trying to keep his voice quiet, "I think security scooped them. With Tara's eca-"

"We can't know for sure." Khalil interrupted. His dark eyes glanced around the group and settled on Raha's warm round face. She returned his intensity and nodded her approval. Khalil took a breath and whispered, "It's not over. Even if we get split, we're still in this together."

~~~

Investigator Ada opened the door to the interrogation room and sat down in the chair opposite Vi, who was still restrained to the chair and had been left alone with hir anxiety for over an hour. Ada's presence made Vi's hairs stand on end.

Without any pretense, Ada focused her eca and pressed into Vi's mind. 'Your friend Tara already told us about the Seds and your plan to reconnect with your father, Zedrik and brother, Xain. You have one chance to volunteer the whereabouts of these encampments.' Ada paused and the room filled with a tense silence.

Vi shifted in hir restraints and squeezed hir mouth shut.

Ada licked her lips and pressed her will in Vi's mind, 'I will tell you where to find the Seds.'

Vi's eyes widened in shock as hir mouth opened, "I will tell you where to find the Seds." Ze took a shaky breath hir eyes pooling with tears, "There's a small base camp along the west perimeter that's hidden in the rocks. Chester set up a wedge in the perimeter to run supplies in and out."

Vi breathed heavily as tears streamed down hir face. Ada looked pleased then used her eca and radiated a wave of reassurance towards Vi. Ze relaxed involuntarily staring helplessly at Ada

"Chester set up a wedge in the perimeter." Ada repeated. Vi shuddered as Ada focused her eca again, "I will tell you about Chester."

Vi's jaw tensed, "I will tell you about Chester." Ze felt the words being pulled from hir, "We've been friends since I was little. We'd scavenge the plastic rubble piles on the banks of the fringe territory. We searched for usable parts for his devices. He makes all kinds of devices. He constructed a hack,"

Vi began to pull on the restraints. Ada pushed on hir mind until ze spoke again, "He constructed a hack for the chips." Vi exhaled sharply and hung hir head.

"Chester constructed a hack for the chips." Ada repeated thoughtfully. She radiated another wave of reassurance at Vi and said, "Thank you for your cooperation."

With that she stood up and exited the room, walking down the corridor to where Stone was waiting at the monitoring station.

"Excellent work, Investigator Ada." He said. "Enforcers are en route to the west perimeter and will walk the border on foot, if need be. We will find this supposed wedge in our defences. We need you back with Controller Tristan to monitor Player Tara. It is essential that we learn as much as we can from her eca."

9

March 9th 2640, new moon

The sky was fading into an iridescent pink as the sun was working its way towards the horizon. The sheen off the shield created tiny orbs of light that sparkled just under the dome. Claudia was linked arm in arm with Tara, her toothy grin sparkled along with her red sequined dress.

Tara felt completely unlike herself. Guardians had dressed her in a blue pantsuit with a cream yellow strapless bodice, her dark hair pulled up in a spiralling bun held by a ruby bejewelled pin. In the pocket of her pants she felt the small tablet that had the image of her mother, her heart expanded to know a part of her was so close.

She had only ever travelled in the security transports. The one in front of her was not designed to be utilitarian, it oozed luxury with its sleek silver and chrome. Claudia led Tara where their driver discreetly waited. He waved a hand over the door to slide it open. Tara eyeballed the soft upholstery inside, *Everything Tristan has is top quality. Am I really part of his collection?*

Tristan strode up to them and gave Claudia a small peck on her cheek. He was dressed in a dark suit with ruby encrusted ribbons adorning his chest. He stood at the door to the transport and gestured for them both to climb in, then he followed.

Tara ran her fingers along the seat, feeling the texture of the stitching. The view was a blur of colours as they travelled along smoothly. She barely noticed the vibration as though the transport was gliding above the road.

She scanned the view of the different residences, some partially embedded in the rock and some planted on top of.

The transport slowed down and Tristan said, "It's a checkpoint. We're entering the PUSH."

Suddenly the view was a stream of lights as the transport travelled through the Pulsating Ultra Speedy Highway. The acceleration only notable from the blur of the vortex propelling them. Tara was mesmerized by the swirl of lights.

"These highways make it faster to travel above ground in any transport. Except by air." Tristan explained. He gained satisfaction from her childlike curiosity as she leaned her head against the window. The transport slowed with ease at the end of the highway before it accelerated on its own through the winding mountain roads.

When they slowed again, it was for the checkpoint entering the Banquet Hall. The enforcer patrol waved their transport through and they pulled up to the main entrance. It was situated on an expansive plateau with dark mountain rock cut sharply on three sides. Holovids animated the rock faces. The entrance had a grand staircase draped with a blue runner.

Tara stared at the height of the mountain as she stepped out of the transport, the dark moonless sky over head blended into the dark rock. Tristan wrapped his arm around her shoulders and pulled her into his body. She watched him link arms with Claudia, their faces overtaken with a pretense of jubilation. In the entrance were a smattering of people lingering on the steps, everyone dressed in elaborate textiles in every colour and pattern. A group of taletellers took sight of them and immediately called out questions. Tristan promptly ignored them and led Claudia and Tara up the stairs.

There was laughter mixed with the rhythmic music that reverberated off the rocks. The sound amplified the instant they crossed the threshold. Tara was bombarded with so many visuals; there were holovids in every direction, long hallways opening to large rooms displaying artwork, colourful sculptures that were taking up the open spaces, people dancing and socializing, a group were roller skating in a rink shaped room, others skateboarding on ramps that wove through the hall, and some were even slacklining from one of the statues to a balcony. Tara glanced up to the balcony where groups of mostly naked people were lounging on cushions. She watched one hold something to their nose, inhale, then lay back with glassy eyes. Others moved in kissing and pleasuring one another. A blush rushed across her face. Tristan steered her into the crowd.

Tara could feel everyone's eyes on them as they approached an elite couple who grinned wildly. They swayed their glasses towards Tara and took a sip of the golden liquid. Tristan gave a courteous bow and they moved on. The next couple were introduced to Tara as, Tristan's old game rivals, Controller Ito and Noble Tofer. Their son Bronik, stood out with his flame red mohawk, face piercings and torn black shirt. He eyed Tara as he flicked his lip ring playfully with his tongue. There was talk of Gerrit and Bronik playing against each other in the Quarter Circuit. They shared in fake laughter and pleasantries before Tristan steered them away. His arm stayed securely around Tara as they met another couple. More idle chatter, then they moved on. He exchanged polite words as he introduced her to Controller Slavik and Noble Zarya, then led her to another couple. This continued as Tristan, linked with Claudia, led Tara around the Banquet Hall to greet various well-dressed elite controllers and their mates. The next couple they reached were introduced to Tara as Tristan's old friend Controller Yoshiro and his mate Noble Haru. There was talk of gathering for a meal together, more congratulations and they moved on. Tristan gave her an encouraging squeeze as they approached yet another couple. Tara didn't need an introduction. Her eyes dropped compulsively to the ground and she wrapped her arms around herself after she realized Controller Pierce and Noble Prudence were the next couple they would greet. Tara could feel them watching her critically behind their delighted party mask expressions.

"Salutations, Controller Tristan and Noble Claudia. What a pleasure to see you celebrating with your new found daughter." Pierce said.

"Salutations, Controller Pierce and Noble Prudence.

Thank you. It is a delight to introduce her to everyone." Tristan replied.

Prudence raised her glass towards Tara and smiled genially. Tristan bowed and led them to greet the next couple. Tara tried not to show how overwhelmed she was by the number of people at the party. Each one wanted to congratulate Tristan and get a glimpse of her. Taletellers with recorders trailed behind them, they captured video and eavesdropped on their conversations.

Tristan continued to keep his arm around her until they arrived at a quiet space with padded lounge sofas and dim ambilights. Gerrit was squished between two beautiful women, one with long silver hair with legs to match and the other with coarse short dark hair, who laughed to reveal a gap in her front teeth. Gerrit was dressed in a fitted black suit paired with a red shirt and black tie. Pinned to his lapel was the an eight-pointed gold star that he earned from his escape course. Noticing them approaching, his grin grew even wider. After a quick word with the women, he stood up and strode over to his parents.

"Father. Mother. It's good to see you." He looked down at Tara, "Salutations, Sister." He said with a wink.

"How did you like my course?" He directed his question to Tristan.

"You performed very well, Son. Our viewership went up and it was highly entertaining. The way you escaped from that pit gripped me with suspense!" Tristan said.

Gerrit leaned down closer to Tara's ear and asked, "What did you think?"

"I was on the edge of my seat." Which was true but didn't reveal how she was terrified of the experience.

Tristan removed his arm from Tara's shoulder and stepped back, "Gerrit, keep close with Tara. Tara, enjoy yourself. Consider this your homecoming celebration." With Claudia on his arm Tristan went back into the crowds of the party.

Gerrit put his arm around Tara's shoulder, and she noticed it carried a jovial brotherly feeling that was different than

Tristan's stoic hold. She eyed him curiously as he led her back towards the padded lounge sofas. The two women had moved and Tara found herself next to Gerrit. She looked out at the rest of the party goers from her cushioned spot.

Gerrit leaned in and focused his eca, 'Smile. You're on camera.'

Surprised, she furrowed her brow at him. He gestured with his eyes towards the recorder hidden in the post nearby. Tara saw it, then spied several others nearby.

"Who views these parties?" She asked.

'Those who wish they could have been invited.' He continued to speak to Tara telepathically. He leaned in closer and flashed her a devilish grin, 'Look around you. Everyone here is on display and is vying for attention. For some, the games are these parties.'

He flicked his eyes up to the balcony then back to Tara. She followed his gaze to the blur of naked bodies all intertwined.

She paled, "They're players?"

Gerrit nodded, 'Most are runner ups from the Interlude. They live in the parks positioned in the VXTC dens. They're a main attraction of these Banquet Hall parties.'

Her body flushed as she looked around at the party goers. Her eyes widened with disgust as she processed what living in the parks meant for those players.

Nervously, she looked back at Gerrit and asked, "What's the Interlude?"

Gerrit suppressed a frown and spoke into her mind again, 'Kragen plays to base human desires. Every two years he selects players for his Interlude, a game where they compete for the chance to mate with him. Winners are taken to his Jardin d'Olympia to join the ranks of his concubines for a chance to produce an heir. The runner ups are given the coveted position of QTpi and serve in parks where they live. Some are chosen by controllers to bond or match with their offspring. That's how my mother bonded with our father. She was a runner up in the first Interlude and the story goes that Father claimed her right after.

Those who don't find a mate come to these parties to be shown off by Baroness Ga or Fixer Locke to mingle among other nets.'

A shiver ran through Tara's body. She hugged herself and dropped her eyes. Gerrit saw her reaction and wrapped his arm around her to warm her up. Startled at his touch she shoved him off.

"Yow! Remember this is a party and we're supposed to be celebrating." He smiled at her encouragingly with his hands up defensively.

At that moment, they were approached by a man dressed in a long red coat and goggles that made his green eyes bulge. He slid close beside Tara showing his ultra white teeth in a lurid grin. Alarmed by his sudden presence, Tara slid closer to Gerrit.

"Lady looks cold. Could she use some zing?" He spoke quickly. He opened his coat to reveal an assortment of colours, there were pill bottles, sniffers, eyedroppers and needleguns. His eyes fluttered between Tara and Gerrit as he went on, "You see something you fancy? Take your pick; luusid, bizzters, hoppies, xos, grip, bogoggles, snap, bluesky, zing?"

"No thanks, friend. We're all set." Gerrit said firmly glaring at the man.

The man eyed Gerrit oddly and asked, "Maybe a vaperz or some herb to smoke?"

Gerrit shook his head and eyed the man back. He laughed like he had just heard a great joke, but bowed and moved away. He closed his coat and blended back into the party. Gerrit let out a slow breath as he peered around. Taletellers had their recorders pointing at them and people nearby were not shy about eavesdropping. His friends Nylah and Prynn, who had been on the sofa with him, were watching them with fascination from a refreshment table.

He ignored them and shifted to face Tara. He focused his eca and spoke into her mind, 'I find the trick to being a player is to look like you're being mischievous but really you're just playing the part.'

She continued to look at him dubiously.

"Here." He sighed and pulled out a small disc from his pocket. Tara leaned into the backrest with her feet tucked beside her and looked down curiously at the disc. He held his hand out over it for a moment and a flame erupted from his palm. Tara's eyes lit up with wonder as she witnessed him using his eca. The flame was warm and the chill left her body. He smirked and let the fire dance between his palm and the disc for a moment longer before he pulled his hand away to extinguish the flame.

"How do you have access to use your ability?" She asked.

"I have a small collection of serums that I obtained after that course. I earned a lot of points." He explained defensively, "I'm not self medicating, but I still struggle coming down from a course like the one I ran today and not have my eca for longer than one dose. Surely you know the feeling of emptiness that follows the serum wearing off?"

Tara nodded as she remembered the last time she used her eca. *I was so close to freedom when the serum ran out. If I didn't have this dank chip it would have worked. I wouldn't be trapped here.*

Gerrit leaned in closer and she heard him in her mind again, 'Don't worry Sis, I'll get you some eca serum. I am super keen to see you use your eca in person.'

Intrigued, she raised an eyebrow at him. *Interesting. Guess I ain't surprised Tristan's son has access to eca serum.*

'What you did to those drones was cracked. Everyone on the channel forums is trying to guess what your eca could be. Most suspect some advanced telekinesis.' A furtive knowing flashed in his eyes as he continued, 'But I bet you're more powerful than that. What is it? Do you speak computer?' His words carried an air of humour.

She shook her head without elaborating. She was not about to share anything about her eca at this huge party, but it was alarming to hear him deduce her ability. *If I had my ability I'd do more than 'speak computer'! I would tune into all the devices and electronics in the building, possibly further. I've been chipped for so long now I don't remember the feeling of my full ability.*

The emptiness of that disconnect nagged at her. Impulsively, she touched the skin on the back of her neck. She felt for the tiny chip deep near her spine. Gerrit watched her curiously but remained quiet. Tara glanced back at him with apprehension, his wry smile suddenly looked just as fake as Tristan's.

"Yow, don't worry, Sis." He said.

Don't worry!? How can I not? I've been thrust into a fever dream that I can't wake from.

Tara sat back holding herself tight and observing the party around her. Everyone looked like they were having the time of their lives, glee seemingly plastered across their faces.

Her eyes were drawn back up to the balcony, a plump older woman with dark hair and bangs wearing a black dress cinched at her waist was directing the naked players. There was a blast of music that drew her attention to contortionists balancing and writhing into knots on a small platform. She was mesmerized by their twisted forms.

When Gerrit's body stiffened it made the tiny hairs on Tara's arm raise. She followed his eyes to a strawberry blond haired young woman. Her peaches and cream skin was covered in a form fitting red dress with diamonds dangling from her ears. She entered the lounge area with an entourage of elite youth and was trailed by enforcers.

His voice sprang into her mind, 'We're moving! I don't want to party with Cari. And I definitely don't want her to meet you.' He stood up, taking a hold of Tara's arm leading her away from the lounge area before Cari had a chance to notice them.

"Cari?" She asked as he led her towards some tables near the large windows that faced the terrace.

"I'll tell you later." He promised.

There was a fountain with shimmering water that poured out of different spouts at its base. A table set up next to it with glasses and other refreshments.

Gerrit filled a glass and handed it to her, then he proceeded to pour himself one. Tara sipped and looked out at the party curiously.

A bizarre rattling caught her attention and she turned around. She saw a tall man staring at her. He locked eyes with her and she felt her surroundings slow down and move out of focus.

The sounds of the party dampened and she could only see this man with warm brown skin, short thick hair and dark brown eyes that were flecked with green and gold.

As the man's penetrating eyes bore deep into Tara she realized that she was not in control of anything she was doing. The intensity of his stare had her placing the water glass down and walking towards him. Finally, she stopped moving and felt the cool breeze of the open air.

His eyes bore into her even deeper and there was a strong sense of safety that arose within her.

His deep voice filled her mind, 'What happened to Vi?'

The question threw her back into the sinking feeling of the fate of her friend. Without hesitation she responded, "Vi was taken to the Research compound. Ze'll be moved to the castle under Kragen's net."

He nodded.

She asked, "Who are you?"

He showed his white teeth in a grin as he pulled a small tablet out of the pocket of his wool coat. He leaned forward and whispered as he passed it to her, "Keep this safe. It has everythin' you need to know."

She took the tablet slipping it into the pocket with the tablet of her mother, feeling them clunk together. Mesmerized by his eyes, she started to hear the music grow louder.

Tara blinked and he was gone. She was alone on the terrace looking around with confusion when Gerrit rushed up frantically.

"Why did you wander off!?" He quickly scooped her under his arm and pulled her back inside. He spoke into her mind, 'You need to be careful! Things are not what they seem and you're too precious. What if something had happened to you!?'

Tara was startled by his protectiveness. She thought about the mysterious encounter she just had and glanced around at all the party goers. *Did that even happen? He appeared out of nowhere and vanished just as quick.* Touching her pocket and finding two tablets were there, her heart sprang into her throat, *That was real! I need to know what's on that tablet!*

She was led through the party until they were reunited with Tristan and Claudia. They were sipping from tall fluted glasses. Tristan flashed an open-mouthed grin as they approached.

"Having fun?" He asked and reached his arm out for them to come close.

He leaned into Tara and gestured towards a man.

Tara followed his direction to the curtained area with a ring of enforcers on the periphery. A bronze skinned man in a sharp black suit with diamond studs along his shoulders and wrists was surrounded by a group of scantily dressed people. Each one was pampering him with snacks while a group was performing different sexual acts to each other as everyone else was viewing. The sight made her stomach churn as she realized who he was.

"Our Sovereign Kragen is there and he would like to meet you." Seeing her apprehension, Tristan took hold of her hand squeezing it tight. He leaned in close so only she could hear, "Don't worry. We will keep it as brief as possible."

Gerrit's arm returned around her shoulders and together the four of them walked up to the periphery of the stage.

Tristan exchanged some words with one of the enforcers who let them enter the curtained stage.

Tara kept her eyes low but saw Kragen shift his position as he watched them approach.

"Ah, Controller Tristan. Good to see you! You've much to celebrate tonight. Noble Claudia, you look lovely as ever. Player Gerrit, my man! The way you got out of that pit, all I can say is, wow! Gold star well earned. Tristan, you must be proud that he made the cut for the First Quarter Circuit." Kragen said benevolently.

"My liege, I am pleased beyond measure." Tristan lifted his chin with pride.

Kragen turned his attention to Gerrit, "Cari was also

thrilled that you made the Quarter Circuit. How does it feel to level up your game?"

"Most excellent, my liege." Gerrit replied smoothly, "It pleases me to hear that Scion Cari is my cheerleader."

"Soon you'll be bonded with my Cari and will make your father and I even prouder. You must be excited." Kragen said.

"Yes, I am. I think about my duty every day." Gerrit said with a bow.

"Good man." Kragen praised. His dark eyes focused on Tara, his honeyed tone set her hairs on end, "Now, you must be the infamous Tara. Welcome to the mountains. I know we will get to know each other better."

Kragen slowly let his eyes trail over her whole body before speaking again, "You're right Tristan, she does look like Sheena. She has her eyes."

Tara stiffened at the mention of her mother. *How does he know what Mama looks like?* She dropped her gaze and hunched forward.

Kragen focused his eca and spoke to Tristan, "I want Player Tara to run the 1st Quarter Circuit."

He spoke with such authority that shocked Tara, she felt her need to obey instantly.

She watched aghast as Tristan nodded curtly, "Yes, my liege."

Kragen looked satisfied as he turned back to Tara and said, "It's going to be a great course and I know she won't disappoint the viewers. Will you, Player Tara? I for one am eager to watch you." He leaned back and turned his attention to the person who offered him a small chocolate.

Gerrit steered Tara away with Tristan and Claudia.

Tristan put his hand out to stop Gerrit once they were outside of the circle of enforcers, "Take her home."

Gerrit bowed and led Tara out of the party.

The night air was cool and fresh as Tara followed Gerrit down the steps, past the taletellers and into a transport that carried them swiftly back to the large house in the mountains.

A Forest Without Trees / JP Solanki-Davie

10

March 9th 2640, new moon

Tara felt wrapped in warmth as Gerrit ushered her inside. They had been silent the whole way back, giving Tara plenty of time to process. Witnessing that scale of excess and debauchery was a shock to her system. Encountering Kragen's power of persuasion had then shook her to the core. *I want Player Tara to run the 1st Quarter Circuit*, his words echoed in her mind.

Gerrit led her down the hall, into a side corridor and descended a flight of stairs. They walked the length of another long hall through a side passage and another hall. When they arrived at a wooden door Gerrit waved his hand over a scanner and it opened. Tara was struck by the few dozen computers cramped in the room, each one buzzing as code ran up the screens. Gerrit drew up a chair next to a cabinet and pressed Tara to sit down.

"This is my den. These computers are running the search that we talked about last night. There's not much information about your mother. All I can find is her processing reports from the raid on the feebler encampment." He gestured to the screens then shoved his hands in his pockets. He locked eyes with Tara, "In order to get what you want you're going to have to keep playing the games. Kragen wants you to run the Quarter Circuit. We don't have much time to prepare. I am going to help you, but I need some reassurances from you first."

He held something hidden in his fist when he pulled his hand out of his pocket. His eyes were intense and hopeful. She regarded him attentively. All his manufactured expressions were gone.

"I believe your mother is alive and has left the Federation.

If I give you the serum, you need to promise me you will not use your eca to try and leave before the Quart-C. And that when you do leave, I go with you." His blue eyes were dead serious.

Tara stared at him shocked. *He wants to leave the Federation!? He wants to help me escape? Would that be possible?* She eyed his hand, *He's got eca serum.* Her ears burned as she asked, "You want to leave the Federation?"

Gerrit nodded, "It's my only option I have left."

"Only option? You got a gold star on that course. You're well liked. You'd throw that away? Why?" She wanted to trust him. Her heart ached to embrace him as the sibling he was, but a tightness in her chest made her hesitate.

"It's true I was born into privilege. My eca aside, I have more than anyone could ever need and it's all due to my father. Our father." He corrected himself. "I enjoy this lifestyle, don't get me wrong. But our leader is bent, and too many are following blindly. I've kept my feelings to myself because no one will hear it, and too many that have spoken out have been silenced over the years, or have disappeared. Kragen has everyone caught in his net and no one opposes him. I don't think Father even realizes how twisted he is or maybe he truly believes in the games. Either way, our father is as selfish as everyone else."

Tara studied his face, traced his angular features down to his black suit with the eight pointed gold star on the lapel, *I don't know. He reminds me too much of Tristan.* She challenged, "So, you wanna leave? Sounded like you're due to bond with Kragen's offspring. Why would you want to leave her?"

He slouched as he offloaded out his secrets, "I was born into a role I don't want to play. When I was ten, I was given the position of player and started running courses. I saw first-hand the lifestyle I was being groomed for and it freaked me out. All pubescent aged players train together at Velvet Lake in the summer months. We're given a chance to flex our eca and to mingle outside of our controller's division. That's where I met my friends, Prynn and Nylah. That's also where Cari noticed me."

He shivered as he said her name, "She's never been shy

about her interest. A few summers ago, Kragen hosted a dinner party at his villa that's on the lake. Father was pleased when Kragen announced to everyone that we would be an ideal match. It doesn't matter that I have no interest in this relationship. Whatever Cari wants, Cari gets. She's a scion. Actually, she's the eldest of Kragen's heirs, which is why Father was eager to promise me to her. He's securing my future with a prestigious position in the Federation. I'm supposed to be flattered to be chosen to continue Kragen's legacy, but I think he sees me as a way to keep Father under his thumb."

"Dank, that's turdz. I'm sorry. Did you explain how you felt to Tristan?" She couldn't bring herself to call him, Father.

Gerrit shrugged sorrowfully, "I begged him to intervene, but he was already reaping the benefits of me being Cari's promised mate. He just gave me luusid to shut me up. So, I learned to stay quiet, to keep my head clear. I learned how to pose like a player." His face seemed to morph as he smiled wryly. Just as suddenly, his face relaxed. He let out a sigh, "It hasn't been easy to play along, but what choice do I have? I reach the age of maturity in June, then Cari and I will forge our bond. I really don't want to be bonded with Cari."

Tara stared at him with astonishment. His conviction was undeniable. *He's trapped here too and wants a way out. But I dunno. Should I trust him? He puts on a convincing act. What if this is a trick?*

Gerrit took a shaky breath and went on, "The way Kragen eyed you tonight. Tara, you don't know what he's like. My own mother was one of his potential mates, and she has since served well in her position to Father as his perfect pixie mate." He rolled his eyes and stooped further, "Kragen's whole Jardin d'Olympia and the Interlude are justified by his desire to procreate the perfect heir. He's obsessed. Cari is being groomed for private channel games. As her mate, I would be pulled into these games, where all our coupling rites would be monitored and available for private viewers. It's heinous! Be wary, Tara. You're of the age of maturity already and he hand picks players for the Interlude. We need to get you out of the Federation before he has that chance."

Tara stiffened as she remembered how Kragen had looked at her. *Is he serious? Fek! I have to get out of here.* She steadied herself and asked, "What about Tristan? What will he do if you leave?"

"That's just it, I don't know. But I really don't care." Gerrit said with desperation, "He has a lot to answer for already with the work he does for Stone and Kragen. Father is responsible for those sniffers being so widely used, for the serums and for me getting hooked. It was his labs that developed them in the first place! He over sees production of all the narcotics that man showed you tonight. That's how he earned his elite status of Platinum Knight Division Ruby rank."

Tara blinked. *Tristan makes those drugs that were pushed on me tonight? And he cautioned me about using. Oh, Source fend! What kinds of games is he playing?* She cautiously asked, "What do you mean Tristan got you hooked?"

Gerrit's expression dropped as he shared, "Luusid can be ultra addictive. Father dosed me when I was resistant to playing games. He kept me dosed to keep me in line with my training. But I was hooked. It's like a foggy blanket that you can't unwrap. Eventually you never want to get out from under it. It took everything I had to secretly ween myself off it and just act glassy-eyed. Most can't cope and are pixilated just to get by." Gerrit locked eyes with Tara, "Father's been a pompous pisser my whole life. A total sycophant. His actions have directly caused the rise of the parks and the Arcade. He doesn't even realize how Kragen has played him since they were young. They'll call me a feebler for quitting the games, but I don't care. I want to leave."

Tristan dosed his own son so he'd play games? Sodz! Would he have dosed me if Ada hadn't manipulated my words? How can he value the games that much? She scrutinized Gerrit again. Her heart raced as she filled with hope, *Gerrit's trapped here like I am. If we work together that would increase our chances, but if we get caught, we'd be collared and that would be the end of it. If we do this, it needs to be timed right. Just like at the Training compound, these serums never last long enough. Still, he's willing to leave and help me find Mama. I'll need to trust he's being honest.*

Tara eyed him seriously, "You have my word. I won't use my eca and try to leave before the Quarter Circuit. You wanna break out? A stick in a bundle is unbreakable."

His face lit up with excitement.

"How big a dose you got?" She asked.

His eyes twinkled and he opened his fist to reveal a vial of blue serum in his palm. Her eyes shot down to the vial, her heart pounding.

"It's a partial dosage, it's what they gave me to come down from the course today. I don't know how it compares to the doses you've had before." He said.

"Acha, do it." She stood up.

Gerrit produced a needlegun that had a slot for the vial.

In the next moment, he had the needle against the flesh of her upper arm. She inhaled sharply as the surge of energy spread through her bloodstream. She felt the energy of Gerrit's lab grow inside her. The chip in her neck hummed in her mind and she remembered her conversation with Tristan from earlier that morning, about it being implanted near her spinal cord.

She shifted her focus away from her chip, the temptation to shut it off was too great, but her fear of what could happen if she did won over. Tara took a calming breath. For the first time in six years she would be able to experience her eca without fear of persecution from the enforcers.

A smile spread across her face. Gerrit's eyes lit up as he gestured towards the screens. Tara closed her eyes and sensed all the devices within her mind. She focused her eca and tuned into the system in front of her.

She navigated the security system and bypassed the security walls with a simple thought.

Gerrit's eyes glowed as the screens switched from code to images, videos and reports on an escape from a work camp five years ago.

He glanced at Tara in amazement and said, "Looks like a group escaped but security tried to cover it up. They didn't recover any of the workers and from this report it looks like they tried to sweep the whole thing under a rug. Security was increased for all compounds. They planted nanokbot detonators and installed motion sensor blasters."

Gerrit scanned the document, "That's it. The group that escaped were known Seds but they aren't listing any names here. Do you think your mother was with them and is with the Seds still?"

Tara shrugged her shoulders and turned her attention back to the system. She focused her eca and the screen switched to an aerial view of the work camp. An explosion tore open one of the buildings. A moment later a group of more than a dozen people jumped out and ran towards the treeline.

Tara paused the video and zoomed into the group. There was a woman with a long dark braid down her back - her mother. Tara's heart floated into her throat. *Mama!* She scanned the group and recognized Bricker, Trace, Aria and Viera among them. *Thank Source you're safe!* She let the video play; a team of enforcers chased after the escapees.

"Whoa! Your mother got out! Dank! What caused that explosion? How did they deactivate the security protocols to escape so smoothly?" Gerrit stared at the screen astounded.

"Yah." Tara said, relieved.

"She's with the Seds. You don't hear much about them on the recreation channels. There have been a handful of these work camp escapes over the years. I know some people who've told me some things. First-hand accounts." He said as if to brag.

Tara didn't look impressed so Gerrit went on, "The Seds went deep underground after the feebler encampment raid. I remember the winter when it happened, that raid where you and your mother were detained. I was young, but I remember Father was busy at his lab manufacturing the chips for all those detained without them. At the time I didn't understand, but as I got older and was thrown into the lifestyle of a player, I realized that these chips are simply a means of control. It's mind-boggling how few people seem to recognize this."

Tara pursed her lips. *I remember that day like it was yesterday. That's when I was cut off from my eca. When I was torn from my family. And that was the day I met Vi.* She gasped as the memory of her friend surfaced. She focused her eca on the computer in front of Gerrit and pulled up the channel for the Research compound. The screen switched to an aerial view of a large grey building surrounded by a large fence and a field similar to the one surrounding the Training compound.

Gerrit looked at the screen, "The Research compound?"

Tara didn't reply as she pulled up the file report on Vi. The image of her friend filled the screen. Her heart sunk as her mind processed the report.

Gerrit read out loud, "Detainee Vi. Level 2 ability status. ECA - telepathy, telekinesis, enhanced sensory-motor ability. Extreme strength demonstration caused structural damage to grade F Training compound. Assisted escape attempt of Trainee Tara (Levelled up to Player). Known family ties to the Seds, father is Zedrik and sibling is Xain. Maintain collared. Considered high risk."

"Is that your friend?" Gerrit asked.

Tara nodded.

"Vi's Zedrik's offspring? He was an infamous player. He played with our father and Kragen back when they were pubescent. Zedrik was levelled up to be a Top Player in Elbion's castle when he reached maturity. He's famous for rage quitting during a Quart-C before Kragen came into power. That video has been banned from view." Gerrit explained with concern, "Father said he stayed at the festival grounds for a time, when he met your mother. He would have been there with Zedrik then. No wonder Father never speaks of him or his time at the festival grounds! After the fires, Zedrik was declared deceased and became the figurehead of the Seds. The Federation condemned any of his supporters and spent over a decade trying to weed them out of the fringe territory."

Tara looked alarmed, "They thought he was dead!?" Her heart sank, realizing she'd revealed the truth to Ada and Tristan earlier that day. "Vi was detained with me and ze sacrificed hirself so I could escape and link up with Zedrik. I failed. I can't abandon hir or any of my other friends from grade F."

"I get it. There's a lot of pieces to this puzzle." Gerrit said as his mind worked through a plan, "Getting you out of the Federation is still my primary goal, then we link up with the Seds. From there we will be able to form a plan to help your friends."

Tara was filled with a surge of hope, "Yah. Get to the perimeter woods and contact the Seds."

She remembered the tablet in her pocket. *That man from the party asked about Vi. Why would he want to know unless he's with the Seds? Was that Xain?*

"Into the woods?" Gerrit asked. "There's nothing out there. Security drones patrol the forests regularly. All along the perimeter of the Federation is nothing."

"Yes." She said.

If that was Xain, he risked coming to that party to give me that tablet. Can I trust Gerrit? I don't even know what's on there. But Gerrit said his goal is to get me out of the Federation. Fek it.

Tara reached into her pocket and pulled out the two tablets. She picked one and held it in her palm, it instantly lit up as she used her eca.

A holovid of her mother appeared. She was looking around anxiously and filling a bag with supplies.

Tara watched as her mother tied a knot on the bag, nodded at someone from behind the recorder and squared herself in front of the lens. Tara held her breath as she prepared for what happened next.

"Tara, my sweet child. I'm sorry I didn't keep you safe. We tried to get to you but failed. If you're seeing this then I know you're free of that training compound. I trust you will be in the company of Zedrik and the others here. You need to trust them to get you safely to the Cullis then they will guide you home."

Sheena's words reverberated around Tara's mind as the

holovid disappeared. She closed her eyes and connected with the tablet again but there was nothing else stored on it. *Mama made it out. Thank Source. I knew it. I need to believe they all made it out.* Gerrit gaped at her in shock.

"Mama escaped with the Seds and left the Federation." Tara said, "Xain was at that party to give me this message. I can't explain it. He was there, then he wasn't. But if we can get to the perimeter woods, we'll find them. I know it's true now because I've seen proof. Mama is alive and waiting for me to come home."

Gerrit closed his mouth and swallowed with astonishment. He ran his hand through his hair, "Let me get this straight. Xain came to the Banquet hall tonight and delivered you that tablet from your mother?"

Tara nodded.

"No one saw him!? I wonder how he did that? Not that it makes a difference, you've linked up with the Seds. Whoa!" His eyes popped wide with the realization. "If we get to the woods, they should be able to trace us with that tablet. I wonder if it could be that simple? Just get into the woods."

"It could be that simple." Tara repeated.

Gerrit blinked and asked, "What's the Cullis?"

Tara hesitated. She chewed her lip, *How do I answer without telling him? What if he tells Tristan or Ada?* She slowly said, "It's hard to explain. Maybe one day I'll introduce you."

Gerrit eyed her sideways before he said, "Here's my idea: after the Quart-C the drone transports fly us out, that's when we make our move. If we're in a transport together you can bypass the drone and steer us to the perimeter. Once we get to the woods, we ditch the drone and seek out the Seds. We'll have a stash of serums from the course that we can use to evade any patrolling enforcers. We won't have long before they suspect you're trying to escape again but maybe if you're with me we can play it off as sibling mischief. It's a long shot."

"Yah. It'll be a fluke," she said.

A Forest Without Trees / JP Solanki-Davie

11

March 9th 2640, new moon

Xain hid in the shadow of a boulder waiting, tapping his foot impatiently. *Chester's right, it's much harder to get outta the party. But, if Bhyt had stuck around I wouldn't get my time with Flo.* He kept his eca focused to maintain the mirage of his invisibility as a transport slowly passed. The line of transports that carried guests to and from the banquet hall were a constant procession. He waited for a gap to dash across the road and scrambled up and over the steep hill opposite. The sounds of the ongoing party rang in his ears as he ran along the bank to the back entrance to find his ride.

There was a group of guardians socializing at the door to the kitchens. Parked further away tucked in the shadow of a boulder was Flo. She was looking down as Xain quietly crept around to the passenger door. Peering through the window he saw Flo drawing on her tablet. Her shoulder length dark brown hair streaked with blue and purple fell over her pale round face as she concentrated on her craft. She wore a clinician's uniform, a simple white jumpsuit that hid her curves. The blue and white patch on her shoulder indicated her status as a care clinician.

Carefully, he waved the door open while he maintained an illusion that the door was still closed. Without a sound he settled into the seat and closed the door.

"Greetings, my sweet blossom." He said as he released his mirage.

"Ahhh!" Flo jumped as Xain suddenly appeared in the transport. She glared at him and smacked his arm, "Oh! Stop doing that!"

Xain chuckled, "But where's the fun in that?"

Flo rolled her eyes and Xain smirked lovingly. They leaned for a kiss and as they pulled away Xain caressed Flo's cheek affectionately. She brought her hand up to his leaning her head further into his hand.

"I missed you." She said softly.

"Same." He took her hand and brought it to his lips, "Let's get to our spot."

She smiled flirtatiously. Xain maintained an illusion around himself to keep himself invisible at the checkpoints while Flo drove. As Care Clinician Flo, she was able to travel above ground throughout the Federation. They travelled down the mountains, along the PUSH towards the Arcade. The clinician apartment complex that Flo lived in was between the Arcade and a security outpost near the perimeter. Before they entered the apartment complex checkpoint, Flo slowed the transport and parked it off the road near some slender cedar trees. Xain jumped out and placed a device on the roof. Instantly, the transport was hidden behind a holo-effect.

Flo retrieved a bag with their supplies and they headed out. Following the stream into the ravine along a familiar path. They used a secret cave for their stolen time together. From the bag Flo brought, they set up the cave with ambilights, an ambifire to keep warm and a padded mat for them to spread out on. There was a basket of snacks and a corked bottle marked with a D^2.

"Have I told you how beautiful you are." Xain said and pulled Flo into an embrace.

She smiled up at him and wrapped her arms around his neck. He leaned in and they kissed.

"Yes. But tell me again." She purred.

~~~

Three scrappers carted away three large bins from the banquet hall. Their plain brown jumpsuits making them seemingly invisible, but each one was rather unique. Berwyn's ear held a dangling earring and was clearly the oldest. Kohl had a partially shaved head with the rest brightly coloured, pink and lime green. And Mo's head was fully shaved which highlighted his bushy eyebrows, he was also covered in tattoos. They descended to the lowest floor where they continued on through a dingy tunnel. Their bins hovered onto a cart and they climbed into the magrail cabin. They travelled smoothly at top speed. Berwyn quietly chewed his pick while the other two cracked jokes.

"Yah, ite. How'bout this one? Did you hear how the zombie bodybuilder hurt his back?" Mo asked.

"No." Kohl replied hesitantly.

"He was dead-lifting." Mo laughed.

"Ha! How'bout this one? Light travels faster than sound, which is the reason that some people appear bright before you hear them speak." Kohl said and elbowed Mo lightheartedly.

"Ha, ha." He shoved Kohl playfully and countered, "What do you call someone with no body and no nose?"

"What?" Kohl played along.

"Nobody knows." Mo chuckled.

"Yah, ite. How'bout this one? What are the three parts of a wood-burning stove?" Kohl asked.

"Wood burning stove?" Mo repeated, "What's that?"

Kohl threw his hands up and rolled his eyes, "Never mind."

"Come on! You know I ain't seen real fire. What's the punchline?" Mo pleaded.

"Fine." Kohl shrugged, "Lifter, legs and poker."

Mo nodded as though he understood, "Oh. Haha!"

Berwyn glanced over his shoulder and said, "You don't get it. You've never gotten a chance to use your poker."

"Oooooh!!" Kohl goaded.

"How about this one?" Berwyn joined in, "You know there's no official training for trash collectors?"

"Trash collectors?" Mo asked, "You mean scrappers?"

Berwyn pulled the pick from his mouth and answered, "They just pick things up as they go along."

Kohl and Mo chuckled.

Kohl lifted his hands up in defeat, "Grand Père wins."

The magrail came to a stop, they deposited the bins of scraps in a large chute before proceeding through a series of intricate tunnels that created a network just for scrappers to use.

They entered the scrapper lounge. There was a racket from music and a group that were dancing and singing along to an old era rap track. It played from a refurbished jukebox; the faux wood shimmered as the band of rainbow lights glowed along its edges.

The dance floor was creaking from their jumping as they threw themselves around. Small round tables filled the rest of the space, each one covered with a delicate table cloth and surrounded by mix-matched chairs. Tea cups on saucers were laid out, each one a different pattern and colour; they were scraps from elite homes that were repurposed by the scrappers. The room was decorated with an assortment of antiques, on the walls were rusted road signs, photographs, small paintings, velvet curtains. There were chipped marble busts that lined a shelf hung over a bulky screen that played a screensaver, a sequence of images from the old era in loop.

Berwyn, strode to the corner where a kitchenette was set up. He filled a kettle with water and turned on the warmer. It clicked and he proceeded to brew a pot of tea. Several scrappers noticed him and hovered nearby. He retrieved a metal box from his bag and opened it beside the teapot. He cleared his throat. Someone paused the track on the jukebox and the room quietened down.

"Heya'll. My niece delivered a tin of her biscuit squares. Come have one and some tea." Berwyn took a biscuit and popped it into his mouth. They passed the tin around, filled their dainty teacups and settled around the tables. Berwyn punched the jukebox and the room filled with music again.

12

March 10th, 2640, waxing crescent moon

    While it was still dark in the early morning, Xain and Flo packed up their bag and hiked back to the transport. They embraced one last time before Flo climbed into the transport and drove away. Xain compulsively reached his hand to the back of his neck and adjusted the band held against his skin.

    He pulled out his hoverstream and set out for the perimeter. From their secret spot he was only a short distance from the shield, but he had to double back several times as he kept running into security. He avoided the enforcers as he navigated the rocky terrain until he reached a sparse forest. Once under the canopy of leaves he relaxed a little. He folded the hoverstream into its shell and straightened up to his full height. Holding a small device in his hand and checking the direction, he ran, working his way between the slender trees toward the perimeter.

    The sound of voices made him freeze on the spot. He focused his eca and blended into the trees around him. He held his breath as two enforcers walked past. One said, "Can you believe we have to walk! Operator Stone won't even let us use our hoverstreams." The other responded, "Shuddup! Just keep your eyes open. The sooner we find the Seds the sooner we can both get outta here."

    Xain kept still until their voices were in the distance again. He cautiously released his mirage and continued slower through the forest. Once he got to a large boulder, he scanned the treeline. Not seeing anyone else, he knelt down reaching his hand under the rock. His finger found the button, the sound of the latch released behind him. Under a moss-covered faux rock was a metal door that revealed stairs leading underground. He quickly checked over his shoulder one last time before he stepped inside and closed the door behind him. The sound of the lock resetting reassured him before he started down the dark steps. The smell of damp earth filled his nostrils as he reached the bottom of the tunnel.

He climbed into the magrail that carried him at top speed through the Seds underground network. When he got to the end, the tunnel opened up into a plemp lined foyer that connected with other tunnels. A small closet appeared after he tapped a wall. He proceeded to unpack his coat and placed everything on a tray on the top shelf. He exchanged his outer coat for a grey wool sweater full of patches, kicked off his boots and slid on some canvas shoes.

With his satchel over his shoulder, he approached the only door in the room and held his hand over the scanner. A robotic voice came through the speaker, "Speak your password"

Xain replied, "Blossom."

There was a click and the door slid open. The long white corridor led to a larger hall with several white doors along one wall. He walked straight through the one furthest to the left and continued through another shorter corridor with several passages that stemmed off from it. He walked to one door and entered.

Inside, was a small kitchen with an ambihearth glowing in the corner. Xain inhaled the familiar surroundings, that morning's breakfast was mixed with the earthen undertones of their subterranean refuge. From under her short brown hair Lyra's dark eyes shot to Xain but her hands remained focused on chopping vegetables. Adeptly, she yielded the sharp knife with her prosthetic arm that attached above the elbow. When the corners of her lips turned up slightly it tugged at the burn scars around her jaw. Her sibling Zara was busy stirring a pot of porridge and Bo was preparing tea while humming to herself, her voluptuous curves were swaying in rhythm. With their heads down at the far end of the long table playing a holovid game were Nester and Liss. A meal bar was clutched between Nester's teeth, the wrapper hung off the end, while he played.

"There you are!" Bo exclaimed.

"Heya! There's a lot more enforcers patrollin' the woods than usual. Had to double back heaps." Xain explained.

Zara caught his attention and winked. She brushed her light brown hair off her face to reveal the gnarly scar that led down her neck to her back and snickered. Lyra pressed her lips between her teeth to suppress her comment. He blushed slightly as he sat down.

Bo placed a mug of tea in front of him and touched his shoulder lovingly, "I'm glad you're home safe."

"Thanks. Hope you didn't wait up for me." Xain replied.

Bo shook her head and squeezed his shoulder. Xain pulled the metal tin from his satchel and handed it to her. She eyed the tin knowingly and pursed her lips.

"And how is Flo?" She asked.

Xain smiled bashfully without reply. Zedrik walked in with Silas and Chester, he spotted Xain at the table and grinned broadly.

"Yow, Xain! How's it?" Zedrik asked.

"We've linked with Tara." Xain said.

Silas slipped next to Bo and they exchanged a loving kiss and a hug. She handed him a mug of tea and he turned to address Xain, "Good job. Now, we just wait until the right time for her to activate the tracker."

Silas patted Xain firmly on the back before he pulled up a chair. Zedrik sat next to Xain on the other side, his long grey locs hung over his shoulders and framed his long face, which was covered by a dark warm brown bushy beard. He bit his cheek as he turned to Xain, his brown eyes asked the question.

"Vi's at the Research compound, but will be at the castle under Kragen's net." Xain said frowning.

Zedrik pulled Xain in under his arm and they hugged tightly.

"You think Vi's gonna be a player?" Chester asked.

"If ze is, that might be more of a break than you'd think." Zedrik said. "With Vi in the castle, then maybe we can finally get a message to hir."

"How's that?" Xain asked and pulled out of Zedrik's hug.

"Do you remember Rainn?" Chester's crystal eyes sparkled with fond memories.

Xain eyed Chester suspiciously, "Rainn. Yah, I remember. Why?"

Zedrik answered, "Rainn is positioned at the castle. She was one of my guardians, back when I was a Top Player in Elbion's castle. After I quit, Rainn stayed linked. She even visited us once at the festival grounds. She and Chester have a –well, wachu call it Chet?"

Chester shrugged and occupied himself with his drink.

"So we have an insider in the castle that can get a message to Vi. That's aces!" Xain said optimistically.

"I'll get a message to Rainn as soon as possible." Chester promised.

"What else did you learn?" Zedrik asked.

Xain took a deep breath and shared what he overheard from the party, "I watched as Tristan showed Tara off and Gerrit lounged with her. I slipped her the tablet on the balcony. Then I followed her to Kragen's stage. He ordered she play the Quarter Circuit and Gerrit took her home."

"Tara's gonna run the Quarter Circuit?" Lyra asked with concern.

"The Cullis needs to be informed." Bo said.

"Kesia will have reached Adrshy by now. She will deliver our message and they will relay it to the Cullis." Silas said reassuringly

"That reminds me, I delivered Bhyt the package when he picked me up. Here's ours." Xain pulled out a black case from his satchel and handed it to Silas, "But gettin' outta the Banquet Hall was a trick. Doubled back heaps on the hoverstream. The fringe is lurkin' with patrols."

Silas pulled out a tablet and scratched the grey stubble on his square chin thoughtfully, "There's heightened activity along the west perimeter. We'll add extra defences, which should scramble their searches."

"How'd they know where to patrol?" Xain asked.

"Most likely grilled Vi or Tara for info," Silas replied with a sigh. "They must know about the wedge. The Feds will know that you're alive, Zed. It's likely they know that Vi's your offspring."

Zedrik stiffened but remained silent.

"Sodz! If that's true, then they'd know about me." Xain said bleakly.

"Maybe even the chip hacks." Chester added.

Xain's face dropped as he realized, "Vi's going to be used against us. Isn't ze? Kragen and Stone know about us and will parade hir on view to force us out of hiding. Will they use Mom too?"

Zedrik nodded solemnly.

"So, what then? Kragen is obsessed with bloodline. Will he bring Vi into his fold? What about Mom? She's in the castle isn't she? Maybe, I could use my eca and slip in. Wait! Why can't Rainn get a message to Mom?" Xain spoke his thoughts as he worried for his sibling and mother.

Chester shook his head and explained, "I'm sorry Xain. Rainn told me that Tristan dropped her off and left, but then it was like Remi just vanished. The domiciliary sector has limited access to the castle towers, only platinum guardians with security access gain entry. Stone personally selects them and Rainn has never made the cut. What we know is Rhyzo have not cared for Remi. Trust me, we've been tryin' to communicate with your mom since she left."

Xain slumped his shoulders with disappointment, "Tristan dropped her off at the castle? That piece of turdz!" He shot an accusing look at his father adding, "You never told me Tristan was the one who took Mom. What happened?"

Zedrik avoided Xain's stare as he said, "I don't know what he said to make her leave. She just told me Kragen needed her urgently at the castle."

"I bet Tristan lied to her. He was too slick at the party. The way he paraded Tara around, like some kind of ornament for his collection. Fek! He's gonna pay for what he did to our family." Xain said with conviction.

"Yes, he will." Zedrik agreed.

Silas caught Zedrik's attention and added, "Now that Kragen and Stone know the truth, I think it's time you tell Xain the whole story."

Zedrik glanced around at everyone nervously and took a deep breath, "You're right. Xain, it's time you know."

"What?" Xain asked.

"I never shared this with you because your mother never wanted people to know. Once your mother left, I couldn't bring myself to tell you because it didn't change anything for you to know." Zedrik went on.

"What are you talking about?" Xain asked uncomfortably.

Zedrik lowered his gaze to his hands, "You were too young to understand and you already had enough reason to hate Stone."

"I was too young to understand, what? Understand that I have my enemy's blood in my veins? What didn't you tell me?" Xain demanded.

Zedrik took a deep breath and held Xain's eyes in his, "Stone violated your mother when she was young. She fled with me to the festival grounds for her protection."

Xain's face dropped in horror, "What!?" He looked around the group, Chester, Liss, Nester, Lyra and Zara were as mortified as he was. Xain swallowed thickly as he realized, "Mom's been in that castle all this time. With him."

Zedrik nodded sadly. Xain knocked his chair over as he jumped to his feet. Overcome with rage and grief he staggered back with tunnelled vision. His breath was ragged, "That fegal!" His stomach clenched violently. He doubled over struggling not to vomit. When the sensation passed, he blew out his breath and looked around. Everyone was watching him with concern. Chester came closer offering him a comforting arm but Xain shoved past him without a word storming out of the kitchen.

13

March 11th 2640, waxing crescent moon

The grey walls of the compound pressed in on Tara as she walked the long corridor. A distant echo beckoned for her to come closer, to follow. She tried to run but felt glued in place. She looked up; there was Vi at the end of the hall. Hir dark eyes pierced into Tara, she suddenly filled with terror. Vi let out a low growl and Tara turned to run away.

Tara was moving as fast as she could. She was trying to escape. Slender trees grew in lines that she wove through. Consumed by the urgency to flee, she kept moving. She looked around frantically.

Which way do I go?

The scene changed and she was surrounded by people with exaggerated smiles that made their teeth seem excessively large for their faces. She bumbled through the crowd. Trying to find an exit, she felt a pull on her arm causing her to fall deeper into the crowd. She spun in a whirlwind until she faced Kragen. He was like a statue; his condescending expression carved into his angular features.

Suddenly, she was back at the compound. She was running through the grey halls in a panic. She could hear the enforcers getting closer. A hiss came into her ear and she spun around to face the grey-eyed enforcer. She gasped.

The scene changed and Tara was in a white room full of monitors and screens. There was a persistent beeping coming from the machines. The room was full of clinicians. A sudden flash and everything went red. Wires were coming out from the back of her head, attached to a computer beside her. The room swirled like water in a drain.

Tara's eyes opened wide, the room still shrouded in darkness. She threw the covers back and rubbed her face, bringing herself back to reality. She looked around with confusion, *How did... What? Where am I? Oh, right. Tristan's house. That dream was strange.*

She drank a cup of water and bathed, dressed in loose fitted grey hemp pants and a relaxed long sleeve linen shirt. She grabbed a blue wool shawl and wrapped it over her shoulders. The view from her window called for her to go outside, *Is it too early to be out of my room? No. I'm not at that compound anymore. I'm a player now. I start training today.* Tara sighed heavily.

Creeping through the dark hallways, she quietly retraced her steps from the day before. Finding her way to the kitchen and slowly opening the door, Tara was struck by the bustle of guardians hard at work preparing the morning meal. She inhaled the freshly baked bread and stepped in further. A guardian carrying a basket of chicken eggs narrowly avoided bumping into her.

"Sorry." Tara shrunk back nervously.

The guardian smiled politely and went about their task. *Guess I'm allowed to be here.* She scooted into a corner and observed with interest. Each guardian wore the same pale blue uniform with a darker blue apron on top, a ruby coloured pin on the chest pocket and their hair tucked under a blue wrap. They moved around the kitchen in a well rehearsed dance, their heads down as they busily attended to their tasks. Tara was mesmerized by them, *I've never seen guardians working.*

At that moment the back door opened and Kohl, the scrapper, entered carrying a large basin. He set it on the floor and announced, "Here to collect the food scraps!"

The guardians paused from their tasks and promptly dumped in their scraps, before returning to their work. Kohl ran his hand through his strip of pink and lime green hair before he picked up the full basin. He glanced briefly at Tara, then left.

The cold outside air wafted in and Tara wondered, *Can I go outside on my own?* She eyed the busy guardians. *Tristan never said I couldn't.* She edged towards the back door timidly. When the guardians didn't react, she waved the door open and stepped out into the fresh dewy mountain air.

Her skin tingled and she gazed around the beautiful scenery. The sky was aflame with red and orange as the sunbeams cut through the clouds. The sheen from the perimeter shield seemed to ripple as the light passed through it. Tara set out for the meadow that Tristan had shown her the day before, the grass crunched from frost as she walked.

Once there, she lay her shawl on the ground and sat down, crossed her legs and rested her palms down on her knees. *Greetings, mountain friends, it's me Tara.* She gazed out towards the horizon; the light danced off the craggy mountains. She quietly sang one of the songs her mother sung to her as a child, "Be still. Feel her in the breeze, blowing with ease, with ease, with ease. Be still. Listen to her voice. Calling to us all, us all, us all. Be still. Trust in her love, flowing with grace, with grace, with grace."

When she finished, she closed her eyes and tuned into the gentle movement of her breath. The inhale sipping in through her nostrils, filling her lungs and expanding her chest, and the exhale emptying her body. After several breathes, her mind raced,

I still can't believe I'm here among mountains. The air is so fresh. It's not fair. It was my fault. I was too slow to get out. Lino would have been faster. The others were counting on me and my eca, and I failed. They're still stuck there, while I sit on top of a mountain.

Tara's heart twinged. She focused to keep her breath steady while mentally reciting a mantra her mother taught her. Yet still, her mind jumped to her worry,

How could Mama be attracted to Tristan? He's so fake. The act he put on last night. Oh, Source fend! That party was heinous. But Gerrit seemed genuine. Can I trust him? I really don't want to be a player.

Tara tried to resettle her mind. She stayed this way for some time as the sun illuminated the sky in a gradient of pinks, oranges, with blues and purples that rippled through the shield. The frost melted from the grass as the sun warmed the morning chill. The regulated weather from the perimeter shield allowed for more comfortable living conditions.

By the time the sun was above the mountain peaks, Gerrit was walking up the grass towards her carrying a pair of lace up shoes. She blinked open her eyes. Taking a moment to let them adjust to the view, before looking at him.

"Heya, Sis." He was smiling down at her, holding the shoes out as an offering. She took them, removed her shoes and started to lace up the new ones. He scratched his head and asked, "What was that you were doing, sitting with your eyes closed?"

She regarded him with surprise and answered, "Meditation. You never seen it practised?" Growing up with her mother and others in her community, meditating was a fundamental practice. She had shared what she knew with those at the Training compound, as much as she could. *Bizarre. So few know about meditation under the shield.*

"Oh, I've heard of that. Um. No, I've never seen it practised." He said uncomfortably. Stretching his arms over head he added, "Come on, Sis. Time to get moving."

They set out at an easy pace. The trail wove around the meadow and through the hills of the mountain. *This place is so beautiful! I feel so blessed to be here right now.* Each turn Gerrit led her around, revealed another mountain expanse that stole her breath away.

14

March 11th 2640, waxing crescent moon

Nestled within the dark granite on another mountain, stood Kragen's castle.

The catle's interconnecting buttresses created a lace like appearance with eight towers thrusting up towards the sky. The walls were high and strong. Most of the new-build technology in the Federation was made from plemp bricks, manufactured from repurposed plastic waste and hemp.

Kragen peered out of a window from his tower room, the beauty of the morning sky did not calm his nerves. He had woken from a nightmare and could not get back to sleep. He had been trapped by thick vines that wrapped around him. And there were flashes of lightning showing a pair of eyes. *Her eyes.*

His mind filled with memories from decades ago at the festival grounds, *That summer I visited Cousin Rawlyn to get away from Ella, and her failings.*

Putting on a costume and pretending I wasn't the Main Operator gave me a chance to escape the duties that I've been carrying since I was 15. Rawlyn understood this and let me camp with him. He had been visiting the grounds for years, since they started. I wanted a piece of whatever made him so happy. Only, I wasn't expecting to meet her.

That day, Rawlyn told me he was heading to the outskirts of the festival grounds. So, I followed him. He'd been so secretive about who he was meeting. Of course I needed to secretly follow him. He went deep into the forest where there were only a few campers. I lost him in the woods but that's where I met Sheena. She was gathering some plants or something when I was wandering through. She stopped and stared at me. Her dark eyes drilled into me. I wanted her.

My costume worked and so did the fake name I gave her, Alban. She was timid but I could tell she was interested. That was the only time I'd ever explored the wilderness, and I fumbled through the thick brush. I bet I could have won her had she not seen past my disguise and recognized me. The way she turned on me still stings. I went home that night. Ella became pregnant. But when it was stillborn, I couldn't. I was done.

I focused on completing Uncle Stone's construction of the perimeter shield. The festival grounds continued to sprawl through the fringe, it expanded beyond Federation territory. We needed to protect the border and put an end to the camps. Tristan was playing his own games with his buddy, and had learned that Zedrik was in fact living on the grounds. So, the summer before the fires I sent Tristan into the feebler camps to entice Zedrik to be a player. I thought having Zedrik on my team again would put an end to the camps.

I had not anticipated Tristan would meet the same woman I had years earlier. I certainly didn't expect her to fall for him. But when I visited to inspect the shield tower construction, I knew he was distracted. Tristan was always a player in the old-era sense. I was curious what woman had enticed him this time. I put on my disguise and tailed him back to his tent. That's where I saw her, Sheena. She smiled at him and they embraced. I couldn't let him have her! Not when she rejected me! Not when my mate was failing to birth my heir. No. If I couldn't have her, then neither could Tristan.

I waited for our next tower inspection to set the trap. Wearing my disguise, I let Sheena see me as Alban walking by. Her curiosity led her to follow me to my meeting with Rawlyn and Tristan. Of course, once she realized Tristan had lied to her, she blew up. Tristan chased after her, but she didn't come back. He had it coming. He'd been chased by too many girls and never got burned. Now, I learn Sheena had Tristan's baby? That twat coupled with her! He has no idea that I saw her first, but I won't let him win again. Not after producing a male heir before I was able to. Not when destiny has gifted me with Tara. Her likeness to her mother is striking. I will enjoy getting closer to her.

But first, there's the problem of Zedrik surviving those fires. He hid himself away all this time, and calls himself a leader? Ha! More like a feebler to the end. He and Remi coupled and had Xain and Vi, that muddies things. Hmmm. Tristan didn't notice that? He truly was distracted by a girl. Pfft! The primary concern is that Zedrik's been colluding with wild people outside of the Federation. Sheena is one of them. She is more dangerous than I originally thought. Who is she really? And where does she come from?

He pulled his plush robe around him more snugly. There was only one person close to him who would know those eyes. He walked out of the tower room and down the spiral stairs, through long corridors until he came to a guarded door.

The enforcer kept his stare directed straight ahead as Kragen nodded at him in his casual attire. He walked through the door to another spiral staircase.

Climbing the stairs and arriving at a dark wood door, Kragen swiftly placed his hand on the scanner to unlock it.

"Dear Remi, it's me, Kragen." He announced.

The room was small but fully furnished with a luxurious bed, sofa and chaise, dining table, a desk with chairs, a bookshelf full of antique books. An ambihearth was glowing, there was a large window opposite, and a door that led to a private bathroom which was closed. The sound of the bathroom door opening made Kragen turn.

"Oh! I didn't expect you this early." Remi said meekly.

He smiled and gestured for her to sit. She did so stiffly, adjusting the hem of her linen skirt around her willowy legs and keeping her eyes low.

"How did you sleep?" He asked.

"As well as can be expected, dear Brother." was her reply.

Kragen sat down on the edge of the chaise, leaned his forearms on his legs and clasped his hands intently.

Kragen held Remi's eyes in his stare and focused his eca. She surrendered as he penetrated her memories. Kragen recalled his encounter with Sheena at the festival grounds, those smoky eyes that had stirred his soul.

Remi's memories shuffled as Kragen watched her mind and waited for the memories to settle.

The scene materialized in his mind, the tall trees and colourful tents, laughing faces blurred past his vision until her face came into focus. Sheena sat in a circle of people, her dark brown hair pulled back by a yellow headscarf. He watched as she laughed and gestured to the person to her right. The group looked oddly dressed, as though they had tried to fit in. Kragen looked around the circle but didn't recognize anyone except for Tristan and Zedrik. Kragen watched as memories flew past his mind, they settled inside a green tent with Zedrik and Remi. Kragen heard Zedrik say, "This could be our only chance. We need to trust the Cullis, take our babies and get outta here. Hush! I know this saps you, but your brother is dangerous."

Remi's memories fluttered by Kragen's mind again, this time paused on Sheena with a grey shawl over her head. She spoke quietly to Remi, "I can't stay any longer, I'll be returning to wilderness tonight with Aria." She handed a small disc to Remi and closed her hands around hers. "When you're ready, seek out the Cullis and give them this. Those ready and willing to leave the Federation only need to cross the expanse."

Her memories swirled away as Kragen pulled out of her mind. She let out a heavy sigh and slumped forward.

Kragen glared at her while his thoughts raced, *Zedrik brainwashed my sister and forced her to live with him in those derelict areas of the festival grounds. They broke all the bonding laws starting their undocumented family. All because he was a feebler player and couldn't handle the games. He was supposed to be dead. They all should have been killed in those fires.* He considered his words carefully, "Remi, when you lived in the festival grounds, did you ever voyage deeper into the wilderness? Did you ever go beyond Federation territory?"

Remi shook her head and kept her eyes low.

"If I hadn't sent for you, would you have gone into the wilderness?" He pressed.

She slowly licked her lips before she spoke cautiously, "I am loyal to the Federation and the legacy of Kharis the Great. Whatever may have happened in the past does not change the fact that I am here with you now. I stand with you, dear Brother."

Kragen pulled on his eca as he spoke sternly, "I want that disc Sheena gave you."

Remi looked stunned, "I gave it to Zedrik before I left the grounds with Tristan."

Kragen's nostrils flared as he used his eca, "I want to know about the Cullis."

Her eyes widened with fear as she felt the words pulled from her mouth, "The Cullis are a group who live outside of the Federation. They are guardians. They only allow those with permission to cross the expanse. They protect the communities thriving beyond." Tears pooled in her eyes, "We met them at the festival grounds and Zedrik formed a friendship with Bricker, who is their leader."

A hardened expression flitted across Kragen's face as he focused his eca, "I want to know if you ever left Federation territory. I want to know if you've ever been in the wild."

Remi's lip quivered as she answered, "I've never left Federation territory. I've never been to the wild."

Kragen huffed and released Remi's mind. He chewed on what she had just told him. *Remi kept her offspring a secret from me. She thought they died in the fires with Zedrik. And she still wouldn't tell me? She's such a liar!*

She kept it a secret that communities existed outside the Federation. She was working with them to leave! This Cullis is a security risk and Sheena is a part of it.

Did Rawlyn know anything about this? The Cullis has stayed linked with Zedrik and the Seds.

What were the Cullis doing at that feebler encampment all those years later? They weren't just meeting the Seds. Why did

Sheena bring Tara with her? She would have been so young. Could it be her eca is unique beyond the Federation as well?

Tara is special. To think what we could have accomplished if we had known who she really was. Tristan doesn't yet understand the magnitude of Tara's importance.

"Have you heard?" He asked candidly, "Tristan made a love child with Sheena."

Remi looked up surprised as he continued, "I met her last night at the party. She has the same beauty as her mother."

Remi's brow creased with worry.

He chuckled, "Turns out she was among the youth detained from those feebler encampments and Tristan never knew she existed until the other day. She'll be the perfect addition to my collection. Don't you think?"

Kragen let his words linger in the room, while Remi fiddled her fingers anxiously. He pushed himself up to stand and strolled toward the window.

Peering down into the private scion gardens, he could see some of his offspring already playing games. He put his hand in his robe pocket and gripped a luusid sniffer.

"For your stash." Kragen said and dropped the sniffer in her lap.

With a smirk, Kragen walked out and locked the door behind him. He messaged Stone to be prepared for his arrival.

~~~

Remi quivered and looked down at the luusid sniffer. She fought her desire to use it. Her mind whirled, *Tristan and Sheena have an offspring? They coupled!? And they were at Kragen's party last night? Was Sheena there? Kragen knows her?*

Easy. Kragen likes to play mind games.

He wanted to see my memories of Sheena. Now, he knows about the Cullis, if he didn't already. When Sheena and the rest headed back to the wild, I wasn't ready to leave, but I knew that's where we were headed. And now Kragen knows it.

He knows about my babies too. He glossed over that

detail. *He knows something he's not telling me. If they're alive, Zedrik could be alive too. Source, may that be true!*

She thought back to the festival grounds, *I didn't see much of Tristan, he focused his coercion on Zedrik. When I did see him snooping around, I hid my babies as best I could. I didn't want him seeing them. Of course, now Kragen knows anyway.*

She let out a heavy sigh, *What was Sheena doing with Tristan? She must not have realized who he really was. He's such a charmer. I didn't know they had developed any real connection, or coupled. She had his baby!*

I should have heeded her words and left when we had a chance. Tristan was playing us the whole time! Had he known Sheena was part of the Cullis he would have told Kragen everything then.

Tristan's always been in Kragen's pocket. I was a fool to trust him when he said I was needed back in the mountains. That evening when he came to our tent, he told me a devastating story that convinced me there was an emergency in the castle and Kragen needed me.

I trusted him and he walked me into my prison. I bet he forgot about me like he forgot about Sheena, distracted by his games and his lab.

She looked down at the luusid sniffer with disgust, a metallic taste filled her mouth. She swiped the sniffer across the room.

"I haven't forgotten, and now I'm done getting pixilated to cope." She whispered harshly, "Tristan has a daughter. Kragen wants her in his collection. He wouldn't want her for one of his concubines, would he?"

Remi caught sight of a group of birds out the window and held her breath, *Kragen's an insatiable brute who is gearing up for a new game.*

15

March 11th 2640, waxing crescent moon

Gerrit had just given Tara a tour of the different buildings on Tristan's residence. The gym, the library, the main house with the laundry building in back near the garage. And of course, Tristan's lab that was partially built into the rock and faced the rest of the property.

"Here is Father's lab." Gerrit told her as they stepped into the plemp brick building with yellow tinted windows. She nervously looked around the room, she sensed the familiar buzz of Ada before she noticed her beside the desk. Tara averted her eyes from Ada's sickly sweet expression.

Tristan sat at the desk and regarded them warmly, "Ah! There you both are. Do you like the residence, my dear?"

Tara nodded but kept her eyes low.

"Player Tara, come in. We have much to cover before your first course." Ada was by Tara's side leading her by her forearm to a chair in the middle of the room. Ada's eyes were sparkling with excitement, "I want to know how you communicate with electronics. So, we are going to give you a low dose of serum and take some readings." She pulled out a tray with a pink serum in a needlegun and a wrist device that she handed to Tara, "Put that on." Tara did as she was told. Ada held her arm and injected the pink substance. "This is to track your vitals."

Gerrit moved around the room and leaned up against the wall. He caught Tara's gaze and mouthed the words, 'Don't fake it.' Tara swallowed thickly, but didn't acknowledge him.

"Let's get started." Ada approached Tara with the needlegun and quickly injected eca serum in her upper arm. Tara inhaled slowly, it was a smaller dose than Gerrit had given her.

But she could feel the tablet in front of Tristan and the hum from several other devices in the room.

Ada walked across the room to face Tara, she tapped her tablet a few times and said, "Let's start simple. Speak to me, telepathically."

Tara blinked slowly. She set her jaw and focused her eca into Ada's mind, 'You gonna tell me your secrets, Investigator Ada?'

Ada's eyes lit up and she replied in her mind, 'No. But how are your reflexes?'

She threw a rubber ball at Tara's head. Tara caught it right before it struck her in the face.

"Whoa!" Gerrit chuckled.

Tara eyed him and held the ball up on her palm. He smoothed out his face and watched her carefully. Concentrating on the ball and removing her hand, the ball remained hovering in the air.

Ada snatched the ball and pocketed it. "Moving on. Let's asses your telekinetic ability." She tapped her tablet a few times then picked up five darts. She handed them to Tara and pointed at a target on the wall, "Throw a dart with your mind."

Tara looked at the darts then at the target. She concentrated her eca and levitated a dart in line with the target. The dart flew across the room into the target just right of centre.

Ada tapped on her tablet again then ordered, "Throw the remaining darts with your eyes closed."

Tara obliged and was surprised to see she had hit the bullseye a couple times.

"Good shot!" Tristan exclaimed.

"Now let's test your electromagnetic ability." Ada said with a nod to Tristan.

He retrieved a game console, which he placed on the table. He removed the hand controller and pocketed it. Then tapped the side and a holovid emitted with several orbs of colour that hovered playfully.

"Do you think you can beat the high score on this game?"

Tristan asked as he pointed to the green orb on the projection.

Accepting his challenge and focusing her eca on the game station, she felt the system hum inside her.

She activated the green orb. The holovid switched to an open range with several targets interspersed among other shapes that moved from side to side.

Tara tuned into the trigger and began to hit the targets, each exploded one after the other. More targets would appear as Tara worked speedily through the levels.

Gerrit stood next to Tara, stunned as the score added up. Ada was in awe as she read the data from Tara's eca. Soon the holovid erupted in confetti and the words HIGH SCORE flashed in red and orange.

Tara paused the game and looked up at Tristan expectantly. Deep in thought, he had his arms crossed over his chest while one hand stroked his chin.

"That's cracked, Tara!" Gerrit laughed.

Tara smiled weakly at him.

"Let's try something else." Ada tapped her screen again and stated, "I have a random image generator; you are going to tell me what image appears."

Tara focused her eca on Ada's tablet. She saw the program running. Ada tapped the screen to start the random generator.

"Bread." Tara said. The image changed again and again, each time Tara spoke, "Chair, Tree, Map, Mountain."

Ada paused the program and asked, "What's the next image going to be?"

Tara focused her eca to take control of the program then said, "Pillow."

Ada tapped the screen and the random generator rotated through images until it stopped on one of a pillow. Ada looked up at Tara impressed. Gerrit let out a small chuckle.

"That's enough." Tristan commanded, "Gerrit, take Tara to train in the gym."

Ada took the wrist device from Tara, "Very well,

Controller Tristan. Until our next session, Player Tara."

Tara eyed Tristan as she stood and followed Gerrit out of the room.

Once they were outside, she grabbed hold of Gerrit's arm and put a finger to her lips. She closed her eyes and focused her eca on Ada's tablet, a smile flit across her face as she sensed the connection.

She tapped into the microphone and could hear the conversation from inside the building in her mind.

"We have enough data for you to be salivating for months." Tara heard Tristan say.

"Hmm, yes. I have already forwarded the data to Operator Stone, and I have no doubt he will want Tara transferred to the Research compound. Or probably the Arcus. It is only because she is your offspring that Our Sovereign Kragen has even considered her staying here with you." Ada's voice resonated in Tara's mind.

"She will stay under my net so long as I have a say in the matter." Tristan said.

"Yes, of course, Controller Tristan." Ada said in her contrived melodious tone.

Gerrit was watching Tara with bewilderment having not heard anything. Tara heard static then felt her connection to Ada's device break.

Gerrit looked at her quizzically, "I know that face. Your serum just ran out. What were you doing?"

She considered him for a moment then said, "Just eavesdropping."

Amused, Gerrit grabbed her arm and led her toward the gym, "Oooh! You little sneak!" He threw his arm around her shoulder and added, "If that's just a demo of what you can do with your eca, you're going to lead the Quart-C!"

16

March 11th 2640, waxing crescent moon

The sound of the door opening startled Vi awake. Ze readjusted in hir restraints as best ze could as Kragen sat down in front of hir. A chill poured down Vi's spine as ze recognized who he was. A vile smirk spread across his face at hir reaction. Without a word he focused his eca to invade hir mind. Vi groaned as ze tried to resist. Ze shut hir eyes tight, turning hir head down to the ground.

Kragen's voice echoed in Vi's mind, 'Lift your head and open your eyes.'

Vi's head lifted as though someone forced it up, hir eyes stretched open. Kragen looked deep into Vi's dark brown eyes. Entering hir memories, he thought about Zedrik and let Vi's memories shuffle in his mind.

The memories settling on Zedrik squatting near a fire, stirring a pot with a spoon and speaking over his shoulder, "Xain, we can't go back to the grounds, the fires were too widespread. You know the feds are blamin' it on us non-conformers. They called it an act of sedition! We're better off if they think we're dead." Kragen heard the small voice of Xain in his mind, "So what we doin'? What about Mom!?" Zedrik hung his head as his face screwed up in pain. He looked at Xain through tear filled eyes and said, "I dunno."

Kragen watched as memories flew by until Zedrik stood around another fire with a group. Kragen heard them discussing the energy pulse and the side effects. The memories fluttered forward again, stopping among chaos. Zedrik was being subdued by an enforcer. Vi's memory showed the view from the ground as ze lay next to hir father in the dirt. The memory stuttered to white tents outside, a stumbling memory of Vi moving towards Zedrik and Xain who each had a patch over the back of their necks. The memory flew forward again and settled at an encampment where Zedrik was hugging Vi and saying, "Be easy my child. The feds seemed more concerned with gettin' everyone chipped than properly identifyin' anyone. Hush! They didn't even recognize me. But, we were lucky to get out together. We'll go deeper into the western fringe with the others. They're already buildin' a new camp."

Memories shuffled forward as Kragen paused on different moments of Vi's life in the encampment with Zedrik. He saw time move forward and Zedrik grow grey hairs. The memory paused, Xain climbed over a pile of plastic, "Yow Dad! Would this work?" Zedrik's head peered out from behind some rubble, "Add it to the collection for Chester to sift through. I hope he's right that he can hack these dank chips."

The memories moved forward again and settled on a quiet conversation under a green tent. Vi was playing with a device to the side of a group talking around a table. Kragen heard a man with burn scars covering his neck say, "Chester says the wedge is holdin' in the perimeter shield. If we keep the frequency low enough, they don't seem to detect it." Another man with a rugged build said, "Soon a scoutin' group'll head out to seek the Cullis and some of us can migrate out to Adrshy."

The memories flew forward again, finally settling with Zedrik sitting at a small table under an orange canopy in an open-air eatery. A gentle breeze was building up the snow on the ground at the base of the tents. Vi's memory was playing a ball game with Xain on a nearby field. They slid on the icy grass, laughing as they did. Kragen watched as the encampment erupted in chaos. Security was raiding the camp. One explosion separated Vi's memory from Zedrik and Xain, ze stumbled into an enforcer's grip, then sat in the back of a security transport.

Kragen relaxed his mental grip. Vi slumped forward into the restraints and gasped for air. He assessed hir silently as ze glared back at him.

An obnoxious grin flitted across his face as he focused his eca again, "Welcome to my division, dear Vi. I want you to feel proud to be a part of my collection. You will earn my gifts as you work to please me."

Vi's chest swelled at his words. Ze tensed hir shoulders as hir heart ached through the forced pride.

"I will enjoy watching you play the games for me. I've always wanted to be an uncle." He leaned forward on the table between them and spoke slowly, "Your mother was overjoyed to know that you survived those fires at the festival grounds. Had we known you and Xain had survived all those years ago, we would have brought you home sooner."

Vi stared at him, speechless. Hir heart ached both with grief and pride. Ze watched helplessly as Kragen stood up without another word and walked out the door.

~~~

"Bravo for your new collection, Nephew." Stone said lifting his glass.

Kragen tilted his glass and savoured the golden liquid. They were in Stone's den at the Research compound. The ambihearth was glowing warmly next to where Stone and Kragen sat. The only window was covered with a heavy burgundy curtain that blocked out the light. The flicker from the ambihearth was the only source of light.

"Yes, I will enjoy watching Vi perform for me." Kragen gloated, "If Zedrik won't give himself up after all this time, then I will use his offspring to force him out. He has been subverting my authority for too long, tarnishing the legacy of Kharis the Great while acting the part of a martyr."

"Quite right." Stone replied, "Vi shared that the wedge was in a rocky area. Patrols will run further subterranean searches of the western perimeter. The woods are empty. The Seds have gone underground."

"Oh! Really? Knowing Zedrik has been stuck in a hole in the ground, hiding like a coward, just makes it all the better."

Kragen chuckled. Stone smirked at his reaction. Kragen went on, "Vi shared the memory of some hack the Seds have devised for the chips. This confirmed what Investigator Ada found, right? We need to find this, Chester. We can't have this spreading."

"Yes, Nephew. I have already been researching." Stone said, "Although, I have yet to find anything on these hacks, I do know that Chester was positioned as a player. He played a few games as a pubescent, but didn't score that well. His mother Bo, was a clinician at the Medbay. His father Silas, was an enforcer positioned in Bright Mountain Park. The whole family fell off the map after the pulse and I suspect they joined the Seds. I've placed a flag on their retina scans, so when they cross a checkpoint we can track them. Once we locate their underground base, we need to cave it in."

"Cave it in? I don't know. Is that necessary? Sure, seal off the wedge, but I thought we could chase them out. The whole Federation would tune in to view! Let's make an example of them." Kragen said.

Cold radiated off Stone in waves as he fixed Kragen with his stare, "You will take your responsibility more seriously. Zedrik and the Seds need to be squashed. They don't deserve to be on view in some game of yours. We need to shut down this wedge immediately. You would be pleased to oblige."

"Yes, Uncle." Kragen said and compulsively sipped his drink. He eyed Stone worriedly, "What of these communities in the wild, that Tara spoke of? Vi showed me the Seds set up a cmap in the wild called, Adryshy. Remi showed me that Sheena was part of a group called the Cullis. Supposed guardians of communities beyond the expanse."

Stone cleared his throat and picked a piece of lint off his dark pants, "Kragen, you always get so worked up. There's no fire. I doubt there is a large community in the wild, but we can't afford to discount it. You will remember, I was there with your Grandfather Kharis when he was injured in the wilderness." He paused as a shadow moved across his craggy face, "We had taken a surveying trip around the perimeter. The Federation declared sovereignty over land from the last stragglers of the climate refugee camps. We had ventured out on foot and it was there in the deep woods, the storm started and we saw it. I still don't know what it was. A beast is what we told the children to keep them from venturing into the woods, but you know I saw something that day, your father saw it too. The storm was brewing and there we were, caught in a heavy rain, with it lurking through the trees. The troops openly shot at it, and chaos broke out. There was a horrendous flash flood. That's when your Grandfather fell. Your Uncle Clifton perished. Almost all the troops were killed as the water rushed into us. The beast vanished and we collected our survivors. We carried Kharis the Great back to the Federation camp, but he died shortly after from his injuries." Stone held Kragen in his intense stare, "That thing is out there, Kragen. We need to hunt it down and destroy it."

"Yes, we will." Kragen returned his uncle's intensity, "Sheena is one of them, and so is Tara. Tristan has no idea that she will be the key to our success. Her eca is intriguing. Did you see the data that Investigator Ada collected?"

Stone nodded, "I am eager to test her eca."

"I am eager as well." Kragen smirked and dropped his eyes into his drink, "Tristan won't have any choice but to agree to my terms after the obstacles I have planned for the 1st Quarter Circuit."

"Quite right." Stone agreed. He relaxed back in his chair and asked, "What of Remi?"

Kragen carefully formed his next words, "Remi has had ample opportunity to prove her allegiance to the Federation. She is a traitor who broke the law and bonded illicitly with Zedrik. They produced two undocumented offspring! I don't trust her. She's still blind to Zedrik's blatant control over her. He forced her and all this time she still defends him!? She willingly withheld the fact she had two offspring! The example I could have made of her if I had known at the time..." His eyes darkened with his unfinished words. He took another sip of his drink and licked his lips bitterly, "She has been a thorn in my side. Keeping her in the castle all these years has been a strain. If she would have just agreed to play, to opt-in. She could have assumed her role with grace." He let out a frustrated sigh, "She doesn't even view them! She's always shied away from the spotlight despite her theatrical talents. Her lack of participation in the games shows her true nature. She's worse than a feebler, she's conceded her position."

Stone remained silent as he listened to his nephew vent. A chill seeped off him from his eca that pressed his will on those who felt it.

Unlike Kragen, Stone's ability did not directly force someone to speak or act to his will. His eca let him steer another person's eca, and he could drain one's eca through his breath. It was through Stone's eca that the chips were developed and the anti-eca technology.

Kragen had always depended on Stone's guidance since he was a young boy and especially after his father died. Stone took his role as caretaker seriously; raising the offspring of his older brothers, Elbion and Clifton, was his primary concern. He had been waiting patiently for the right opportunity to remove Remi from her tower cell. Now was that time.

"With Vi in my collection, I am done dealing with Remi. I can use Vi to get to Zedrik and lure him out of his hiding hole." Kragen went on as he stared into his drink, "Remi will stay where she is until after the Quarter Circuit. Then if you want her to still move in with you at the Arcade, so be it. Your direction always kept her behaviour in check. She'll no longer be given a choice whether she is to partake. She will play the role she was born to play."

17

March 12th, 2640, waxing crescent moon

Time ceased to make sense for Vi, ze was exhausted from too many sleepless nights locked in the windowless cell.

Ze hugged hirself tightly and squeezed hir eyes shut. Hir heart ached with grief, hir stomach was queazy, ze was overwrought with anguish, *Stone knows where to look for Dad and Xain, if they find them it'll be my fault. Ugh! They know about the hack for the chips and the wedge. Fek! They've got powerful eca! I couldn't stop them.*

Lifting hir heavy head ze stood stretching hir stiff body. Ze eyed the recorder in the top corner of the room as ze paced to keep warm and to not give in to boredom or anxiety.

Vi's memories wandered to hir mother, *I was so young when she left. I was sleepin' and she was gone when I woke up. Xain reminded me of her as we grew, but I was so little, I barely remember myself. Dad never talked about her. He was still heartbroken that she left.* The thought made Vi's heart hurt. *Why would she abandon us like that? Leavin' Dad alone? Maybe she never really loved Dad.* Vi shook hir head. *No! She loves him. Kragen twisted her, like he does everyone. Like he did with me.*

Kragen's voice echoed in hir mind, *I want you to feel proud to be a part of my collection. I will enjoy watching you play the games for me.* Vi shivered. Ze knotted hir hair back and continued to pace.

He's gonna make me play his games and there's nothin' I can do to stop it. I'm supposed to feel proud to be in his collection. Ugh! Am I actually feelin' that? I'll be forced to perform for Kragen's viewership. With a smile on my face, no doubt. I wonder, will Mom be there?

Vi stopped and leaned hir forehead against the wall. Ze tried to block out hir thoughts.

The sound of the door opening made hir jump and turn around. Three enforcers rushed into the room followed by Operator Stone. Hir heart leapt into hir throat and ze braced hirself as they came at hir from each side.

Grabbing Vi's arms and holding them behind hir back they swiftly laid hir onto hir stomach. The third enforcer knelt on Vi's legs pinning them down. Ze let out a grunt and tried not to struggle.

"Attach the electronic ankle cuff." Stone ordered.

The device was strapped around hir right ankle. There was the sound of a lock tightening then a loud click. The enforcers yanked hir to hir feet.

"You will be transported to Our Sovereign Kragen's castle. That ankle cuff is a monitoring device. It also will prevent you from leaving the castle grounds without permission via an electric shock." Stone sai.

"Furthermore, it is now programmed to subdue you if needs be, when you've been given an eca serum, which means you will no longer be required to wear that suppression collar."

An enforcer removed the collar and Vi took a deep breath in as it was lifted away.

"Let's test it to make sure that it's working." A wave of cold radiated off him.   The two enforcers let go of Vi and Stone tapped his wrist device. Vi screamed as a jolt of energy surged through hir body. All hir muscles went into spasm. Stone tapped it again and Vi crumpled to the floor, unconscious.

"It's working." He said.

The enforcers grabbed Vi and dragged hir limp body out of the room. They carried hir all the way to a transport and strapped hir in before ze regained consciousness. When ze realized what was happening ze began to struggle.

Stone, who stood at the door of the transport, said, "Uh-uh" and gestured toward his wrist device.

Vi became still, eyes wide with fear. Stone nodded his

head approvingly, then slammed the door shut. Vi was left in darkness.

The transport carried Vi for the better part of a day. It was nightfall when they finally arrived at Kragen's castle.

When the door opened two enforcers removed Vi's restraints and steered hir into the lower levels of the castle.

They marched quickly through the cool dark hallways until they reached a small cell.

There was a square window high on the wall, a sink and floor toilet in one corner and a thin mattress in the other.

A clinician stood with a case hovering beside her, a scanner in her hand.

The enforcers shoved Vi into the room and left. Vi waited nervously while Stone leaned his bony shoulder against the door frame and crossed his arms over his chest.

"This is your Care Clinician, Max." He said, casually gesturing to the clinician.

Max approached Vi with a needlegun and a few vials. She withdrew samples of blood and placed them in the case.

"Provide a urine sample." She handed Vi a lidded cup and averted her eyes.

Vi tried to ignore Stone's stare as ze walked to the floor toilet in the corner of the room.

Ze pushed away the feeling of humiliation and undid the crotch of hir green jumpsuit. Sealing the cup and handing it back to the clinician, ze kept hir eyes low.

Max waved the scanner from Vi's head down to hir feet then looked at the readings.

"When was your last menstrual cycle?" Max asked.

Vi shrugged.

"Alright. I have everything I need." Max said.

After placing everything in the case, Max shot Vi a stiff look and left.

Stone studied Vi's face as waves of cold seeped off him. Vi's ears burned while the rest of hir was frozen.

"You resemble your father." Stone said with distaste,

125

"Your father is a traitor to the Federation. But you will not be held accountable for his treason. Our Sovereign Kragen has declared that you will only be responsible for your misdeeds and for now, your debt will be worked off as a player. Your first course will be in the Grand Hall next week. Our Sovereign Kragen would like to see a demonstration of your strength, for himself."

With that he closed and locked the door.

Vi looked around the small room, it was dimly lit from a green bulb by the sink and the moonlight from the small window.

Ze walked over to the sink and washed hir hands, then hir face. Ze leaned against the sink and let the water drip off hir face along with hir tears.

Well, I'm here now. A total effn mess! When will this be over? I had no guess this is where I'd end up when we made our plan. I wonder what happened to Tara. I can't tell what was true and what was them playin' mind games with me. Ada said, Tara told them about Dad and Xain. But then she got caught.

No! Tara had to have made it out. Source, may it be true. Ze splashed hir face again then let hir locs hang lose.

Vi gazed at the moon as it poked out from the dark clouds over the mountain scene.

Ze sighed heavily and lay down on the thin mattress. Laying there sleeplessly, hir mind continued to race, *Kragen's gonna have me be a player in the Grand Hall? That will be visible on the public channels. He's gonna use me to entrap Dad. Fek! I'm bein' used as bait. What can I do to stop him?*

A knock on the door pulled hir from hir thoughts and ze sat up abruptly.

A stout woman with warm dark skin and tightly braided hair walked in with a kind smile on her face. She was carrying a tray with a steaming bowl on it and had a blanket under her arm.

"Heya, Vi. I'm Guardian Rainn. I brought you some soup. You must be hungry." She placed the tray on the floor next to the mattress where she had placed the blanket. She stepped back and knelt down on the floor.

Vi took the bowl sipping the soup and enjoying the warmth running down hir throat.

"There." Rainn said once Vi had finished. Her brown eyes twinkled as she added, "You have your dad's eyes."

Vi looked at her startled, but before ze could ask a question Rainn explained, "I've been a guardian in this castle for a long time. Back when your dad was a top player and things were different, Zed and I had become friends. He introduced me to Chester." Her eyes dropped and she blushed.

She then cleared her throat and became serious. "That's who contacted me and told me you were coming. Your dad knows you're here. I can get messages to him for you, and he has a message for you."

Vi's eyes widened in surprise and ze rose to hir knees. Ze reached out hir hands, Rainn took them in her own and squeezed back.

"What?" Vi asked in a whisper

"They want you to know they're working on a plan and you're not alone in here." Rainn said warmly, "I've gotcha, kid."

~~~

Operator Stone's boots echoed while he marched. With a short nod to the enforcer guard, he climbed the north tower.

When he arrived at a dark wood door, he placed his hand over the scanner.

The door opened and he quietly entered.

Remi was sitting by the large window looking out at the night sky. She didn't hear Stone walk in.

There was a collection of poetry books beside her. Her eyes were distant as she was lost in thought, *The sky is staying light much longer. Is it already another spring? Yes, of course the next Quarter Circuit approaches. Wow!*

The stars are really bright tonight. Where's the moon? Hmmm, the moon was dark the other night, so it is waning now. Still, it must be out there somewhere.

She sighed deeply as her thoughts shifted to her love, *I*

wonder if Zed can see the moon and stars from where he is?

He always told me that he would love me as long as there were stars in the sky. He's alive. They all are. They have to be.

Stone remained silent as he watched Remi. His eyes lingered over her dark silky hair, the colour reminded him so much of her mother, Isolde. Her hair, her eyes, her skin. When they were young, Stone and Isolde would play and talk of a future together. It was a young love, but not meant to be.

An involuntary twitch ran through his neck at the thought of his dead brother's late wife.

He focused his eca on Remi. Her eyes widened and she let out a gasp. The familiar feeling of Stone invading her mind made her sit bolt upright.

'Remi, it's time for your walk in the garden.' He commanded telepathically.

Remi stood up immediately. She avoided looking up. She grabbed a shawl from the back of the chair and hugged it tightly around her shoulders.

After many years of solitude in the castle, she heeded her uncle's words without hesitation.

Stone ushered her in front of him, he guided her with a hand on her low back.

He led her down the tower stairs and straight out to a garden enclosed by high walls. The spring bulbs were spotting the garden with flecks of colour and even at night the trees were showing their young leaves.

Remi breathed in the crisp spring night and looked up at the starry sky.

The crescent moon was above the tower that was her prison. The sight tore at the scars of her heart. She dropped her eyes and pushed away her feelings.

She was guided through the dimly lit garden to a bench. Her breath was shallow as Stone sat next to her.

"This year marks the seventy-fifth anniversary since your Grandfather Kharis the Great founded the Federation." Stone said casually, "The festivities and courses will be monumental. If you play your cards right with Kragen, maybe you could attend a party this year. I have a feeling you will want to be cooperative and eager to play along when you see the new player in his collection." A wicked grin spread across his face but Remi remained silent with her eyes lowered.

"I know you don't like to watch the screen in your room," Stone continued, "but you won't want to miss the channels on the days that lead up to the Quarter Circuit. Kragen has acquired a new player that may interest you."

Stone leaned back on the bench and crossed his bony knees. "Turns out Tristan isn't the only one benefiting from his daughter's spectacle at the Training compound. Her accomplice will be a valuable asset in the Federation's fight against the Seds."

Remi's curiosity was piqued. *Could that be one of my babies? Why else would he tell me?*

She tried her best to keep her face emotionless as she spoke in almost a whisper, "Sounds like Kragen will be pleased."

Remi stiffened as Stone's arm draped behind her and rested on the back of the bench. He leaned closer, inhaling her scent.

His breath was hot on her skin as he spoke in her ear, "Yes, he will. You should know, Kragen has given his blessing for you to join me in the Arcade. I will be taking charge of your care."

Remi closed her eyes consumed by the familiar numbness of her body. They were both quiet.

Stone tilted his head toward her and stroked his fingers under her shawl to reveal her soft skin.

Sitting motionless, she was trying not to feel anything. *No! I cannot despair. Not when my family might be alive. Though she be but little, she is fierce.*

18

March 15th, 2640, waxing crescent moon

"My dear, you are already passed the age of maturity." Tristan explained, "The bonding laws state that players in the recreation sector must bond with a mate within the year they turn 18. You'll be 19 before the next round of bonding games where a mate would be chosen for you."

Tara filled with worry as Tristan informed her of the importance for players to bond with a desirable player. Gerrit wore his characteristic wry smile like a mask as he stood stiffly beside her in Tristan's den.

"Typically, if a player fails to secure a mate in the games, they are demoted to a maintenance worker, building and repairing courses." Tristan said, "Do not fret, you have been granted special consideration, which provides me some extra time to find you a suitable match. It will be a challenge with you not being groomed properly, but I've secured Gerrit to forge his bond with Scion Cari, I am certain I will secure a mate for you."

Bile rose in her throat at the thought. *A mate? Ew! No! Gerrit was right, I'm gonna be pushed to bond.* She kept her eyes low and tried not to look at Tristan's fake expressions.

"Now, onto the topic of your reproductive health." Tristan went on, "All players are assigned a personal care clinician. Gerrit, for example, visits with his care clinician each month. Once he bonds, his reproductive health will be monitored to ensure proper coupling. This is all part of the position of a player, my dear. Your reproductive health is paramount to Our Sovereign Kragen's vision for the future of the Federation."

Tara's body involuntarily shuddered, as the reality of life as a player in the Federation weighed down on her, *How does*

Gerrit keep up his façade?

"Your menstrual cycle will be monitored and games assigned according to your cycle. Typically, you would not be running a course without knowing when your next period will start," Tristan cleared his throat, "Your care clinician will arrive shortly and will answer any of your questions."

~~~

Tara found herself waiting in her room gazing out the large window. The sun was low in the sky and shimmered off the snow-covered mountaintops, the clouds were painted pink and purple. Tiny orbs of light sparkled under the sheen of the shield.

She let herself get lost in her thoughts while watching the day give way for the night. *What am I doing here? I don't belong here. I don't want to be a player. I don't want to bond with anyone. Why is Tristan in such a hurry to push it? Can he really expect me to play along with a smile on my face? My only hope is to get out with Gerrit. I've got no choice.*

There was a knock on the door.

Tara took a slow steadying breath before saying, "Yah?"

Tristan's voice carried in, "Tara dear, this is Care Clinician Flo. She will oversee your healthcare program."

A well-rounded woman followed Tristan into the room. She wore a crisp white hemp uniform, her dark hair with blue and purple streaks was pulled tightly into a bun. She smiled kindly at Tara as she strode over to the desk and set up a case.

Tristan lingered in the doorway as Flo gathered a few empty vials, a small cup with a lid and her scanner. She gestured for Tara to come forward, but Tara remained a statue.

Tristan cleared his throat, "Would you like me to stay?"

Tara shot him a mortified look, but it was Flo who spoke, "No need, Controller Tristan. This consultation is not complicated. I will meet you in the main foyer when I am finished with Player Tara."

Tristan bowed and shut the door as he left. Flo let out a sigh and flashed Tara a reassuring smile.

"Some men just don't understand." She gently said, "Greetings, Tara. My name is Flo," She gestured again for Tara to come forward.

Tara kept her eyes low as she approached.

"Here, we'll get through this business, then we can have a little chat. Please provide a urine sample." Flo held out a cup.

Tara shuffled to the washroom and returned shortly after, her eyes still low.

"Thank you." Flo said and placed the sample on a scanner in her case. She turned back to Tara with a needlegun and a few empty vials, "I need some blood samples. Please, sit down."

She gestured to the chair where Tara could rest her arm on the desk. Tara sat hesitantly and offered her arm. Flo drew the blood samples and inserted each one into a device in her case. She scanned a code on the side of each sample and placed them all methodically on a tablet set out on the desk. She tapped the screen and placed the samples away, before pumping sanitation gel onto her hands from a tube on the side of the case.

Turning to Tara once again, she held up the scanner, "I just need to run this scanner over you. Alright?"

Tara nodded and watched Flo wave it over her body. When Flo was finished, she looked at the screen and scrolled through the data. Her brow furrowed with concern at the readings.

"They really just barely kept you nourished, didn't they?" Flo sighed.

Tara thought back to the grey sludge she'd eaten for years and shuddered at the memory.

"They recycle food scraps from the higher levels to be produced into meal drinks and other supplements for the lower grades of the Boost Academy and the Manufacturing Division. The Federation's version of the food chain." Flo explained with a hint of sarcasm in her tone, "Players require more calories for their games, therefore they receive the highest quality of food."

Oh, Source fend! I saw that scrapper collect those kitchen scraps. They processed it into the sludge I was forced to eat all these years!? Tara's worry grew with this information, *Everyone I left behind in grade F will be eating my scraps from Tristan's table.*

Flo pulled out a smaller case with different pills inside, selected several pale pink ones and transferred them into a smaller bottle. Again she used the scanner and took a log before she handed them to Tara.

"These pills will help your vitamin levels. I want you to take one with each meal until the Quarter Circuit." Flo explained, "The initial scans of your blood show your levels are a touch low across the board. The urine sample looked good though, no signs of infections. My main concern is to keep you hydrated on the course and your nutrients in check. Game rules allow for you to have enough meal bars and water for the duration. It's vital that you remember to drink and eat. The vigour and endurance needed means your system will be pushed to the limit. When you return from the Quarter Circuit, I will reassess your levels. As your care clinician it is my responsibility to keep you healthy and keep you playing."

Tara looked down at the small bottle of pale pink pills and closed her fingers. *I've never had a clinician treat me this kindly before.* She lifted her eyes to Flo and nodded gratefully.

Flo pulled up a chair to be at the same level as Tara. She reached into her jumpsuit and pulled out a small parcel wrapped in a cloth.

"This is a family recipe. Eat it now, it will help." Flo offered it to Tara.

Tara hesitantly took it and unwrapped a square biscuit. *It's a biscuit?* She glanced at Flo, said, "Thank you," and shoved it in her mouth. It was soft, not too sweet, and almost melted on her tongue.

"Now, we need to discuss your menstrual cycle. Can you tell me when you started your last cycle?" Flo asked gently.

Tara flushed and she bit her lip before answering, "I dunno. It was hard to track it there. I think I'm due soon? But I really don't know." Tara felt like a dolt for not knowing more about her cycle. She had started menstruating in the wild and her mother had taught her the importance of caring for herself throughout her cycle. Once she was taken to the Training compound, she was denied this consideration. She, along with all the others who menstruated, struggled to endure the sanitation bathing rooms.

"It's alright. Priorities are different for players. When it starts, we will begin tracking it. For now, we will focus on getting your levels up and get a base line for your cycle." Flo took a deep breath and chose her words carefully, "I've reviewed your file from the Training compound. I'm sorry for what happened to you. Also, I'm sorry there will be no reprimand for those enforcer's actions."

Tara's eyes dropped and her shoulders tensed.

"If you ever need to talk, I am here to listen." Flo said kindly. She leaned forward and spoke quietly, "I realize this is all new for you, and that so much as changed so quickly since you came under Controller Tristan's net. Life as a player is drastically different than that of a trainee, especially from grade F. The Federation games can be a head trip in themselves. Add in your status as daughter of an elite controller, and you're going to be playing serious effn mind games. Just remember Tara, whatever happens, I am here to support you."

Tara was filled with an odd sense of safety. She looked into Flo's soft brown eyes with gratitude.

~~~

Vi stood awkwardly as Max, ran the scanner over hir body. Two enforcers stood guard at the door watching Vi closely.

"You said your period is usually this light?" Max asked.

Vi nodded.

"Alright, that's all I need." Max said and left.

The enforcers stepped in and took hold of Vi's arms.

One leaned in, she whispered in Vi's ear, "You know, enforcers aren't like players. We don't care if you can reproduce, we just like to have fun."

Vi flared hir nostrils in disgust as they snickered. Ze was

led through the castle down into the dungeon to one of the eca research rooms.

Waiting for them was Stone, who was reading from a tablet and took no notice of them.

Vi was steered to a table with restraints. The sight made hir skin crawl and ze shifted hir weight back.

"Whachu you gonna do?" Vi asked.

Stone looked up annoyed with hir comment. Cold radiated off him as he gestured to the table harshly.

The enforcers proceeded to shove Vi to the table and strap hir down. Hir breath quickened with fear. A clinician approached with a helmet and another had an eca serum loaded in a needlegun.

"We will be testing your eca. Your strength is obvious, but I am curious about the extent of your enhanced sensory-motor ability. This helmet will induce your eca and provide us with what we want to know." Stone explained.

The helmet was placed over Vi's head, wrappings were fastened around hir neck and everything was secured to the table. Vi's eyes darted to the clinician with the needlegun and held hir breath with anticipation.

"Let us begin." Stone stated.

19

March 25th 2640, waxing gibbous moon

Tara was sitting with her friends from the compound, a bowl of bland mush in front of her. She felt sick. It was eerily quiet except for the increasingly audible click-clack sound of Caretaker Bridget's shoes. A glint caught Tara's eye and she looked down the long table. The glint grew into a bright light that hurt her eyes.

She was walking an endless spiral hallway. Her feet felt like they were trudging through mud. The walls were grey except for the circular windows showing a greasy sky. Tara felt someone creeping up behind her. Panic rose from within her chest. Enforcers' voices were getting louder. She kept moving forward, feeling lost but the urgency to flee consumed her. She was running as fast as she could, searching the crowds of terror-struck people in the market. She felt a strong wind blow into her, she fell forward.

Mama! Where are you?

Tara was running away from the compound. The smell of fresh air fuelled her hope. The forest drew near. She could see people waiting for her among the slender trees. A whisper came through the wind, patience. She kept running towards the forest until it changed into a rock cliff.

She turned around. She was at the base of an escarpment. Somebody was there, his grin large as though he wore a mask. He was jumping from one foot to the other in a strange dance. The sky was full of colourful lights. A low growl sent a chill through her body and she spun on her heel. Vi was glaring at her. Hir eyes solid black and ze barred hir teeth.

Vi?

Tara was running. Dodging the rows of slender trees, trying to get away from the enforcers' chase. Their snickers echoed off the rocks. There was a flash of light from her left and she was tackled to the ground.

The scene changed and Tara was in a white room full of monitors and screens. A persistent beeping sound was coming from a machine behind her. There were clinicians everywhere reading monitors and hovering over her with scanners. She looked down at her body strapped to a medical table. A clinician injected a blue vial into the IV. She stiffened at the sight of a bone-thin grey-haired man standing at the foot of the table watching her. His hazel eyes drilled into her and everything faded to white.

Tara woke with a start, sitting upright in bed.

Her heart pounded in her chest as she heaved in deep breaths. *What's with my dreams?* Throwing back the covers she stood up stretching her body. Her muscles were aching from the daily endurance training. She bathed, dressed and drank some water, then poked her head into the hallway. *It's still dark out. I can probably sneak outside before others wake up.*

She found her way to the kitchen and entered cautiously. A guardian came up behind her with a bag of flour.

Startled by her closeness, Tara jumped back, shoulders tense and eyes low. T

he guardian went about her business and Tara relaxed a little, *This ain't the compound. I'm allowed to be here.* Carefully, she wove her way through the busy guardians to the back door.

She walked to the meadow for her meditation practice. The sun was still below the horizon, the sky shrouded in clouds. The air was cold so that her breath fogged.

Her mind was unsettled. It replayed her concern for her friends, her fears about the Quarter Circuit, her hope of escape, mixed with her distrust of everyone around her.

When she noticed her mind distracted from the present, she would take another deep breath. *Inhale one, two, three, four. Exhale one, two, three, four.*

It was there, in the meadow where Gerrit found Tara. He

approached her quietly as he had the other mornings. Only today he sat down beside her and copied her breathing.

The sun remained hidden behind the clouds as the soft light filtered through the shield. Before Tara opened her eyes, she listened to the bird song.

She could feel Gerrit's presence and hear his breathing beside her. *I really hope he's not setting me up.* Tara opened her eyes and glanced over at him.

"Morning." He said with an oddly calm expression. "I've never breathed like that before." Tara lifted her eyebrow at him, amused by his reaction. He shrugged and stood up, "Come on, Sis. Players need to run."

They ran through the mountain trails and continued down a different trail until they were in a small valley.

An elaborate wooden agility obstacle course was erected among the rocks and trees. Tara eyed it nervously. Tristan and Ada were by the obstacle's start. A short guardian stood to the side, holding a tray with two tall cups of green smoothie.

"There's my progeny!" Tristan called, "Did you have a good run?"

"Yah." Gerrit replied.

The guardian offered them each a smoothie, Tara gratefully accepted. At first, she sipped the drink. But as the sweet flavour hit her tongue and her hunger overtook her, she chugged the whole thing in one go.

The guardian collected the cups, Tara wiped her mouth with the back of her hand. She noticed that Tristan watched her closely. *Why does he look at me like I'm a sapling?*

She turned her attention to Ada who observed her keenly with that unconvincing smile. *Ugh! Her look is so much worse.*

"We have a lot to cover today, so let's cut right to it. Player Gerrit, I want you to run the course, then Player Tara you can follow. Once on the other side we will go over some defence drills in the clearing." Ada said.

Tara watched Gerrit, who had just been injected with eca serum, move smoothly through the course.

He jumped from one platform, flipped to the next, swung from high bars and balanced along a high beam. Once he made his way back to the start he was panting.

"Your turn!" He said.

Ada handed Tara a wrist device to track her vitals, which she put on. Ada pulled out two vials, one pink and one blue.

Tara gritted her teeth as she was injected. She immediately tuned into the chip at the back of her neck along with the others, including the tablets in Ada's and Tristan's hands.

As she approached the first obstacle, Tara looked up with hesitation at the large wooden trunk that she needed to pull herself up to, high above her head. *If I use my eca I can do this. But I have to let them see me. If I try to hide it, they'll know.*

"Just do your best. Remember this is to help you prepare for the real course, which will be an endurance course as much as anything." Tristan said encouragingly.

The real course is putting up with these dank games. Tara thought. She focused her eca and gripped the wood. She stepped her feet up and in one fluid motion pulled herself up.

As she jumped, she could feel her mind bend the course for her to reach it with her small frame.

From a viewer's perspective, Tara was moving with confidence and grace. When she reached the end Tristan applauded her loudly.

"You aced that! You truly are full of surprises." He said.

Ada led them to the far side of the course where there was a clearing with large boulders scattered around. Ada motioned that they each climb a boulder, which they did.

She tossed them each a long wooden staff. Tara gripped her staff looking down from the tall boulder she had just flashed. Her heart was beating fast but she felt razor sharp as the serum ran through her body.

Gerrit was on the boulder to her right, he was in a wide stance, spinning and thrusting the staff around him.

Mesmerized by his movements, Tara only noticed at the last moment when the resin balls flew towards her head.

Instinct and muscle memory took over, she shifted her weight and spun the staff to block three of the balls. She crouched low and ducked the last one. In the next moment another volley of balls came towards her.

Tara pivoted and spun the staff again. She continued to block the balls with her staff and from the corner of her eye, saw Gerrit was doing the same.

Tara crouched down low as a ball flew past. Breathing heavily, her eyes darted around the small clearing until she could trust there were no more balls.

She straightened up and noticed Ada keenly immersed in her tablet. *C'est ça. I can't hide anymore.*

Ada pointed to the ground in front of her and ordered, "Come here."

Tara watched as Gerrit swiftly performed a forward flip off the boulder and performed a series of flips until he landed on the ground in a crouch. He stood and walked up to Ada without missing a beat.

Tara's eyes were wide with shock at Gerrit's display, *What the fek was that?* She darted her eyes to the ground, *Serum or not, I won't jump down from here. It's way too high up.* She rolled her shoulders back, tossed the staff down then lay on her stomach to swing her legs over the side of the boulder.

Carefully, she lowered her body, she reached out with her toes for a foot hold. Her body bent to the shapes needed to safely descend, her eca guided her to sense the rock until her feet safely hit the ground.

"You may not be a trained player, my dear, but you are a strong climber." Tristan's voice rang out in the clearing.

"Your unconventional approach will surely draw a large viewership. Don't doubt yourself, don't hesitate. Use your instincts during the Quarter Circuit and you will play a most excellent game."

A Forest Without Trees / JP Solanki-Davie

20

March 31st 2640, waxing gibbous moon

On the evening before the course, Tara was trying to relax in her room after another full day of training under Ada and Tristan's close watch. She stared into her mother's image, her thoughts wandered, *Does Mama know? I need to trust the Cullis are coming. They would tap into the Federation channels from Adrshy.*

Dib would have something set up to monitor within the shield. Maybe, he even figured out how to bring it down. No. If he had, they would've done that already. Wouldn't they? But what if they didn't all make it out? No. They made it. I have to believe that. Vishal would be working to mitigate the waste run-off being dumped by the Federation. He'd be close, Mama might even be with him. Maybe Bricker has already crossed the shield to come for Hami, Hori and me. Source may it be true. They must know by now. There would be footage from that party, and definitely of me in the field with the drones.

They would know I'm in the Quarter Circuit. Ugh! How is this my reality? Mama, I hope you've seen it and are coming for me. I'm ready to come home.

There was a knock at the door. Tara shut down the tablet immediately and sat up straight.

"Yah?"

Gerrit poked his head into the room, the rest of his tall frame followed. He had a mischievous look on his face, and a leather jacket in his hand. He whispered loudly, "Want to get out of here?"

Tara stood apprehensively, "Wachu mean? You said, wait until the course. That's tomorrow."

"Yah. I mean, get out of the house. I want you to see my favourite hang-out." Gerrit offered the jacket to her and grinned playfully, "Come on! Let's go have some fun."

Tara accepted the jacket; the leather was soft and smooth. She bit her lip as she considered her response, *He wants to get me out of the house. And go where? A park? I've never seen one. Might as well.* She pulled the jacket on and said, "Gare. I'm game."

He smiled his inimitable smile, "Keep quiet now, we'll head out the back door."

They snuck out of the house and into a garage full of luxury transports. He strode up to a motorcycle parked near the back. After he pulled on a leather jacket himself, he grabbed two helmets and passed one to Tara.

"This was a prize I won from one of my games. Pretty sweet, huh?" He tipped his head at the bike, all black leather and chrome.

"Acha. Let's go," she said and put the helmet on.

They set off, weaving through the mountain roads. Tara clung tight to Gerrit's muscular back as they rode the PUSH. This time she kept her eyes closed. There was no sensation of wind within the vortex, making the speed imperceptible.

They sped across the Federation to the eastern mountain parks. When they arrived at the final checkpoint Tara opened her eyes again.

"State your purpose for being out this late," the enforcer demanded.

Gerrit flipped up his visor and said, "We're heading to Prominence Park for some suds."

The enforcer held a scanner over them and read the screen. Without another word he waved them through.

Gerrit pulled forward slowly, then picked up speed along the meandering mountain roads.

They finally stopped in Prominence Park.

When Tara climbed off the bike her legs vibrated. She took a deep breath of the crisp night air, elated by the change of scenery and to be free of Tristan's paternal authority. Gerrit curled his arm over her shoulder. She eyed him and reminded herself, *Be easy. He's just trying to protect me.* He steered her along the cobble stone streets, the façades animated by holovids. She stared around her, astounded by the excitement of the late-night games at play. There was a game of keep-away with a glowing orb as the object to keep. An eatery on the corner was switching out the evening meal for an open bar. Viewers were betting on the race that was playing out on the screen above. Another screen showed a baseball game where a player slid onto home plate. The viewers cheered as they jumped and hugged each other. Other screens were promoting upcoming Rumble matches, with cuts to taletellers gabbing and spotlighting players.

High above the street was a large orange sphere made of plemp, holovids on the lower half were detailing player rankings. There was a ticker scrolling around the centre of the sphere listing upcoming courses open to levelled up players. A taleteller was enthusiastically announcing the next heat of players to enter the ProPod.

Gerrit followed her gaze to the sphere and explained, "That's a ProPod. Players enter for a chance to boost their rank and potential of entering larger courses, like the seasonal Quart-Cs. It's dodge ball on grip, so players can crawl the walls and get a leg-up in the games."

Tara frowned, *I didn't understand half of what he said. But I know, I don't like the idea of a ProPod.*

A group of players took notice of them and pointed. Gerrit urged her along before they approached or drew any more attention. They passed a VXTC den with a sign that flashed a promotion, Doors to Compromise program available for all mates needing a hook-up reboot. The windows were translucent pink, holovids of dancing figures in silhouette. Tara watched with astonishment as they passed a salon. A clinician dropped something into a person's eyes and their hair changed from black to a vibrant yellow with glittering hot pink tips.

Tara noticed an archer taking aim in a side alley, she tried to hang back to watch but Gerrit moved her along. They passed a serene looking young player as he left a den with darkened windows, a grey D^2 over the door. Gerrit led her down a side ally. She noticed a splash of red colour on a building and spied a graffiti tag that read: /me eyes clear>. They walked to a door painted dark purple with gold trim, the words 'Kijami' written above it in lights. He knocked on the door three times. An eye-hole opened.

A voice spoke through a speaker, "Password?"

Gerrit glanced down at Tara with a sly grin and replied, "Cherry Pie."

The eye-hole slammed shut, and the door opened. The social was dimly lit with music playing through speakers. A dance floor surrounded by a scattering of tables with chairs, each with a small ambilamp.

A long bar covered the length of one wall, a large screen above it showed several different channels. Tara cringed when she noticed one of the channels showed footage of her. She pulled out her braid to hide her face. Gerrit ordered two drinks from the bartender as Tara surveyed the room in search of the recorders that were everywhere else in the park.

"Are the recorders hidden?" She asked.

Gerrit shook his head, "This is a private social. No recorders. See why it's my favourite hang out?" His smile was casual and genuine.

Tara relaxed a little and looked around the social again. A few people were playing gaming stations along one wall. A group with their cards face down on the table, failed to remain discreet as they watched her. She shifted her attention to another table, a group with brightly coloured hair, blue, green, pink and purple. A mix of clinicians and plain-clothed people absorbed in conversation. She caught sight of a deep brown skinned man in the far corner of the room, his stare was fixed on her. Tara averted her eyes uncomfortably and watched a couple dance together on the otherwise empty dance floor.

Gerrit left a few credits by waving his hand over the scanner and took the drinks from the bar. He led them to a table near the back and Tara settled in.

A couple of guardians entered from a side door to join the group with colourful hair. She glanced back at the man in the corner, he wore a well-fitted black suit with a bronze pin on his lapel. He raised his glass in a salute. Tara dropped her eyes to her drink nervously. When she looked up again, the man was still staring at her.

She elbowed Gerrit and asked, "Who's that man?"

"That's Controller Kayn. Prominence Park is in his division and Kijami is where he controls his net." Gerrit lifted his glass towards Kayn and added, "Don't worry, Sis. It's all good."

Tara forced herself to look away. *Don't worry? He says that a lot. He acts like Tristan too, so sure of himself. Easy. He brought me here to have fun. I can do that. Right?* She glanced back at the group that she noticed before; they had returned to their card game. Scanning the room again, she saw everyone minding their business. A group of scrappers entered from a different door and settled in at a table tucked beside the bar. They all wore the same brown jumpsuits but each had a unique style, they were a mix of shaved heads, locs, tattoos and piercings. *I've never seen a group of scrappers before. I guess this social is open to everyone.*

"So, this is your favourite hang-out? Is it because there's no segregation between sectors?" Tara asked with a nod towards the scrappers.

"What? This is one of the few places I don't have to act my part." Gerrit said quietly.

"So can scrappers?" Tara pressed.

"What scrappers? No." Gerrit looked around confused.

Tara directed him to their table, "Over there."

"Oh. Huh. I didn't notice them. Guess so." Gerrit shrugged.

Tara eyed him, *No, you wouldn't notice scrappers. Would you?* Gerrit shifted uncomfortably in his seat and occupied himself with his drink. Her attention was drawn to the large screen, and soon she was absorbed by one of the channels. Gerrit noticed her gaze and followed it to the screen. They both watched as a tall figure with long locs emerged from a door at the back of the grand hall. Vi was dressed in a black jumpsuit with a sparkly white trim. Tara's eyes widened in recognition.

"Is that Vi with the dreadlocks?" Gerrit asked.

"Yah." She stared at her friend on the screen, "They're called locs. Not dreadlocks. That's an antiquated term."

"What?"

"Locs" Tara restated, "There's nothing to dread about them."

"Oh." Gerrit said.

Vi approached the first obstacle, a pile of large masonry blocks to be carried one at a time to the end of the track and stacked neatly. There was a wrangler next to Vi riling up the crowd. Vi patted chalk on hir palms and approached the first block. Ze made it look effortless as ze quickly carried the heavy block to the end of the track and placed it down gently. Back and forth ze went, until finally there was a wall of bricks built. The crowd cheered and the wrangler directed Vi to proceed to the next obstacle that was on the other side of the newly built wall. Vi moved back from the wall several paces and sprinted towards it. Ze leapt into the air, gracefully flipped over the wall and landed with barely a sound. The crowd erupted with cheers. Vi approached a rope suspended from the high vaulted ceiling. Ze climbed the full height until ze reached the top. From there, ze grabbed a hold bolted to the arched ceiling and proceeded to climb its length. The audience cheered excitedly as Vi returned to the ground and a guardian fitted hir with a weighted vest. Ze climbed the rope again and scaled the ceiling.

Gerrit leaned over and whispered in Tara's ear, "They'll have Vi climb that course with increased weight until ze uses up hir eca. Main Operator likes to push his players to their limit. Ze'll be given another eca serum, maybe some snap, then run some other course or maybe spar with another player or something."

"Why!? Is this entertaining?" Tara was shocked.

"You saw hir flip over that wall ze built!" Gerrit exclaimed, "Vi already has an additional 70lbs on hir as ze climbed that ceiling. That's right cracked! Viewers live for players that are superhuman."

Tara gaped at him and he laughed at her reaction.

"Look. This is the recreation sector and viewers eat up anything where someone's eca is pushed to the extreme. I didn't say I agreed with it, but you have to admit it's impressive to witness." He said.

Tara leaned her arms on the table and rubbed her forehead with frustration, "They're celebrating synthetically induced eca. What about letting people have full access to their abilities instead of injecting a false cure in their system for entertainment purposes? Why can no one else see this?"

"Why indeed," Gerrit replied. He leaned in again to whisper in her ear, "This is exactly why we are leaving the Federation. Things are not what they seem." He looked at her knowingly. In a hushed voice he explained, "Our plan will only work if we both get to the flag together with enough serums in reserve. When the transport carries us out of the arena, we should be able to get deep enough into the fringe from there."

Get to the flag? That's not my goal. Why does he want the flag?

"I was wondering, would you be able to deactivate our chips?" He asked quietly.

"It'd be risky. Tristan said it's implanted in the spine." Tara said.

Gerrit nodded and took a nervous glance around, "Well, we'll just cross that bridge when we get there. For now, we need to get through the course together so we can get out of there together."

"Why do you want to leave? I get what you said before. But what makes you think you'd like living outside the Federation? From what I've seen, you like the games and the big life." Tara said.

"What?" Gerrit's eyes widened with surprise, "You know why I need to leave. I'm sick of acting the part. I bet I'd surprise you in the wild."

She looked at him skeptically and countered, "Oh yah? You know nothing of life outside the shield. You were bred for this life. There are no games for show beyond these borders. There's no such thing as a player where I'm from."

"I don't want to be a player! I want to leave. I don't care that I've never been in the wild. Anything is better than living here." Gerrit pleaded.

"You say this now. What happens when you miss this life? You don't realize how different it is in here. You have no idea what is beyond the perimeter shield." She said glancing around the room nervously, "There's a whole world out there, and none of it is for show."

"Trust me Tara. I'm ready for it." He said.

"Trust you!?" Tara laughed, "How!? I hardly know you! You wear your mask well, like Tristan. You keep telling me to, not worry. How can I not? I don't know if I can trust you."

Gerrit sunk back in his chair, his eyes drooped sadly.

Tara sat up straighter and added, "It's probably better if you stay inside the shield."

"No!" Gerrit looked up in a panic, "Tara, please. We've talked about this. I need you to take me with you."

She eyed him doubtfully, "But do I need you?"

His features hardened as he spoke, "Yes, you do. You're still inside the shield and here we play games. You're right. I am a good player and I wear a convincing mask. Underneath it, this is me." He held his hands out to the side, "I'm not like Father."

Tara sighed and turned away. *We'll see about that.*

Gerrit leaned in, "I'm not like Father. We didn't come here to sip drinks and watch the channels. We're here to meet a friend. He is one of the few that I trust."

Tara looked at him seriously, "How do you know you can trust him?"

"He's a player turned bookmaker. I've known him since I

was young. We'd frequent the same socials and over the years we've come to know one another. I've made him a lot of credits. And he's helped me get through some rough patches." He explained.

Tara looked at him dubiously, but didn't say anything. Gerrit added with a whisper, "He's got maps of the fringe so we can navigate it after the course."

Maps? Does he not realize I can access any Federation system with my eca? Tara bit her tongue keeping her thoughts to herself.

"Tara," Gerrit said urgently, "I may not know anything about the wild. But I do know how to help you get there. Please."

If I go it alone, I'm sure to get tracked by security. Would having Gerrit on my side change that? I don't know. He says he wants to help me leave. I'll have to trust that for now. She took a deep breath and said, "Yah. We're on the same team."

Gerrit sighed with relief, "You won't regret it. I promise." He sat up straight as he noticed someone enter the social, "There he is. It's ok."

He smiled reassuringly. Tara followed his gaze to a thin pale man with light brown hair that bounced as he walked. Dressed in an oversized dark grey wool coat with a high collar. He spotted them at their table and walked straight up.

"Salutations, Gerrit." He said.

"Good to see you, Dillon." said Gerrit and gestured to Tara, "This is Tara."

Dillon glanced at Tara and nodded politely. Tara pressed her lips together into a tight smile, *This is Gerrit's friend? He looks like he's hiding something.*

"What's the word, kip?" Gerrit asked.

Dillon pulled up a chair and sat down. He leaned his forearms on the table, the glow of the ambilamp illuminated his bony features as he spoke, "Word is, Main Operator planned a course that's set in a new arena. From the leaked images, the course will be an entire old-era city. Expect to be camping and to have night drills. The robotics factory has upped production of all

Kbots. There's even rumour of new mega and nanoKbot models."
He looked Tara directly in the eyes and said, "Bet you 1000
credits, you make short work of those kreepbots."

Tara averted her gaze nervously.

Dillon continued in a hushed voice, "But I'm sure you
know all that already. Here's what you wanted to know."

He pulled out a tablet from the inside pocket of his large
coat. He slid it towards Gerrit, who reached out and took it into
his lap.

Dillon turned his attention to Tara and eyed her
questioningly, "Wanna see a magic trick?" He pulled out a deck of
cards, a playful glint in his eye.

Tara glanced at Gerrit immersed in the tablet, then
returned her attention to Dillon. *Do I want to see a magic trick?*
Tara noticed a tattoo on his inner right wrist as he shuffled.

He caught her and teased, "My, what sharp eyes you
have."

Her shoulders tensed and she looked away.

"Feel no way. It's nothing more than a pubescent getting
inked." He pulled up his sleeve to show her. An elegant R in the
centre of two intersecting circles in grey, black and white. While
Tara admired the artistry, a woman wearing a grey hooded cloak
entered the social and joined the group with colourful hair. Dillon
quickly glanced at their table before he pulled his arm back.

"Arite, arite, arite. Simple draw card. Let's see if I can
remember." Dillon said as he shuffled the cards. "Pick a card, any
card."

Tara shrugged and said, "Five of spades."

Dillon stopped shuffling and placed the deck down on the
table in a neat pile. He folded his hands in front of him, "Choose a
card."

Tara furrowed her brow, reached forward and cut the deck
at a random spot. She chose the card below with her other hand.
He smirked at her hesitation. She turned the five of spades card
face up on the table. Tara's eyes opened with astonishment then
she glared at Dillon. He tried to suppress a grin as he gathered the

cards and shuffled them again. Gerrit placed the tablet back on the table and nodded his gratitude. Dillon returned the deck back in his inner coat pocket along with the tablet.

"Your ranking is looking good for the course," Dillon said to Gerrit, "but hers has already licked all the other players." he tilted his head at Tara.

"Wachu mean? My ranking?" She asked.

"Players are given a ranking for the course based on their average viewership." Gerrit explained, "It determines where we are dropped in relation to the goal of the course. Think of it like a proximity advantage. The lower the ranking the further back you start the course. The Quart-C will have 12 players,"

"13 players." Dillon interrupted. A smile lit up his face as he nodded toward Tara, "This one's breaking all the rules. First time in history a Quart-C will have 13 players. These are the other players."

He reached into his coat and pulled out another tablet that he placed on the table. A holovid cycled through each player in the Quarter Circuit with their names and their rankings: Angelik(7), Bronik(6), Delia(13), Gerrit(11), Mikhail(2), Nylah(4), Prynn(9), Reese(8), Reilly(3), Syrene(10), Tara(1), Yane (5) and Ziggy(12).

Tara flushed as she took in the information. The weight of competing against these trained players was overwhelming. *They've been groomed for this since puberty. How can I compete with that when I've been locked up for the last six years? I'll have my eca, but if I use it they'll all know what I'm capable of.*

"Your rank is number one. Your projected viewership is off the charts." Dillon said.

"This can't be happening." Tara slumped back in her chair. The idea of being watched by so many viewers made her head spin. *Oh, Source fend! If it was only the course and not the constant surveillance. How do they expect me to be so casual about being on view?* She sighed with frustration as the words of Controller Bridget echoed in her mind, *It's not just about finishing the course, it's about putting on a good show.*

"Don't worry, Sis." Gerrit said. Tara pursed her lips and glared at him. He cleared his throat uncomfortably, "You'll get used to the recorders. Just focus on the goal of the course."

"Yah! Zactly, feel no way, Tara. You're already trend-z, just finish the course and watch the credits roll in." Dillon said.

"I don't want any effn credits! Or to get used to being on view!" Tara huffed and crossed her arms over her chest.

Gerrit took a sip of his drink and scanned the room anxiously. Dillon replaced the tablet in his coat pocket and glanced past Tara to Controller Kayn. He focused back on Tara and leaned forward on the table.

"You know, not all eyes viewing are watching the same show." He let his words linger.

Tara furrowed her brow, *What did he mean by that?*

Dillon turned his eyes to the large screen where Vi was still climbing the ceiling. Tara followed his gaze and frowned; her heart ached for her friend. *How many times will they make you climb? Oh, Vi. Why did you have to be the one to cause the distraction? I'm so sorry that I'm here and you're there. When I get out, I'll come back for you.*

"Vi's been getting a lot of attention too. You two stirred things up supremely. If you stick around, remember to keep your eyes clear and mind free. I know a winner when I see one. I'm betting on you, Tara. Be easy." He winked at Tara. She stared back at him startled.

He stood up and straightened out his coat, "Now, if you'll excuse me. I have to visit my flower's sister." He gave a small bow and walked over to the table of people with the colourful hair.

There was an awkward silence between Gerrit and Tara once they were alone.

"Best we head off. We have an early start tomorrow." Gerrit said.

Tara let out a quiet sigh and replied, "Yah."

21

March 31st 2640, waxing gibbous moon

The energy of the room shifted as Gerrit and Tara left Kijami. It was as though a bright light had gone out, people were no longer distracted by Tara's flame.

Stella ran her hand through her wavy green hair watching them go. Across from her was Dillon who had just joined Flo. With an adept slight of hand, he slipped a TokPuck into Flo's cloak pocket before he sat down. He adjusted his wool coat and laced his hands on the table.

"How's it? Everyone enjoying this lovely evening?" He asked the group.

Stella eyed Relt before she leaned over to speak in a hushed voice, "What's she like in real life?"

The group of clinicians and guardians all leaned in closer to listen. Their positions within the Federation were associated with the security sector versus the recreation sector. This gave each one more access to players and secure information than others from the domiciliary sector. Tara's presence at Kijami stirred their interest as gossip had spread about her eca.

Dillon glanced around the table and said, "Well, she's adamant about not being a player."

"Why wouldn't she be? Players are always on view. " Relt screwed up his face with distaste, "Plus, I wouldn't want to play if I'd been in grade F all this time."

"Agreed." Rabi chimed in with a nod to his older brother. His light brown hair contrasted to his brother's vibrant blue hair, "Relt's right. She's not meant to play games. She's too important."

"No one is meant to play these games." Stella added.

Yeva tucked a purple curl behind her ear and subtly

glanced around the room. She quietly asked the group, "So, does she have any idea?"

"Maybe." Dillon kept his voice low, "Best she knows as little as possible."

"Agreed. She's better off going in blind. We leave in a couple days. That should be enough time to prepare." Relt said in a hushed voice.

"About that. How'd it go with el Dentista?" Dillon asked.

Stella nodded as she ran her tongue over her back molar. Her older sister Roo wrapped her arm around her lovingly. Roo's dark brown eyes smouldered with intensity as she looked around the group.

"Eyes up, friends. Hold steady. I see the tide turning and we're riding it." Roo said.

~~~

Remi stared at the screen, unblinking as Vi moved along the ceiling climb again. Her leg bounced with her distress. The last time she willingly watched any game was when Zedrik had been a player, in those days there were no eca and the games were less extreme. She was wrapped in a blanket and stared in disbelief at her offspring, *That's my baby. That's Vi. Vi's alive! Then, they all must have survived those fires! Wow! How many times are they going to make hir climb? The castle games are different with eca. Kragen certainly has twisted them to his own liking.*

In the balcony observing was Kragen, and the woman doubling as Remi. Seeing her double made her insides burn with her helplessness. *Kragen's been keeping up appearances. Vi will think that's me. It looks like I'm endorsing Kragen.*

She watched as Vi descended the climb and crumbled to the ground exhausted. The weighted vest was removed and a clinician injected Vi with another vial of serum and one of snap. *No! Let hir rest!* Vi jumped from columns that were towering in the room. Ze flipped from hir hands to hir feet over and over again.

Kragen is using Vi to get to Zedrik, and to get to me! He thinks this will defeat me and force me to step back on view. He wants me to play his games. Oh! If I be waspish, best beware my sting. My dear brother, you have no clue what you have done to me!

Remi threw the blanket off, moved to the desk and pulled open the bottom drawer. She held a small cloth wrapped package and took a slow breath, *It's been years since I dared look at this.* Her fingers trembled as she unwrapped a small tablet. Holding it with both hands she tapped the screen. It was a still image of her holding baby Vi in her arms, Zedrik standing beside her holding a smiling Xain on his hip. She let her eyes linger over the smiling faces and the bright eyes until she felt lost in them. *I miss you. I'm sorry my family. I didn't intend to abandon you. We could have escaped to the wild when we had our chance.*

Remi's heart panged and she sunk into a chair. Her eyes filled with tears as memories from her life in the festival grounds overtook her mind, *We had so many blissful years together away from Kragen's castle, away from his twisted games. I loved feeling your strong arms wrapped around me. We dreamed under the stars. The nights in the tent with the babies, you would always get up and grab me another diaper or some water. The day time was filled with friends, warm meals, poetry, singing songs, rhythmical music and plans for a better life.*

Back then, I had hoped to leave the Federation and go deeper into the wild. To escape the rise of the parks. To escape Uncle Stone and Kragen's grip on my life. We wanted to get out before the perimeter shield went up. When Bricker and the others were leaving, we should have left too. I wanted to wait until our babies were older. Zedrik said we should just go, but I was afraid.

Remi let out a groan, filled with regret, *There was the night that Tristan had come to our tent and told me that Kragen needed me. "It's an emergency!" he urged, "This may be the last chance you have." Like a dolt, I believed him. Tristan was just doing what he was told, like he always does. I went willingly and left my babies. Once I realized what had happened it was too late. Before I knew it, this room had become my prison. They thought I would cooperate after the grounds had been burnt to ash. They told me everyone had died. They wanted me to just forget and move on. I never wanted to believe them. And now, I know they're alive.*

The crowd's reaction to Vi falling off a column brought Remi back into the present. She saw Vi standing up like ze hadn't fallen from such a height and the wrangler gesturing for hir to climb back up again. Clutching the tablet of her family photo, Remi wanted nothing more than to hold Vi in her arms. She watched until Vi was so exhausted ze had to be carried out of the hall.

They know about my family now. I have no more secrets. Kragen wants to play games, and he thinks that he can force me to play his way. What he doesn't realize is now I know my family is alive, where I once felt lost and filled with hopelessness, I now have a reason to fight again. There is a world beyond the Federation and that is where the future lies. Her thoughts played back to when Zedrik had quit playing and gave that historic speech, *Our future is not in hiding from nature but learning from her! We reject the laws of the Federation and refuse to play!*

She was overcome with inspiration as she contemplated what move she could even make from her position. She walked to the door and tried to open it. *Of course,* she rolled her eyes at herself as she realized it was locked, *They've never given me any opportunities to escape. Especially after the energy pulse when I never developed any eca. It was all too simple to hide me away.*

She dug her fingernails into her palms and paced the room. *They've been using me this whole time and I've had no cards to play. But knowing my family is alive gives me an ace up my sleeve. If I can somehow get a message to them. I always told myself I would rather die than exist in the Arcade living out Uncle Stone's demented fantasies.* She moved to the window and stared into the night sky. The waxing gibbous moon was shining through the shield with an iridescent glow. *Could that be what I need to gain my freedom? If I know that Zedrik is watching, then maybe – just maybe.*

22

April 1st 2640, waxing gibbous moon

The morning of the Quarter Circuit, Tara woke from a dreamless sleep. The room was shrouded in darkness before the dawn. She curled into a ball and pulled the covers tightly around her.

Filled with dread, Tara was lost in her thoughts, *I don't wanna do this. How am I supposed to? I just wanna go home. I have to run the course before I can escape. Just like before. The others are still trapped. How can I help them if I'm a player?*

Is Vi a player too? It looked like that on the screens. But something tells me there's more going on than we saw. They know Zedrik is hir father. Ugh! That was my fault for talking. That was a narbo mistake. If I'm not careful they'll know about the Cullis.

I need to stay strong. Once the course ends, I'll sneak off in that transport and find the Seds. Gerrit said we just need to stock pile serums from the course. That should be simple enough. I just need to hold out until the end.

When the sun warmed the room, Tara peeled herself off the bed and headed to the bathroom.

When she stepped out after her shower, she was greeted by a meek guardian who offered her a black jumpsuit.

"Thank you." Tara said quietly. The suit was made of hemp with the emblem of Controller Tristan's Platinum Knight Division on the sleeve with ruby coloured trim. She ran her fingers over the emblem as butterflies danced in her stomach.

The guardian bowed and left her alone again.

"I don't wanna play these games. I just wanna go home." Tara sighed.

Begrudgingly, Tara pulled on the jumpsuit and strapped on the boots. She retrieved her two tablets, slipped them into the chest pocket and zipped it shut.

She calmed her nerves with a few deep breaths and left her room.

As she made her way, she gazed at the artwork on the walls. *This is it. I will leave this house and never come back. Source, please make it true.*

When she walked into the dining room she paused in the doorway. Tristan was absorbed in his tablet, Claudia idly played with her Mochipet, Gerrit ate with his eyes low and Ada worked on her tablet by the window. *I'm gonna get out of here. I have to.*

"Ah. There you are, my dear." Tristan said looking up with a grin, "Come. Eat. You will need your strength."

Ada was by Tara's side, waves of reassurance radiated off her as she encouraged Tara to sit. Tara did as she was told and tried to ignore Ada's presence.

Gerrit glanced up from his plate and smirked. *He's just acting his part. He wants out of here too. I can trust him.* Tara reassured her self as she ate her morning meal.

When Tara finished, Tristan explained to her the rules for the course, "You will gain points when you perform well, and you lose them when you get hit with a paint ball or some other such thing. The obstacles are designed to slow you down, same with the drones, the Kbot interference will drain you of serum and can ruin your day. You will lose points for these run-ins on top of the detrimental effects that you suffer. None of them are long lasting or permanent. Also, if any other player wants to challenge you,"

"Challenge me? To a fight?" Tara blurted out.

"Yes, other players could challenge you to a sparring match." Tristan regarded her with endearment, then went on, "You have to accept or you lose 100 points. Remember that your goal is to get to the flag first, but if you don't have enough points then a player with more points could also challenge you for the flag."

Tara slumped in her chair and gazed out the window. The sun was hidden behind clouds which diffused the daylight. *I don't care about earning points or the flag. Makes no difference to me if someone else wins it.*

She ignored Gerrit's attempt to catch her attention as Tristan continued to outline the game rules.

"The course should only take three days. If all goes well, Gerrit will catch up with you early on. You are allowed to work together, yes, players can team up." Tristan said cheerfully, "I know you will do great!"

They headed out and walked past the garage to a landing pad where two air transports were parked. A guardian who waited off to the side, handed them each their backpacks. It contained the allotted provisions, except anything they could pick up on the course; the meal replacement bars and water rations to last three days, one dose of eca serum, sniffers of both luusid and snap, a rope, a knife, a baton, a sleeping bag, a roll of meditape, and a sanitowel.

Tara clung to her pack as she was ushered into the transport.

Gerrit turned to Tristan and extended his hand, "Good bye, Father. I will play my best."

Tristan clasped Gerrit's hand firmly and pulled him into a hug. He whispered in his ear, "I know you will. Take care of her, Son."

Gerrit nodded curtly and pulled away. He climbed in next to Tara and Tristan leaned in from the doorway. He smiled one of his manufactured grins and faced Tara, "I am sure you will have fun!"

With that, he patted the side of the transport twice and stood back. Tara felt the ground move away from her as she was lifted into the air.

23

April 1st 2640, waxing gibbous moon

There was a gust of wind when the transport lifted off, it made Ada's fine black hair blow in her face. As she brushed it away, she fixed a pleasant smile and turned to address Tristan, "Thank you for your hospitality, Controller Tristan. It is time I depart as well."

He bowed deeply. Ada turned on her heel and climbed into the other transport. It took off and carried her over the mountains to Baroness Ga's residence. While en route, she read the message from Operator Stone:

Due to new information attained from Trainee Nebba in Grade F, Caretaker Bridget has isolated Tara and Vi's accomplices. Trainees Khalil, Desma and Pin were slated for collection but now will be transferred to the Research compound. The others will be shipped to the Manufacturing Division. Report to Investigator Tirich to process the detainees when you are finished with Baroness Ga.

Ada was raised within the Boost Academy after her family perished. Due to her abilities, she was placed under the care of Baroness Ga, the caretaker of the security sector orphaned youth. Each sector cared for these children while grooming them for their future responsibilities. For Ada, this was as close to family as she had. It was under Ga's guidance that she excelled in her position of investigator.

The transport landed on the narrow strip of rock in front of Ga's residence, the building was built into the side of a cliff. The high walls that faced the landing pad only had a few slits for windows and a long terrace that extended out from it like a plank.

The familiar aroma of Ga's home enveloped Ada as she entered.

She could hear the others in the viewing lounge, gearing up for the drop as she made her way through the hallways she knew so well. The click of her shoes echoed off the vaulted ceiling of the gallery, a grand room with ionic columns. The walls were decorated with dark trim moulding and elegant sconces, portraits hung in the spaces between. She gazed at the paintings of the Main Operator's family; Stone with Elbion and Clifton when they were young, Elbion with Isolde and Remi, Clifton with Ga and Rawlyn. She paused to admire the portrait of Kharis the Great, posed in a flowing blue mantle. A shadow caught her eye and she spun around as someone was startled from the room.

"Must have been one of Auntie Caretaker's special cases." Ada whispered to herself.

The hoopla spilled out as she entered the lounge. There was a group of pubescent enforcer trainees egging on Duncan and Daq in their game of slapsies. The viewing lounge had a large screen on one wall, a bar with tables and sofa chairs throughout. At one of the tables were Dale and Covi throwing cards down in a game of war. Laying with their limbs entwined on a sofa was Vyn, Peach and Brody. Their giggles mixed with the hard slap from Duncan as he defeated Daq.

"Oww!!" Daq cried.

"Stop your whining, Daq! Just face it. You're not ready to play with the big kids." Sung-Hyun teased from off to the side.

The group laughed and moved on to other games. Ada slid up next to Sung-Hyun and nudged her with her elbow. Sung-Hyun's warm brown mono-lidded eyes lit up at the sight of her orphaned sibling.

"Ada! Thank Source you're here." She said linking arms with Ada. She turned her nose up at the room of enforcers, "This lot can be a bit much without you."

"Oh, you love us." Duncan said. He jabbed Konnor on the shoulder and added, "You're just wishing more of your siblings proved their worth and levelled up to investigator by now."

Konnor remained firmly unbothered by Duncan's dig and simply lifted an unimpressed eyebrow. Duncan chortled as he walked away. Sung-Hyun turned back to Ada and tenderly tucked a strand of Ada's stray hair behind her ear.

"Missed you too." Ada said warmly.

Everyone turned their attention to the screen as the players gathered at the helipad. The footage flew in from above, circling the players as they prepared for their jump. Guardians were equipping them with parachute packs and securing their harnesses. The video zoomed in on Tara, her trepidation apparent on her face.

"Yow Patton! Ain't that the one that got away?" Covi teased.

"Shut it, Covi! Unless you want your nose broken again." Patton threatened, his hooded grey eyes dared Covi to test him.

"Now. Now. Don't be lewd boys." Baroness Ga scolded in her deep voice as she entered the viewing lounge. The room quietened as her pleasant aroma wafted over them. She surveyed the room from under her dark bangs with her deep-set brown eyes, "These viewing parties are for your benefit. This is not some social in a park. This is your home. I will not tolerate bad behaviour." She smiled sweetly and changed her tone, "Now let's watch the players drop!"

~~~

Kijami was quiet, most of the usual patrons were either attending a viewing party or were on duty. There were a couple clinicians at one table, Controller Kayn was in his usual spot in the back corner, and Bhyt was sipping his drink alone at a table. He was staring at the screens above the bar in a multi-screen panel view that was showing the Quarter Circuit players being outfitted with their parachutes. Bhyt was in the Monster Truck Derby and he also served players under Controller Kayn's division as a driver. He was off duty and waiting for his mate. When Knut entered, ze was accompanied by a young pubescent geek whose eyes bulged with excitement as he took in the social.

Bhyt rose to his feet and scooped Knut into his lean arms. He nuzzled hir neck and said, "Let's skip the drop and go play our own game."

"Stop!" Knut giggled and shoved Bhyt off playfully.

He pouted and noticed the blonde long curly haired pubescent Knut had with hir, "Who's this kid?"

"Tommy." Knut replied and pulled Tommy under hir arm affectionately.

"Why'd you bring him here?" Bhyt muttered between his teeth. He had planned to spend the night alone with his mate. Not playing a parental figure to some naive kid.

"Don't be a gnashgab! You know geeks don't get out much. How could I not bring him to Kijamji for the Quart-C player drop?" Knut countered, "Take my word, he's got enough grit."

"Oh?" Bhyt scrutinized Tommy again as they settled into their seats. Tommy was distracted by the wall of gaming machines.

"Yow kid, can you hear me?" Bhyt waved his hand and caught Tommy's attention, "How'd you end up a geek? You seem keen on the games."

Tommy shrugged, "I didn't want to climb the rope."

"Ah." Bhyt chuckled, "Most popular players are more brawn than brains."

"Yah. Knut already explained it." Tommy's eyes were wide with excitement, "As a geek, I get access to all the parks without being on view. Who'd pass that up? Plus, I get to play with cracked gadgets."

Bhyt lifted his glass in agreement. Knut's attention was distracted by Eric, as he entered the social. His orange basketball jersey was stained with his sweat. A grey cloud hung over him as he dragged his feet across the room. His curly red hair covered his downcast eyes.

"Yow, Eric!" Knut called, "How was the game?"

"Does it matter? It's just a narbo game." Eric replied flatly and headed straight through the door beside the bar.

"He always says that when his team loses." Knut muttered.

Tommy leaned over and asked excitedly, "That was

Player Eric? Of the Flaming Globes, Eric?"

"Yah." Knut replied.

"Whoa!" Tommy stared at the door amazed.

"You ain't seen nothing yet, kid. Stick with Knut and ze'll network you with all the key players." Bhyt said.

He turned his attention to Knut and leaned in closely to hold hir hand in his.

Ze pulled hir hand away and quickly tucked a strand of hir light brown hair behind hir ear.

Bhyt straightened up in his seat rejected. Across the table, Tommy practically bounced in his seat as his eyes spotted the pinball machine. Knut noticed his reaction and smiled endearingly at him

"Go get that high score." Knut encouraged.

"Yah?" Tommy jumped to his feet and nearly ran to the machine. Soon the social had the added pings from the ball as it ricocheted off the flippers.

Knut shrugged at Bhyt and said, "He fancies himself a pinball wizard."

"Oh, Source help us." Bhyt rolled his eyes.

"Be no way, Bhyt. His eyes are clear." Knut reassured.

"I'll get you a drink." Bhyt said changing the topic.

Before Knut could reply, Bhyt stood up and headed to the bar. He leaned against it next to Burke, who nursed his drink.

"How's it, Bhyt?" Burke asked gruffly.

"It's been better." Bhyt said.

"Knut didn't come alone again. Guess your plans for tonight changed." Burke remarked with a nod towards Tommy.

Bhyt ran his hand through his thick hair with annoyance, "Yah. Ze's been avoiding me since I drove Nylah to her park that night. Knut doesn't understand about Marri and ze's better off not knowing."

"Yah." Burke agreed. "Be no way, kip. Knut's no dolt. Ze'll come around."

"I know. Ze just takes it so personally. But what about you? You're here alone. Where's Avis?" Bhyt asked.

"She's not here." Burke shot Bhyt a dangerous look that told Bhyt not to push it.

Bhyt diverted his attention to the screens above the bar, "Game's getting interesting."

Burke looked up as the players prepared to board the air transport. The tension from the players was palpable through the screen. Angelik was flanked by Reese and Reilly, they eyed Tara with interest. Tara was shrinking behind Gerrit as he was trying to deflect their attention.

"That's one way of putting it." Burke said.

24

April 1st 2640, waxing gibbous moon

"Ooooh! Little Ger is gonna try and take us on." Angelik teased, "You're just a flopdoodle!"

"Don't push me, Angelik." Gerrit said steadily. He was standing at his full height trying to shield Tara from view.

"Come now Ger-ger. Don't take life too seriously, you won't get out alive." Angelik lightly threatened, "We only wanted to greet your sibling. We won't hurt her."

"Ha!" Bronik's laugh pulled everyone's attention to him. Syrene stood beside him; her sharp dark features expressed her apathy about the other players. He tilted his head to her as though to whisper while he spoke loudly, "I don't have the energy to pretend to like them today."

Syrene turned her deep brown eyes to her mate and smirked devilishly. Angelik let out a huff as she turned away from Gerrit to preoccupy hirself with hir gear.

"Do your best to avoid a challenge from Angelik." Gerrit whispered to Tara.

"Yah. No problem." Tara muttered sarcastically. She eyed the other players nervously. Each was dressed in a black hemp jumpsuit with their controller's division emblem and different coloured trim. None expressed any of the apprehension that Tara was consumed by, *Why is this happening? I've never parachuted before. They expect me to compete with them. Gerrit was right. I do need him to get through this. Do I even stand a chance against these players?*

"Players load up!" the pilot called.

Gerrit ushered Tara to climb into the passenger cabin. She planted her feet and gripped a strap. The other players stared at her as they all crammed in. Once they were all aboard, they lifted up into the air with a rush. Tara kept her eyes closed as she felt the earth move further away and focused on her breath, *Inhale one, two, three, four. Exhale, one, two, three, four.*

A clinician stood by the open door of the cabin, strapped in with a harness so they could use both their arms. They gestured for Tara to move closer and prepare to jump. Gerrit nudged her forward. They were approaching the first drop zone and because of her ranking she was to jump out first. With trembling hands she gripped a bar next to the open door. The clinician held her arm and injected the blue eca serum. Tara inhaled sharply as she felt it move through her body.

It was a larger dose than she had expected and she immediately sensed the transport and all the electronics within it. She focused her mind on the view in front of her. They were above the clouds within the shield, but she could make out the ruins of an old era metropolis city below. There were some tall buildings scattered throughout trees and rubble. The sound of a buzzer startled Tara and made her freeze on the spot. There was a ripple of laughter from the other players. Before she could react, the clinician pushed her out.

She was falling, fast. The wind on her face pulled at her cheeks and she felt the pressure as her body moved quickly towards the earth. Her body spun and flipped a few times as she tried to steady herself. Suddenly, she felt the jerk of her chute automatically opening at the safe altitude. Her body whipped up then decelerated as the earth came closer. With her eyes trained on the ground she focused her eca to steer her fall to the open rooftop below. As the concrete met her feet, the impact rippled through her body. She kept moving forward, stumbling onto her front with the chute draping over her.

With a rush of adrenaline, she struggled to untangle herself. She released the straps and stepped out of the harness. Crouching low and gathering the chute, the helmet and the harness into a pile, Tara's heart was racing. She took several deep breaths to calm down before she stood up and looked around her surroundings.

The urban sprawl was much more intimidating from the ground, a grid of grey buildings in different stages of decay. Rubble blocked roads along with old-era trucks. A few tall trees were the only green she could see. *Oh, Source fend! This place is huge!* She could see clearly the path to the final obstacle, a red flag mounted on top of an obelisk marked the goal. The road to the flag was blocked by piles of old era vehicles. She focused her eca and tuned into her wrist device for the map of the course. She studied it for a minute, trying to figure out where she should go to find Gerrit. Tara leaned over the edge of the building and saw a fifty storey drop. *How am I gonna get down? It must be faux-old new build, there's no way these are ruins from the old era.* She turned her attention in the other direction and saw the last players diving from the transport in the distance. *I don't want the flag, but I don't want any of those players to challenge me either. Best get moving and hope Gerrit catches up.* She focused her eca to tune into nearby electronics. Sensing all the recorders, the circulating drones, kbots, holograms and the shield generator for the course gave her a thrill having not used her eca like this in years. She pushed away her temptation to deactivate everything. She looked down at her wrist device, her eca serum level was down to 86%. *Sodz! I only have one serum. Gotta keep an eye on that.*

She hooked her thumbs in the straps of her bag and surveyed her options. There was no obvious way down and the idea of moving along the lower levels seemed riskier. Tara noticed a metal beam that extended across the alley to the next building. A glint of light caught her attention, she glanced to the left and spotted the lens of a recorder protruding from a pole. *Ugh! I hate that I'm being watched for their entertainment.* She refocused her attention on the beam and climbed onto it.

Once she was halfway, she heard a high-pitched whirring sound and a small drone hovered into view. Tara considered her options for a moment and focused her eca. She saw it loading a volley of paintballs. They flew towards her and she lifted her hand creating a telekinetic shield. The paintballs struck her shield and fell with a splash of colour. Tara saw the drone reloading.

Gripping the air with her hand and focusing her telekinetic ability, the drone flew against the building, shattering to pieces and falling to the paint-stained ground.

She clenched her jaw and reset her eyes on the adjacent building. Crawling a bit further she heard another whirring sound from an approaching drone. She quickly shifted so her legs could grip the beam and focused her telekinetic ability to knock the drone against the building. It fell next to the other one. She hastily scanned the sky as she crawled the rest of the way. When she reached the other side, she crouched down behind a half-broken wall. She shook her head when she saw her eca level had dropped to 42%. *This is ridiculous. I need more serums. They want me to show off my ability. Can I hide it? Does it matter? They already have an idea of what I'm capable of. If I play this game right, I won't be here for them to manipulate once it's over.* Tara traced a wispy cloud as it floated by. Her eyes settled on a cable that ran down to another roof. *That looks like a zip-line. I wonder...*

Tara surveyed the roof for a way down, but found none. The closest building was on the other side of the cable. She chewed her lip and eyed the distance needed to cross. *I can do this. It'll be like zipping over the expanse. Only, there's no forest on the other side.* She retrieved the length of rope from her bag and tied it around herself like a harness. The rest she held between her hands as she approached the side of the building. She steadied her nerves and hooked the rope over the cable. Before she could change her mind she focused her eca and jumped. Wind blew in her ears as she slid the length. She swung herself onto the roof landing firmly on her feet.

Before she had a chance to untie the rope, a whirring sound made her spin around. She instinctively focused her eca and deactivated the two drones that raced towards her. They fell instantly. She glanced at her wrist device, her eca level was at 5%. *Sodz! That really used up the serum.* She pulled out her one extra eca serum, carefully loaded into the needlegun she was supplied with and formulated a plan, *I'll take this and be more careful with how much I use. I gotta find a way down without my eca.*

25

April 1st 2640, waxing gibbous moon

Gerrit's feet hit the ground as he smoothly unlatched his parachute and harness, performed a floor roll, took one big step and leaped over a broken wall, landing in an alley between two buildings. He wound his way through the rubble until he spotted a collection of old era trash cans. A hint of blue caught his eye and he kicked the cans to the side revealing a dose of serum in a blue canister. He smiled his fake smile, grabbed the serum and shoved it into his bag.

He looked down at his wrist device to check the map and looked around him to get his bearings. *I need to travel north east and catch up with Tara, which would mean I can cut through here.* He turned his body to face a building that was boarded up with wooden planks. He walked confidently up to the door, which was also boarded up. He placed his hand on the wood and focused his eca. Soon the boards began to vibrate until they exploded into splinters leaving an open doorway. Gerrit waited until the sawdust settled and stepped through the threshold.

Inside was dark and dank with cobwebs stretching across the long wall. Gerrit surveyed his surroundings carefully. The floor was rotted out and the ceiling was caved in from several stories up. He looked up and could see a single beam of light that was leaking in through a hole covered in vines. *How much of this is a hologram?* He wondered.

On the far side of the building, across the open expanse of the floor was a door boarded up with wood planks. Above it was an archaic sign with the word 'EXIT'. As he stood there debating if the floor would support him if he tried traversing the edge, he heard the familiar whirring of a drone approaching. He poked his head back into the alley and spotted it hovering in from above. Ducking back into the door jam as a paintball flew at him, he knelt down grabbing a broken brick in his hand. Focusing his eca, the brick began to glow red hot. Slowly he leaned back into view of the drone, took aim and threw the brick which exploded upon contact. Metal debris showered down to the ground.

Gerrit turned his attention back inside and neared the edge with his foot, *It seems solid enough.* He walked along assessing the flooring with each step. He approached the cobwebs and focused his eca, reaching up with his hand he touched the closest web and it caught fire. A chain reaction happened as the fire spread through the webbing. *It's almost beautiful.* A glint of blue caught his eye in the far corner of the room.

Gerrit carefully edged his way along the side of the floor waiting for it to fall out from under his feet. It held steady as he reached the corner and moved a few planks of wood to find another blue canister with a vial of serum. *Aces!* He thought as he quickly shoved it into his bag.

Gerrit turned towards the exit, which was now only a few paces away. Everything happened so fast that he only realized the giant Kbot in the crater of the floor once it pointed its pulserod directly at him.

"Effn turdz!" Gerrit shouted.

He leaped towards the door in a panic. The red light from the Kbot glowing brighter as it prepared to shoot. He reached the boarded-up door, quickly focused his eca and the wood splintered outwardly. In that moment, he felt the ripple through his body from the pulserod frequency that was emitted by the Kbot.

Gerrit stumbled forward onto his hands and knees, he tried to breathe to calm down the brewing discomfort erupting from his abdomen. He gripped the gravel with his fingers and vomited. It projected out of him, emptying his stomach. Once he was done, he pushed himself away from the mess and heaved lung-fulls of air as tears streamed down his face. He trembled as he fumbled through his backpack for the canteen of water. Once his breath returned to ease, he sipped the water and darted his eyes around him. Through the open doorway into the building he could see the Kbot had retreated into the hole.

Glancing down at his wrist device his eca level was at 0% and was flashing red. There was a new yellow bar that showed the effects from the pulserod. *Effn Kbot!* He was in an alley behind a large metal bin, his sick was spattered over the ground and all over the pile of refuse beside him.

Gerrit pushed himself to stand, and moved away from his mess towards the other side of the alley. Once he couldn't smell it anymore, he grabbed a blue vial from his bag and quickly injected himself in his upper arm.

He felt the rawness from his stomach acid in his throat and drank more water letting his head tilt back. He dumped the water over his face, wiping it off with his sanitowel. He crouched low and dug through his bag again retrieving a meal bar, swallowing it in three bites. *That Kbot fek'd me up. I bet it's gonna move through me again when that yellow bar drops down. I can't be caught off guard or it could all be effn over.* He leaned his back against the wall and drank more water.

As Gerrit was formulating his next move he heard a sound coming from the clearing at the end of the alley. He stood up too quickly and felt another rush of nausea move through him. He steadied himself with the wall and burped. *Yuck!*

Keeping a hand on the wall he edged his way toward the end of the alley and peered around the corner. He caught sight of a player who was flipping, running and jumping towards him. A splash of yellow paint hit the ground where he had just jumped from.

Gerrit looked up to see a drone in pursuit of the player. He ducked low so as not to be seen while he spied on the player who parkoured through the urban decay.

Gerrit shook his head as he caught sight of the player's face. *Yane is such a show-off, but let the viewers watch him instead of me for a while.* He sunk back into the alley to avoid Yane noticing him.

26

April 1st 2640, waxing gibbous moon

The transport approached the work camp gate. Silas lowered the window, flashed a card at the enforcer in the guard booth and focused his eca on him, *The ID is valid. The ID is valid The ID is valid.* The enforcer nodded, the gate bar lifted and the transport moved forward.

The compound was a grid of windowless buildings, each with a loading dock on one side. A series of small roads wove around each building with shielded gates between them.

Silas steered the transport to one of the building's docks, he pulled forward then backed in so the rear trailer doors lined up.

Silas glanced over at Xain who was sitting in the passenger seat. Xain focused his eca to appear like the regular Manufacturing Division transporter, and climbed out. Pulling the collar up on his yellow transporter jacket he walked to the back and unlatched the doors.

As he did, he heard the overhead door roll up and turned to greet the enforcer inside. He pulled open the doors, stood back and handed a tablet to the enforcer.

"Everythin' checks out." said the enforcer, "It's those shippin' crates." He gestured to several large metal crates and handed back the tablet.

Xain tapped a panel on each of the shipping crates. They moved on their electronic dolly and Xain guided them.

Soon, all the crates were loaded. Xain double checked they were securely strapped down before stepping out, shutting and latching the doors.

With a brief nod to the enforcer, he climbed into the cab of the transport.

Silas steered it through the narrow roads between the bleak buildings to the front gate.

Again, Silas focused his eca and lowered the window to greet the enforcer at the guard booth.

The enforcer scanned his tablet and nodded his head.

The gate bar lifted and Silas pulled the transport forward. They travelled in silence for some time, only slowing when they approached the checkpoint. Xain maintained his mirage of his transporter role as Silas lowered his window again.

"Evenin' fellas. Hold for a retina scan." The enforcer said.

"You already did the scan. It all checks out." Silas said using his eca.

The enforcer blinked at his tablet then said, "Right-o! Everythin' checks out. On your way." He tapped the side of the transport twice and stepped back.

Silas moved the transport forward until they were clear of the check point, then picked up speed.

He flashed Xain a knowing grin. Xain occasionally checked his scanner for any indication the Federation had caught on.

Eventually, Silas slowed the transport and Xain pressed a button on a device rigged to the dash. They watched as the trees lining the road in front of them vanished.

The transport veered into the clearing, which was a narrow road cut out of the forest.

They moved slowly forward and Silas pressed another button on the dash.

The ground opened up in front of them to reveal a ramp leading down. The tunnel went deep into the earth, slowly levelling out and opening up into a large room with other kinds of transports parked in a row.

Silas steered their transport next in line then powered down. He flashed Xain a triumphant smile and they both climbed out of the cab.

Xain threw open the back trailer doors, climbed in and quickly read the panel on the side of each crate.

He tapped the panel on the third crate to release the straps and activated the electronic dolly.

Swiftly, he steered the crate towards the door, Silas helped him remove it and tapped the panel to open the crate.

The side fell to the ground with a deafening thud. Five exhausted faces peered out at them.

"Welcome!" Silas was grinning from ear to ear.

~~~

Kragen re-crossed his ankles as he lay back in the lounge chair. He was watching the holovid of the Quarter Circuit.

He mindlessly toyed with a FidgiFlint, the ambilight spun in his palm as it switched on and off, he toggled between the players with his other hand. The statistics for each showed their point score, serum levels and Kbot effects.

Kragen zoomed in on Gerrit, who had just vomited again and stumbled along a deserted street.

Next, Kragen panned to the intersection that Gerrit was headed towards and snickered, "He's going to bump into Angelik. That should be entertaining."

He zoomed out and rotated the view again to scan the course for Tara. When he spotted her, he zoomed in. She was carefully lowering herself down the side of a building onto an overhang.

Her eca serum was depleted and with no reserve serums she down-climbed with the rope tied around her as a make shift harness.

Kragen watched keenly as she cautiously approached the next edge. She rolled onto her stomach and swung her feet over the side of the building. Her toes found the windowsill jamb, she gripped the side jambs to lower herself. Kragen zoomed in further to see the strain lines on her face.

Tara moved from window to window until she reached the remains of a fire escape.

She released the rope and wound it back into a coil. She was crouching down tightly gripping the metal railing.

Aww she's so endearing! Kragen thought, *look how she's shaking. The viewers are going to just eat her up.*

A tone signalled Stone's arrival. Kragen waved his hand and the holovid zoomed back out to show the whole city.

"Enter." he said and pocketed his FidgiFlint.

The door opened and Stone guided Vi by the shoulder into Kragen's tower room. It was a circular walled room with a large window on one side, a desk set up near the window with an ambihearth that glowed beside it.

Stone walked Vi to stand by the holovid and settled into a chair.

Kragen acknowledged Stone and turned his attention to Vi, who stood nervously with hir head bowed. Ze was dressed in a black hemp jumpsuit, hir locs pulled neatly back away from hir face and covered in a silk wrap, ze fidgeted hir fingers.

"Vi, come sit down." Kragen instructed.

Vi sat on the other chair. Ze caught a glimpse of the sun setting through the window and turned hir focus to the mountains.

"Well, isn't this winsome? Us; three kindred together? Enjoying a Quart Circuit as a family." He smiled placidly at Vi.

Ze flicked hir eyes between them anxiously.

Kragen tilted his head to the side and said mockingly, "Surely, you are pleased to be among relatives. But perhaps your discomfort is because you are too used to gathering in underground hovels."

Stone chuckled quietly to himself and crossed his legs as he sat back to watch his nephew.

Vi played with hir fingers and tried to ignore them.

Kragen focused his eca and spoke to Vi, "I want you to address me as, my liege. And, I want you to always strive to please me." He let his words hang in the air.

Vi started to sweat as the power of Kragen's words reverberated within hir.

He cleared his throat and said, "Let's practice. Vi, how do you feel being a player in the Grand Hall games?"

Vi tried to stop hirself but the need to speak overwhelmed

hir. Through gritted teeth ze said, "I am proud to be your player, my liege."

"Good!" Kragen guffawed, "Have a look at this course. It's the first of its kind! We chose a ruined city that was mostly overgrown by plants and installed some jaw-dropping obstacles that the viewers will surely love. Even most recently, with the addition of a new player, we reworked some special obstacles with just her eca in mind."

Vi looked down at it. Thirteen players were spread out in all directions, but all steadily moving closer to the red flag flying atop an obelisk.

Vi watched with disinterest until ze noticed a player that descended a fire escape. Ze gasped in disbelief as ze recognized Tara.

"I'm sure by now you've realized that your friend Tara failed to reach the forest. She put on a spectacle and revealed to the whole Federation her electromagnetic ability. She will be a valuable asset to the Federation. This Quarter Circuit is her initiation as a player. Soon she will also be in my collection." Kragen said conceitedly.

Vi shot daggers with hir eyes at Kragen, biting hir tongue to stop hirself from saying what was on hir mind.

Kragen smiled wickedly and focused his eca, "I want you to lure Player Tara to this point on the course."

He pointed to the holovid and a section on the course lit up with a red circle. Vi dropped hir eyes and nodded, hir fingernails dug into hir palms.

"I want you to refrain from speaking to or communicating with Player Tara in any way. Just get her to follow you." He went on focusing his eca.

Vi nodded hir head and started to breathe heavily.

Kragen went on with no regard for how his words were torturing Vi's mind, "Your aim is to lead her to that location then you will exit the course and return here to the castle. Operator Stone will escort you to and from the course and will monitor you through your electronic ankle cuff. If he suspects you need a nudge along the way, that cuff emits a shock at a lower setting that should be incentive enough to keep you focused on your goal. Understand?"

Vi nodded and bit hir tongue.

"I want you say it, Vi." Kragen focused his eca.

"I understand, my liege." Vi felt the words pulled from hir mouth.

"Good. I know you will make me proud." He praised. His smile was warm as he lay back in his chair crossing his ankles, "Let's watch Player Gerrit's fight before you leave."

~~~

The fading light cut through the buildings with the last remnants of day. Exhausted from the Kbot effects, Gerrit hastily searched for a place to tuck in for the night. He entered an intersection when the rough voice of Angelik made him stop in his tracks.

"Well well! Lookie who! Player Gerrit, I challenge you!" Angelik called out from behind him.

He spun around to see hir approaching swinging hir baton and sneering at him. *Sodz!*

"Gerrit! Gerri. Ger. Gah!" ze teased. "You gonna accept my challenge Ger-ger?"

Hir robust figure stalked towards him, the Silver Bishop Division emblem on the shoulder of hir jumpsuit catching under a stray ambilamp.

Running his fingers through his hair nervously and walking backwards into the intersection, Gerrit's ears were ringing while weighing his options, *If I forfeit the challenge, I'll be docked more points, and I'm already down so many from that effn Kbot. If I accept I'll lose to Angelik for certain. I'm in deep turdz either way. Keep playing the part and hope I don't get hit too hard.*

"Yah! Sure, Angelik. I accept!" He said while grabbing the baton from his bag.

A wicked smile spread across hir face as ze reached hir arms out and beckoned Gerrit to come closer.

They dropped their bags as a drone hovered in over them. It illuminated them with a beam of ambilight as the last of the sunlight dropped under the horizon.

Gerrit tried to focus on Angelik and not the bile that burned his throat.

The fight didn't last long. Gerrit found himself face down, Angelik pinning him to the ground with a baton against his neck. One of his arms braced painfully behind his back.

"I yield!" He croaked.

"Yah!! Wooo!" Angelik cheered and released Gerrit's arm.

As ze stood up ze kicked him in the gut once again before ze stepped over him and grabbed hir bag.

Angelik rushed over to his bag and ripped it open. Dumping the contents out and adeptly grabbing all his serums and sniffers ze cackled maniacally while adding them to hir stash.

Ze flashed him a wide grin as ze swung hir newly stuffed bag over hir shoulder and ran off.

The drone switched off the ambilight, leaving Gerrit in darkness. Still winded, he pushed himself up, grabbed his fallen baton and scurried over to the remnants of his pack.

As quick as he could, he collected his sleeping bag, sanitowel, meditape, knife, rope, and meal bars. *At least ze left me with something to eat.* He thought sarcastically.

Looking at his wrist device with dismay, his eca serum level was at 50%. The realization that he no longer had any in reserve hit him like one of Angelik's kicks.

He threw his pack on his back and looked around in the dark. He spotted an old era vehicle with a covered cab.

Good enough. He thought, climbing in to set up for a rough night's sleep.

A Forest Without Trees / JP Solanki-Davie

27

April 1st 2640, waxing gibbous moon

With only the light from the nearly full moon as a guide, Tara carefully climbed down the pile of bricks and rubble that sloped around an old era dumpster. Without her eca she felt completely lost and vulnerable. She sunk into the shadows of the alley not wanting to be seen. The dark was pressing in on her from all around while she pried open the dumpster. She took a big whiff, *Smells neutral. This should do for the night.*

She grabbed a large brick and climbed in. Her feet thudded loudly against the metal and echoed around her in the darkness. She propped the lid open with the brick. A glint of yellow caught her eye and she reached forward until her fingers wrapped around a canister that glowed brighter as she held it.

She studied the small ambitorch, the light grew as she stroked her thumb along its edge. The empty dumpster interior became visible. Relaxing slightly with the presence of light she let out a sigh of relief to be sheltered. She pulled her pack off and retrieved the water canteen. Her mind worked through her plan as she sipped slowly, *Just gotta get through the night then link up with Gerrit. He'll be doing better than me. With his stash of eca serum we'll steer that transport out. If I hide here, I'll be safe until morning.* Tara stuffed a meal bar in her mouth and chased it down with water. She pulled out the sleeping bag and stretched out with her backpack as a pillow. Dimming the ambitorch and laying back, she put her attention on her breathing to settle down.

Just as she felt the pull of sleep, there were a series of high-pitched whizzes followed by several explosive bangs. Tara's eyes opened wide with fright. Flashes of coloured lights came through the gap from the dumpster lid. She struggled to kick her legs out of the sleeping bag. There were more explosions as she crouched to peer out between the gap, the sky was sprinkled with colours. Again and again the sky erupted in ambiworks. The falling lights flitting down on the urban ruin. She darted her eyes around the alley to double check she was still hidden. Once satisfied she slipped back into her sleeping bag and covered her ears with her hands.

The ambiworks continued until Tara was wide awake. When they petered off, she began to relax and again let her body fall into the pace of her regulated breath. *Inhale, one, two, three, four. Exhale, one, two, three, four.* Just as before, a high-pitched whizz filled the air, a series of bangs followed. Another barrage of ambiworks erupted over the city. Tara pulled the sleeping bag up over her head, trying to block out the sound.

~~~

The aroma of a hearty stew filled the small kitchen. Still riding the elation from their successful mission, the long overdue celebration was lifting everyone's spirits. Silas was sharing a drink with Ulf for the first time since the festival grounds, his bushy beard had grown long and grey. Wolf had young Nelli on his knee as he held his mug up to his father, Ulf. Their boisterous laughter was mixing with all the conversations happening at once. Azim was holding Tobi tightly with Akida's arm around them. They had been separated when Azim was captured two years prior. He was embracing his son tightly after finally meeting him that day. Bo and Greta were flitting around the room, filling mugs and passing out bread. Seeing the kitchen full of life made Bo bounce as she moved. Sonal was preparing a soup with Rohit at hir side. He hugged hir leg from the overwhelm of people. He was not yet a pubescent and had never seen the kitchen so full of people. Two others liberated were Alain and Deni. Their daughters Zara and Lyra hovered over them as they enjoyed their soup and bread. Zara was gently massaging her mother's shoulders while Lyra was encouraging them to eat.

"Papa, there's plenty for everyone. Have another bowl full. You weren't fed enough." Lyra insisted. He looked up with tears in his eyes, the scars on his neck stretching as he did. She added, "Go on, Papa. Eat."

Sitting across the table was Tarak, his thick brown hair hung in a mess over his face. His shoulders were rounded and he leaned on his tired arms. His quietness attracted Ezer to sit beside him. He nudged Tarak with his bony elbow and placed a tablet between them. It showed a list of trainees to be transported to the Manufacturing Division.

"Lino and Brill are on that list." Ezer said.

"My Brill?" Tarak almost whispered.

Ezer squinted his pale brown eyes as he surveyed the room, "Our source said, they'd be shipped later today."

Their conversation attracted attention from Sonal. Hir head whipped around and hir long golden-brown hair followed the momentum. Hir eyes were intense with fire as ze reached across the table for the list.

"Raha is on this list." Ze pointed.

The room fell quiet. Silas leaned on the table and scanned the list. He scratched the stubble on his chin and glanced at Zedrik. They exchanged a look that stated their agreement on what needed to happen. Silas activated the holovid. It showed a road meandering through the hills.

"We've been waiting for this opportunity." Silas said as he looked around the room, "Let's keep the momentum going while they're all distracted by the Quarter Circuit."

"Zactly!" Ezer spoke up, "We can't let them take anyone else to those camps!"

"Yah! I have a score to settle." Ulf said.

"Me too" added Alain.

"Let's get our kids back." Ezer said.

There was a unanimous approval from the group, several hooting and tapping their mugs.

"Let's review." Silas pointed at the holovid, "This is where the transport will enter the hills. Ezer's device will deactivate the transport and Xain will use his eca creatin' the mirage. Once the enforcers are distracted, we can extract our eight people. We'll use those new cloakin' packs you made Chet."

Chester was chewing a meal bar sitting on the floor with

Xain next to the screen of the Quarter Circuit. Xain eyed the map skeptically and stood up to get a better look. For their plan to work, they needed the transport to stop precisely between the two larger hills where the road turned sharply, affording them protection from view. Xain would need to project a large enough mirage to hold the enforcers attention long enough for their people to be extracted safely.

Xain crossed his arms over his chest and said, "What about when they get to the work camp. The transport will be empty. They're gonna notice that."

"Yah, but they won't trace it back to us." Silas said. Xain shot him an uncertain look but he continued firmly, "Ezer's device will scramble their system. They may know we did it, but they won't find us. With Chet's cloakin' packs their recorders won't see us. Trust me, Xain. We've been planning this a long time. These are the one's that avoided bein' collected as players. We have a unique opportunity to extract them all at the same time."

Chester finished eating and balled the biodegradable wrapper into his fist as he stood. He put his thick arm over Xain's shoulder and spoke softly, "I know, we'd hoped to extract Vi with this plan. But plans changed as circumstances changed."

"Yah. You're right." Xaid said and let Chester hug him.

"We leave within the hour." Silas stated and stood up..

"Yow! Look at this!" Zalie exclaimed and pointed her pudgy finger at the screen.

Her father Ezer knelt and wrapped his arm around her attentively. She was watching the Quarter Circuit and pointing at a dark street. Everyone leaned in to watch as Vi climbed out of a maintenance hole in the ground. Hir black jumpsuit hid hir from view when the hole closed shutting out the light. Vi sprinted down the street. Throwing hirself at a building and scaling the side effortlessly, the moon was illuminating hir on the roof.

"Vi's an agent." Xain whispered solemnly.

They watched Vi jump from building to building until ze reached the one that overlooked the dumpster that hid Tara from view.

28

April 1st 2640, waxing gibbous moon

After each volley of ambiworks, Tara peered out nervously into the alley for signs of drones. On and on through the night, the sky exploded with colour that echoed off the buildings. Tired and tense, she poked her head out as another series of explosions quietened down. A figure caught her eye from a rooftop. She squinted as she tried to identify the dark form without lifting the lid of the dumpster. The whizz of another ambiwork filled her ears. As it erupted behind the figure Tara saw her friend Vi, hir dark eyes were trained directly at the dumpster.

Tara dropped back as her heart leapt into her throat. She hastily repacked her sleeping bag, dimmed her ambitorch and slipped it into the chest pocket of her jumpsuit. She peered out of the gap again. Vi eyes beckoned for Tara to come out. *Is Vi a player in this course? What is ze doing here?*

She gritted her teeth, carefully climbed out of the dumpster and crouched low behind the mound of rock and rubble.

~~~

Vi's heart ached as Tara climbed out of the dumpster to crouch behind the pile of debris. *No, Tara it's a trap. Don't fall for it.* Kragen's words interrupted hir thoughts, *Just get her to follow you.* Vi sprinted along the rooftop edge. In clear view, of Tara ze leaped across the gap to the next building, rolled then popped up to hir feet. Turning back and peering over the edge of the roof, Vi saw Tara wide mouthed while running after hir.

Vi focused hir eca and stepped back. With a big push ze sprinted to the edge and leapt across the alley. Vi clung to the side of the building, then pushed off, flipped, and landed on a small overhang on the opposite side. Swiftly ze jumped again to land on hir feet at the end of the alley. Vi stood and looked back to see Tara sprinting towards hir in a panic. They made eye contact. "Vi!" Tara called, her brown eyes pleaded for Vi to wait.

Vi fought the urge to respond. *I want you to lure Tara to this point on the course.* Kragen's voice echoed in hir mind as ze kept steadily out of reach of Tara.

Finally, Vi stopped in the middle of an intersection clear of debris. There were remnants of tall buildings all around with multiple roadways all converging at one spot. Vi waited for Tara to catch up. Ze was desperate to try and communicate that ze had led Tara into a trap.

"Wachu doin' here?" Tara panted.

Biting hir tongue and pressing hir lips together to stop hirself from speaking. Vi shrugged hir shoulders instead.

"You k?" Tara asked worriedly.

Without a word, Vi took off in a run towards one of the buildings, ze threw hirself at it and scaled to the top within a few seconds. Tara stood there in the middle of the intersection completely dazed as hir friend pulled hirself onto the roof. Vi turned back to see Tara alone in the open, like the perfect prey.

Overcome with the urge to signal Tara, Vi focused hir eca and spoke into her mind, 'I'm sorry,' Vi fell to hir knees as the shock ripped through hir. "Ow!" Vi gritted out.

The quiet whir of a transport drone approaching overhead drew Vi's attention. Ze looked up as a harness was lowered down. Strapping hirself into it and holding tight to the rope, the drone whirred away. Tara was distracted watching Vi fly into the night and didn't notice the figure approaching her from the shadows.

~~~

Lost in confusion, Tara watched as Vi was carried into the darkness, *Why was ze here? Sorry for what? Why didn't ze talk to me? Is Vi a player on this course? Why did ze run away from me?*

"Hey there, girlie! What a treat to finally meet the infamous, Tara." The voice was like ice water pouring down her spine. She turned and saw Yane, his dark eyes smouldered with desire as he approached. The pit of her stomach dropped as he licked his lips and made kissy faces at her. In a panic, her eyes darted in search for an escape. His head cocked to one side and said, "I challenge you, Player Tara."

She gasped and backed away from him. Blood was rushing in her ears, *I can't fight him! I don't have my eca. I gotta get outta here!*

His smile spread wider as he focused his eca and spoke into her mind, 'That's it girlie, try and get away. Don't accept my challenge, I want to stalk you instead.'

Tara's brow furrowed with concern. She continued to frantically walk backwards.

'Yah, like that. You run and I'll chase you.' He spoke telepathically

She froze on the spot and glared back at him. *Ugh! Is he serious? I can't let this septic creep track me.*

"Hoooo! You gonna accept my challenge?" He mocked.

Tara jutted out her jaw, *I can defend myself, I hope.* She levelled her chin and spoke, "Yah! I accept!"

Yane's eyes darkened as he straightened to his full height. He made a mock frown face as he said, "Hope you're not gonna make this easy. I like a good struggle. Don't you?"

The light of a drone hovering above lit up the scene. Yane tossed his bag to the side, cracked his neck and stretched his arms over head. Tara slowly pulled off the straps of her bag. Remembering the baton inside gave her a surge of adrenaline while pulling it out. She dropped the bag at her feet. Yane eyed the baton flashing her a playful smile.

Yane stepped in closer, Tara moved to the side to keep distance between them. He pulled a faux innocent face and stepped towards her again. She stepped sideways and gripped the baton tighter. He faked one way then lunged towards her. She swung the baton but at the last moment he twisted out of the way, spun around and shoved her ground.

Yane stepped over her as she pushed herself to her hands and knees. He gripped her arm and yanked her to stand so she faced him. She raised the baton in her free hand to strike him, but he stopped her with his other hand. He snapped it down against his thigh so her grip loosened. The baton flew from her hand, clattering to the ground. Swiftly he was gripping both of her arms at her sides and pulling her closer to him so she could smell his pungent sweat. Tara stomped on his foot as hard as she could and felt his grip loosen. She yanked back hard to free her arms and scurried out of his reach.

Her eyes wide and wild, she awaited his next move. He stood tall, cocked his head and spoke telepathically, 'You know I'll catch you girlie, and the more you fight the better the show.'

Tara swallowed hard. *If I had some serum this would be a fairer fight.* She saw the baton on the ground and ran for it. Yane saw her intention before she moved. He quickly stepped in and took hold of her long braid. "Agghhh!! Nooo!" Tara screamed as he yanked her towards him by her hair.

Tara clawed at his hand but he twisted her around and took hold of both her wrists. Wrapping his arms around her in a bear hug and flexing his muscles to restrain her in his arms. Her feet left the ground as he lifted her up. She struggled to breathe as he squeezed her tightly, his hot breath on her neck.

"Mmmm! You smell like flowers." He sighed into her ear.

Tara reflexively reacted. The heel of her foot swung back hard striking Yane in the testicles. She heard the sickening crunch of impact and felt his arms release her as they both fell to the ground. Tara jumped to her feet. Quickly, she turned to face Yane on his knees, his hands cupped his groin and his face screwed up in pain. As she approached he looked at her pleadingly. Her nostrils flared with anger as she glared down at him. She kicked him square in the chest so he slammed back into the ground.

She didn't wait to see if he would get up, but bolted towards her fallen baton, snatched up her bag and ran. Adrenaline was coursing in her system pumping her legs and carrying her as far away from Yane as possible.

Tara finally rested when her lungs burned. She pulled out her ambitorch and held it up above her. A large tree was growing through a building. Without a second thought, she climbed the tree until she was high above the street and felt the safety of the branches around her. She used the rope to secure herself to the trunk, switched off the ambitorch and fell into a restless sleep.

29

April 2nd 2640, waxing gibbous moon

Tara was running. The sun's warmth made her smile as tall grass waved. It was as though she was soaring. Slowing down and looking around, she saw Hami and Hori laughing with other children from Sundarvan. The vast expanse beckoned her to jump. She watched as one by one her sibling-friends focused their eca and zipped down the cable to the other side. Their laughter echoed through the rocky canyon. As she went to take her turn, a rush of wind blew on her face and she shielded herself with her arm. A whisper in the wind told her, "Tara, keep your eyes open."

The scene changed and Tara was in a white room full of monitors and screens. A persistent beeping coming from behind her. She tried to move, but her body was strapped down. The sight of a bone-thin grey-haired man standing at the foot of the table watching her made her feel like she was sinking. She was enveloped by a heavy feeling that tunnelled her vision. All she could see were the man's hazel eyes as they drilled into her. Everything faded to white.

She was shrouded in darkness. Lost. Panic rose from within her chest as she saw lights behind her and heard the enforcer's voices grow louder. The trees were tall and dark. Long shadows chased her. Her feet sucked her into the ground. Everything spiralled and she was swept onto her back. She slid out of control. Unable to slow herself within a smooth orange tunnel. Looking down past her feet with fear into the dark void she was sliding into.

She landed with a thud. She could sense danger approaching. Her heart was racing and there was a ringing in her ears. She needed to escape. Gerrit was by her side urging her forward. She turned to look at him, he was consumed by a shadow and vanished. A blur rushed past her and she spun around. Vi ran, disappearing into a mist. Where did ze go?

Fumes of burning plastic made her choke. She fell to her knees, scratching the earth with her fingernails. Everything went red. She shuddered as Investigator Ada walked into view. She was smiling pleasantly tapping her tablet. Ada's lips moved in slow-motion as her sing-song voice reverberated within Tara's skull, "Run the script."

Tara was suddenly in the bedroom at Tristan's house. She was sitting on the bed waiting. Everything was still. The familiarity of the room made her blink.

This is a dream.

A sudden panic arose within her. The door opened with a stutter and Kragen stalked in. He pinned her against a wall. His dark eyes were penetrating hers when a gust of wind blew between them.

Tara woke with a start. The branches of the tree swayed in the wind. She felt the grip of the rope around her waist and remembered where she was. She leaned her head back against the tree and thought, *Thank you tree friend for the safety of your branches.* Gazing out to the horizon to the daybreak through the layers of shields trapping her. She scanned the city and worried, *Where is Gerrit? How can I find him? That guy last night was a creep. I was lucky. I need to find some eca serum. Wait, I need to calm down and breathe. Inhale one, two, three, four. Exhale one, two, three, four.*

She untied herself and slowly climbed down into an alley that was overgrown with plants. She stared around her in awe. *Whoa! What's this?* She noticed mullein, a furry looking plant with a stalk of yellow buds growing from the centre. She knelt down to touch the soft leaves with her fingers. *Thank you.* She thought as she plucked a leaf. Tucking behind a plastic bin near the opposite wall, she quickly undid the opening in the crotch of her jumpsuit, squatted, emptied her bowels and used the soft leaf to wipe herself. Stepping out and wiping her hands with the sanitowel with a surprising sense of ease. *These plants are breaking the concrete.* The large tree she had slept in wrapped its branches through two buildings and reached higher towards the sky. Tara looked down at the ground cover and recognized several different plants. She felt a flutter in her stomach as her eyes darted around the green foliage; moss, clovers, dandelion, mullein, mint, lemon balm, yarrow, comfrey, lamb's quarters. Hearing the memory of her mother's teaching in her mind, *Bow and present yourself. Listen for an answer carried in the wind.* Tara breathed deeply, bowed her head and said, "Greetings plant friends. I'm Tara."

She dropped to her knees and touched the tough greenery. *May I harvest?* The wind blew through the large tree and she heard the soft sound of the earth speaking, 'Yeeeaaaasss'. Rising to her feet and walking deeper into the greenery with gratitude. She spotted nettle under a pleachee tree and blinked with surprise.

"Are you real?" She said plucking a ripe pleachee and staring at it in disbelief. She unzipped her bag and pulled out the knife, carefully slicing open the hard prickly husk of a shell to reveal the pale pink flesh. Tara salivated at the sweet aroma and she was flooded with memories from her childhood in the wild. Slowly she raised the fruit to her mouth and slurped the delicious juices inside. She dropped the pit to the ground and went on devouring the fruit. She savoured the moment until she was licking the shell.

A grateful smile spread across her face while foraging comfrey, nettle, mullein and other plants from the alley. Once she was done she sat down and pulled out her canteen. She carefully pinched off a couple nettle leaves, but was still stung crushing them into the canteen to infuse with the water. She sliced open pleachee fruits one at a time and devoured the insides. As she washed them down with the infused water, she sat with her back against the large tree. A few small birds fluttered through the branches above her. *What if I just stay here until the course is over?* She thought as her eyes focused on the tiny clover flowers at her feet. Insects fluttered between the flower pods and she got lost in their dance. Tara was so absorbed that she didn't notice when the player walked into the alley.

"How's it, Tara?" asked the player.

Startled, Tara jumped to her feet to face a muscular woman with short dark hair and warm tawny skin that glowed in the sunlight. Tara stepped back nervously. The player raised her palms up to show Tara she was unarmed.

"Don't worry, I'm not gonna challenge you." She stepped cautiously into the alley, "We didn't meet, but I saw you at the party. I was with Gerrit when you arrived. I'm Prynn." She put her hands on her waist and smiled to show the gap between her front teeth.

Tara thought back to that moment at the Banquet Hall party and the women Gerrit had been with on the lounge sofa. She nodded her head in recognition. Prynn wore the same Platinum Knight Division emblem on her jumpsuit and Tara realized, *She's in Tristan's division, like me.*

Prynn swung her bag off one shoulder unzipping it. She pulled out a green canister and said, "A gift." as she tossed it to Tara, who looked down at it confused. "It's for nighttime shows. Blocks out noise." Prynn explained.

"Thanks." Tara said startled by her generosity. She grabbed her knife and a pleachee and offered, "Want one?"

Prynn nodded enthusiastically. Tara sliced the fruit in half, popped out the pit and handed the rest to Prynn. She took it squishing the insides into her open mouth, then tossing the peel to the ground and smiling gratefully at Tara.

"Just one pleachee? Could eat gobs, they're so addictive!" Prynn said and gushed, "I admit I'm starstruck. You're amazing!" She glanced around the overgrown alley quizzically and asked, "How'd you know that was a fruit tree?"

"What!? You've never seen a pleachee tree?" Tara looked at Prynn baffled then at the tree that grew in a garden among the urban decay.

"Um. No." Prynn eyed Tara with the same curiosity.

"Oh." Tara said uncomfortably dropping her eyes to her feet.

"You know," Prynn said turning her nose down at Tara, "you do things polar to norm. Sleeping in a tree and eating plants.

Everyone's hooked on you and will want more of you after this course."

After this course I'll be going home. Tara thought, but smiled politely and replied awkwardly, "Thanks, Prynn."

"Oohh! I love how you say my name with such a bijou accent!" Prynn giggled.

"So, Gerrit's your friend?" Tara asked and ignored her comment.

"Yah. Ger and I became players in the same cohort." Prynn said with pride, "I was lucky enough to make the cut from the Boost Academy. The scouts recognized my talents and I passed the course to enter the recreational sector. Gerrit was my first friend when I arrived at Velvet Lake."

"You were in the Boost Academy?" Tara was surprised.

"Yah. I started in grade C after I was orphaned. But I was able to level up because of my talent." Prynn shrugged and added, "It was nothing like grade F, I bet. I didn't even know there was a grade F. Most orphaned youth who are player material are spotted early on. I was shocked as everyone when it turned out you were Controller Tristan's offspring! I mean, you fleeing that Training compound and crushing those drones was mad crazy. Then you joining the games at your age, with no experience, and you're acing it."

"I dunno about that." Tara mumbled.

Prynn considered her for a moment, "I saw the way you got played last night. I was tucked up in one of the overlooking buildings. The Main Operator is a big fan of throwing agent traps into games to mess with lead players. I watched that agent lure you to where Yane could challenge you. Yane can be an eager dick. You were proper form. He well deserved it. He's so dramatic, laying there until a clinician checked on him. You're gonna wanna watch your back."

Tara tensed at the memory of the night before, "Thanks for the heads up."

"You're totes trend-z, Tara. Winning against Yane and lasting this far without proper training is cracked." Prynn said.

"Thanks?" Tara raised an eyebrow at her uncomfortably.

There was a sudden crushing sound and they both froze. Prynn darted to the edge of the alley and peered around the corner. She quickly pulled back; horror marked her face as she looked at Tara.

"What!?" Tara asked as she dropped to her knees to gather her things into her bag.

"It's a giant Kbot!" Prynn whispered loudly. "It's crushing everything in it's path and it's coming this way!"

Tara's ears rang out as the ground shook. The ominous sound was rumbling beneath their feet. Prynn dashed towards her as she injected her own arm with a blue vial and she said, "Shoot up, Tara!"

"I don't have any!" Tara said in a panic.

Prynn snatched an eca serum from her bag and tossed it to Tara, "Take it! If we team up, maybe we won't get fek'd!"

Tara quickly injected herself. Immediately, she sensed the Kbot and tuned into it to see from its perspective. She dialed into the pulserod, the weapon was designed to weaken muscular activation. Her gut clenched with fear as she realized the devastation that pulserod would have if it was used on them. Tara set her jaw. She focused her eca on the Kbot's programming, saw the script and let it scroll through her mind until she saw Prynn's name followed by hers. With just a thought she deleted their names. For good measure, she scrolled back up to Gerrit's name and deleted it too.

"It's done." Tara said.

Prynn's eyes were wide with confusion and panic as the sound of the Kbot grew closer.

"It's done." Tara said again reassuringly.

Prynn furrowed her brow not understanding. Tara held up her wrist device and showed Prynn her eca level had dropped to 72%.

"It's done." Tara said one last time.

"Whoa! You're serious." Prynn said in shock.

They both crouched down behind the large tree as the

giant Kbot trampled past. It stopped, scanned the alley and didn't see them. It kept on crushing debris in its path. Prynn stood and stared after it, her mouth agape.

She turned back to Tara, "What did you do? How?"

Tara just hooked her thumbs around her bag straps and shrugged. Prynn smiled wider to show the gap in her teeth. "Well then. Let's team up anyway. I've a feeling you'll help my score." Prynn gestured for Tara to follow her out of the alley.

They set off, Prynn taking the lead, she ran at an easy pace, jumping and volleying over some rubble. Tara followed less gracefully, but still managed to keep up. As they approached an intersection Prynn stopped and held up her arm. Tara heard the whiz of the three approaching drones.

Prynn kept her arm up glancing to Tara, "My turn."

She focused her telekinetic ability on the drones. They all stopped in midair and crushed into themselves before they crashed to the ground. Prynn looked back and gave Tara a wink. She set off again with Tara at her heels.

Before they got far the whiz of approaching drones caught their ears again. Prynn gestured for Tara to step out of the way. Tara pressed her back against a building as Prynn focused her eca and lifted several large slabs of concrete from the road. They flew up in the air as seven drones were approaching. Prynn used her eca and hurled them at the drones until each one crashed to the ground.

Turning to face Tara she said, "Sodz! Guess the Main Operator didn't like how easily we got away from that crushing Kbot." She checked her eca level as she ran towards Tara. She grabbed her arm and steered her into the next alley.

"Com'on! Drones are gonna keep coming for us to drain our eca level." Prynn said over her shoulder as they ran, "We need to throw 'em off our track."

They sprinted down the alley only to come to an abrupt halt as a wall of bars flew across their path. They spun around as another wall of bars burst out from the building, blocking the other way. A shield emitted to seal off the top of their cage. Prynn shot Tara an uneasy look.

"Don't use your eca! The cage will electrically shock anyone who uses their abilities." Prynn said.

"What!?" Tara exclaimed.

"Main Operator's version of a penalty box." She said nervously, "Probably doesn't like you hacking his game. Bet we're already being targeted by nearby Kbots"

"So, we just sit here and wait!?" Tara asked.

Prynn shrugged her shoulders, "Got a better idea?"

Tara walked up to one of the bars and looked at the electronic latch that held it against the building. *I can get us out of this cage. Kragen is trying to force us to play by his rules. Fek that! The electrical shock has to be a scare tactic. Tristan said none of the Kbot effects were long lasting or permanent. I won't sit here and wait for Kragen's next move.* Digging her fingernails into her palms and facing Prynn committing to what she would do.

"How big a shock?" She asked.

Prynn's eyes widened in alarm, "Did you lose a screw? Enough to put you out."

"And a Kbot's pulserod will be any better?" Tara countered.

Prynn glanced at the intersection with only a couple buildings still standing around it. She spotted a Kbot as it climbed through the rubble towards them.

"That didn't take long." Prynn said at the sight.

The Kbot towered over the debris. It was navigating effortlessly, using a swinging arm that was rotating around its middle to lift and propel it over the rough terrain. Tara swallowed her fear and took a deep breath in.

"We're outta time." She said.

Prynn watched in horror as Tara focused her eca and the cage bars exploded out.

"Aaaaaaggghhh!!" Tara screamed as a bolt of energy shot out of the wall electrocuting her. Her body crumbled into heap on the ground.

"Effn turdz! Tara! Sodz! Sodz! Sodz!" Prynn screamed and ran to Tara's body.

Moving as quickly as she could and dragging Tara away from the broken cage just as the Kbot was positioning itself. She gritted her teeth and focused her eca. A large boulder lifted up behind the Kbot and Prynn pulled it forward. She let it drop crushing the Kbot into a pile of metal.

Prynn let out a sigh of relief and turned her attention back to Tara who was still knocked out cold.

"You have lost a screw." She muttered.

Quickly scanning the intersection, the only cover was inside one of the few buildings. Prynn pulled her bag to her front, grabbed a snap sniffer and placed it against her nose. She inhaled sharply. A rush moved through her body and she shook her head a few times. Then she swung her bag on her back, grabbed Tara and threw her over her shoulder. Prynn marched to the entrance of the closest building and tucked into the shadows within.

Prynn assessed her surroundings, there was a gallery of columns in the large space with a few boarded-up windows along the wall and a set of stairs that led down into darkness. Prynn carefully lowered Tara onto the ground against the wall. She returned her attention to the door and focused her eca. She pulled a pile of rocks from the rubble in the street until it fully blocked the open door.

"This will have to do." She said quietly.

She impatiently paced back and forth, being careful to not move beyond the space of floor they were on. She checked her wrist device and scanned the map for where they could go once Tara regained consciousness. She peered between the planks of wood and scanned the intersection for any new Kbots or drones. She moved beside Tara and crouched down, pulled out a meal bar and devoured it in three bites. She glanced at Tara who looked like she was asleep.

"What happened out there? La grande fête turdz, is what!" Prynn spoke to herself. She pulled at her thick hair as she worried, "Com'on wake up. I dunno how long until another Kbot shows up." Her hands were shaking. She stood up again. "That snap gave me the jitters, but I can't leave until Tara wakes up. Com'on dynamo wake up!"

~~~

The scrapper lounge was quiet with only Berwyn tucked in the corner table with his cup of tea and his tablet. He was scrolling through his list of pick ups for the next day. The solitude of the lounge made it the perfect place for him to ignore the Quarter Circuit and all the hoopla in the parks. So, when Kohl entered, he immediately drew Berwyn's attention.

"How's it Grand Père?" Kohl asked.

He pulled up a chair and spun it around to straddle. He was smiling widely and leaning his arms on the backrest, eyeing Berwyn playfully.

"What?" Berwyn asked.

"Word is, those spoofs have been approved. We'll likely get'em next month. It's what we've been waitin' for!" Kohl said.

"You've been waiting for." Berwyn corrected.

"Com'on! It's a game changer! You may remember what life was like before, but I don't! By the time I would have developed my eca I was chipped." Kohl said with anger and stood up abruptly crossing his arms over his chest, "Just thought you'd wanna know, since us scrappers never get access to eca serum. But I can see I've interrupted your quiet repose."

Berwyn lifted an unimpressed eyebrow and leaned back relaxed in his chair, his tone was firm but gentle, "My lack of interest doesn't matter. You have every right to be excited. But remember Kohl, you're talented beyond your eca. Don't forget that just because your siblings are clinicians. You chose this lifestyle, as much as your defiant behaviour placed you here. But your purpose is greater than these tunnels."

Kohl jutted his chin and muttered, "I did choose this. Effn politics on the surface. I'm just eager, is all."

"I know. It's good to be eager. You're right. It's a game changer. But be easy." Berwyn said gesturing for Kohl to sit down again, "We scrappers are playing on a whole other level."

30

April 2nd 2640, waxing gibbous moon

Finally, Tara began to stir and Prynn rushed to her side.

"Yow! Easy, easy." She said as she guided Tara to sit.

"Ouch." Tara winced. She placed her hand to her side where her jumpsuit had been singed.

Prynn's brow creased with concern. She produced Tara's bag and handed her the canteen.

Tara smiled weakly, took it with shaky hands and sipped slowly. She placed the canteen down and opened the front of her jumpsuit to inspect where she had been shocked. She peeled back the material until she saw the red mark the size of her fist on her side, just below her ribs.

"Hand me my bag," she said.

Prynn passed it to her and Tara reached in for the plants she had foraged earlier. Prynn watched keenly as Tara tore a leaf of comfrey and started to chew it, then she pulled it out of her mouth and brought it to her side against the burn. She pulled the meditape from her bag and secured a strip over the poltice. Tara took a slow breath in and let it out resting her head back against the wall.

"You a witch or something?" Prynn asked.

"Yah! Something like that." Tara laughed lightly. She closed her jumpsuit and looked around. "Where are we?"

"In a building next to that alley. I crushed the Kbot and carried you here. We should get moving, but first you need to refuel." She handed Tara a meal bar.

"Thanks Prynn." Tara took it gratefully and slowly began to nibble.

They sat in silence as Tara ate. When she finished, she asked, "So, that was Kragen's reaction to me reprogramming that Kbot. Suppose he'd prefer we had a showdown with it?"

Prynn nodded her head and gave Tara an empathetic look. She focused her eca and spoke into Tara's mind, 'Kragen's gonna keep messing with you. You know? I've seen it before with Nylah. He's testing you, big time. Most play into his hands for the views and the chance to level up or be selected for the Interlude. Only you're super fresh and you're no common player. You're magnetic and trend-z. Kragen will want to collect you for his net, or transfer you into security, or something, if you don't already know.'

Tara listened and blinked slowly, her mind flashed back to the conversation she overheard from Ada's tablet, *It is only because she is your offspring that Our Sovereign Kragen has even considered her staying here with you.* The ball in her gut clenched. She slowly turned to Prynn and said out loud, "I've heard."

Prynn shrugged her shoulders and said, "Com'on Tara. You're trend-z, that means you're heading to the top! Don't be faux like you don't want to win!"

I want to go home. Tara thought, but just smiled politely back at Prynn.

Prynn pulled out a couple blue vials from her bag.

Tara glanced down at her wrist device and saw the eca level was at 0% and flashed red.

Prynn injected herself then offered the other blue vial to Tara, who took it and injected it into her upper arm.

Prynn peered out through the slats of the windows. She grabbed her bag, threw it over her back and looked down at Tara impatiently.

"Com'on, Tara. Let's go." She hissed.

Tara stood up carefully and secured her bag on her back. She looked around the gallery of columns and focused her electromagnetic ability.

She tuned into all the different electrical devices in the

space, all the recorders and traps that were hidden in the room.

"Which way do we go? This place is full of traps." Tara said and glanced over towards the stairs. She tuned into her wrist device. The map showed a lower level tunnel that led from that building and went several city blocks in the direction of the flag.

Prynn followed her gaze towards the stairs and said, "If we go outside, we'll be met with more drones and we'll be too exposed. Whachu think is down there?"

"Those stairs connect to this tunnel." Tara said gesturing to the map on her wrist device.

"Can you sense any traps down there?" Prynn asked with a glint in her eye.

Tara focused her eca towards the darkness below but could only sense the recorders. *Is that the way Kragen wants us to go?* Tara wondered.

"There's no traps I can sense." She said.

"Hmm. Maybe some sputnik style obstacles await? Whachu say Tara, think viewers want us to go down the dark tunnel?" Prynn asked with a laugh.

"Acha. Lemme clear a path to the stairs." Tara focused her eca and sensed several pressure traps on the floor, a few projectiles from the side walls. She tuned into their program and with a single thought deactivated all the electronic traps. *Give the audience a good show.* She thought sarcastically.

The two set off into the darkness of the stairs. Tara pulled out her abmitorch and held it out in front of them. A beam of light was their guide as they descended slowly.

Once at the bottom they saw the beginnings of a long tunnel that was completely intact. Compared to the rest of the urban decay of the course, it seemed oddly out of place.

Prynn shot Tara a quizzical look. Tara focused her eca again but couldn't sense anything but recorders.

They walked at a slow pace, the ambitorch glowed against the endless darkness.

After a time, Prynn focused her eca and spoke into Tara's mind, 'This is raz. There's gotta be something big at the end.'

They continued to walk in silence. *Prynn's right. Kragen wants entertaining content, us walking in darkness is not it. I have a feeling I'm not gonna like what's at the end. Maybe we should go back and get above ground.*

Suddenly a sharp noise filled the tunnel. In the next instant a high velocity anti-eca current rushed into them. Tara felt her eca drain as she stumbled off her feet. When the winds let up Prynn gave Tara a startled look and they stood up. She saw her eca level had dropped down to 0%. Tara held the torch up high but there was nothing around them.

Prynn frantically began to search her bag for another serum vial when they heard an ethereal voice from the darkness, "You do not need your extra cerebral ability here. Come forward, Player Prynn and Player Tara."

They followed the voice to where the tunnel opened up, ambilights switched on to reveal a circular room, in the middle was a small circular table covered in black crushed velvet cloth. Three chairs were set up around the table and one of them was occupied by a woman with long red hair and piercing green eyes.

The woman was dressed in a cerulean robe with the hood drawn up over her head, curls of red fell at her shoulders. She held her pale waif-like hands out, gesturing for them to sit down.

As they did, Tara turned off her ambitorch and asked, "Who are you?"

"The question you should be asking is not 'who are you?' but, 'why are you here?'." Corrected the woman. Her eyes twinkled as she went on, "My name is Seer Freya. The Main Operator acknowledges your cunning evasion of the other obstacles and offers you another challenge. You must accept."

Freya pulled a deck of cards from her robe and shuffled. Tara and Prynn watched with anticipation as she spread the cards into a line with one smooth motion of her hand.

"Each choose one. High card wins." She stated.

Tara glanced at Prynn apprehensively as they each picked a card. The woman gathered the rest of the cards and gestured for them to show what they chose.

Tara turned her card to reveal the eight of diamonds and Prynn laid down the nine of clubs.

"Low card enters the maze." Freya said.

She scooped up the two cards, added them back to the deck and returned it into her robe. With her other hand pulled out a flask along with a small shot glass. She poured a small amount of green liquid and slid the glass towards Tara. Tara's body flushed as she gaped at the drink.

"What maze?" Tara asked nervously.

Freya smiled kindly and explained, "You will drink the elixir and enter the maze to run the virch program. Overcome the obstacles within. You have until the dose runs out to escape the maze and return here to claim your prize."

"You want me to drink this!?" Tara blurted out.

She was in a panic at the idea of being sent alone into a maze after consuming some unknown liquid. Freya nodded her head and interlaced her hands on the table.

Tara turned to Prynn for help, but she shrugged her shoulders as though there was nothing to be concerned with and nodded her head towards the green shot.

Guess I have to do this. This elixir's gonna trigger an effn virch nightmare! Tara clutched the shot glass, licked her lips and resolved to do what she needed to do.

As quickly as she could, she threw the drink down her throat. Her face puckered as she swallowed and her body tingled

Pushing herself to stand, noticing the instant change of the virch activating in her system, she was drawn to a green light from behind Freya.

She slowly approached and the light grew brighter until she could see the wall was not solid but had a low arched doorway. With a brief glance over her shoulder to Prynn, she ducked through to enter the maze.

31

April 2nd 2640, waxing gibbous moon

Composing herself, Tara set out walking slowly to the end of the grey passage with green abmilights lining the seam of the ceiling. It turned to the left. Again, the passage stretched on and Tara walked slowly. She followed a few turns. After another turn to the left she saw a junction up ahead.

A lump formed in her throat as she approached the junction cautiously. She looked both left and right and noticed the ambilights were yellow in both directions. *Hmm. Which way?* She wondered. She set off down the left passage, which went straight for a long time. Just as she was starting to wonder if the other passage was the better choice, she heard deep voices.

"There she is!", "Oooooh!", "Come and play with us, Tara." She froze as three enforcers materialized at the end of the passage. The ambilights switched to red as they stalked towards her. Tara quickly moved backwards. Through the sound of her heart racing, she heard the enforcers teasing, "Oh? Don't go yet.", "Stay with us.", "We've been waitin' for you.", "You're not gonna play with us?"

Tara turned and sprinted as fast as she could back down the passage to the junction, the enforcers behind her keeping pace. When she reached the junction, she turned back down the hall where she came and ran until she couldn't hear the enforcers anymore. Looking back, she saw she was alone. She took a steadying breath, *Alright, I'll go the other way.*

As Tara headed back down the hall to the junction, she saw the three enforcers in the entrance to the passage. Her heart quickened and she froze again. The enforcers didn't move or say anything, they just looked at her. She kept her eyes on them as she turned down the right passage. This one was shorter with a few turns Tara followed until she came to another junction. As she did, she saw the ambilight in the passage switch from yellow to green.

She looked back at the green ambilights lining the ceiling and thought, *So, when I get to a junction correctly the ambilights go green. If I go down the wrong passage, they to change red.*

Tara turned her attention to the new passages to choose from, both with yellow ambilights. This time she chose the right passage and followed along until she came to another junction. Once again, the passage she was in changed to green ambilights and she was faced with another choice, left or right. Biting her lip with indecision and turning right again, she set off reluctantly. She stopped as she heard another voice.

"Well, well, Player Tara. Just look how far you've come from the Training compound, and in such a short time." Caretaker Bridget taunted.

Tara's ears burned as Bridget bared her teeth. The ambilights changed from yellow to red as Tara froze from fear.

"You're still not very bright. Are you? You chose the wrong passage, this is your deterrent." She held up a pulserod pointing it at Tara. "Now is when you turn and run in the other direction." She added patronizingly.

Tara heeded Caretaker Bridget's words and raced back down the passage past the junction. Once she was there Tara turned back to see Bridget in the entrance at the junction. She glared at Tara with her beady eyes and waved the pulserod coyly.

Tara clenched her jaw and turned away from Bridget. *This is a virch hallucination.* She reminded herself that neither Bridget nor the enforcers were real. She set off down the yellow ambilight lined passage, following the turns until coming to another junction. The ambilights turned green and she turned left. Once again, she froze when she heard voices.

"Yow look! It's Tara.", "Com'on let's get her!" They yelled. The ambilights switched to red and Tara saw as a group of players materialize in front of her. She blinked several times as she saw the players who had jumped from the same transport as her. These were the players she was competing against on this course. She sprinted back down the passage, confused as she looked over her shoulder at Prynn and Gerrit's faces among the other players. They were all jeering at her while racing back down the passage. When she got to the junction the group of players crowded around the entrance to the passage. *It's not real. This is virch.* She reminded herself in an effort to calm her nerves. Walking down the opposite passage and turning several times she saw the way opening up into a room. The ambilights turned green and Tara felt a sense of relief as she recognized the centre of the maze ahead. She rushed into the room and looked around the empty space.

In the next instant, an old era game console materialized along with two opposing chairs in the centre of the room. She walked up to them and saw the word, Pong, written in capital letters across the yellow panel on the side, a glass top showed a screen with some basic graphics. Tara marvelled at the archaic dials and the odd faux wood finishing.

"Greetings, Player Tara." Kragen's voice resonated.

Tara gasped and spun around as he materialized behind her. Her stomach leapt into her throat and she fought her impulse to run back through the maze.

"Sit down. We are going to play a game." He commanded and gestured for her to take a seat.

Tara did as she was told. Kragen eyed her keenly. A shiver ran down her spine and her palms started to sweat. *He's just a virch trip. Play the game and get outta the maze.* She reminded herself.

"Winner takes all." Kragen stated.

He flicked a switch and the game started. Slowly the ball of pixels moved from one side. Kragen moved his paddle, boop the ball bounced towards Tara. She moved her paddle - boop the ball returned to Kragen. On and it went, a simple game of pong.

When Kragen finally scored on Tara he boasted triumphantly. *Yah, top points.* She thought sarcastically. He started another round. Each rally dragged on as the ball of pixels seemed to move in slow motion between their paddles. Every now and then Tara would glance up towards Kragen whose angular features stayed fixed, his dark eyes focused on the game.

He's not here, this game's not here. It's all a virch trip. If he's not really here, he can't use his eca. At least my mind is safe from his influence. Why are we doing this? All because he wanted to play Pong? Or was it because it was too simple for me to bypass his Kbot? So, he brings me here where I can't use my eca, but why? Everything else in the maze was to push me here to play this game with him. Why this game? Tara wondered, her eyes now dry from staring at the low-resolution screen for so long.

Other than the persistent boop sound from their paddles, there was silence. Kragen's expression was impassive except after scoring a point when he would look at Tara triumphantly, then he would focus back on playing.

All this for what? His ego? The views? To prove he can beat me? Tara's thoughts continued to distract her. *Fek! I'm the game. He's playing me!*

Finally, after Kragen scored 11 points over Tara, he sat back satisfied and said, "I win."

Before Tara had a chance to respond, the floor dropped out from under her and she was spiralling downwards through a tunnel. She struggled to slow herself on the slide until she was shot out into the circular room with Prynn and Freya.

Tara fell on her bum with a thud. Prynn rushed to her side and helped her to stand.

"Bravo! Player Tara, you escaped the maze! You have been awarded five hundred points and may possess the contents of that trunk." Freya's ethereal voice chimed in Tara's ears.

Tara blinked around as the virch elixir ran out. She followed Freya's hand to a small trunk next to the table. Stepping over to it, opening the latch to reveal five vials of serum and a grey marble with a black line around its middle. Tara held the marble in her palm curiously before depositing all of the trunk's contents into her bag and standing up.

A hole opened up in the ceiling, a beam of natural light was cast into the room and a ladder appeared for them to climb out. Prynn rushed over and held the ladder steady for Tara.

Tara's eyes darted around as she pulled herself into the

middle of a large intersection with buildings on all sides.

The reality of the bigger game crashed down on her. She looked down at Prynn, who had almost climbed out, and mentally urged her to move faster. As Prynn emerged from the hole the familiar whiz of a drone filled their ears.

"Not giving us much time, eh?" Prynn said tartly.

Suddenly Prynn pulled out a vial from her bag and injected her arm. In one fluid motion, Prynn scooped up a large rock and hurled it towards the drone, which exploded into pieces upon impact. Prynn looked over her shoulder at Tara and winked.

"You gotta fill me in on what happened in that maze later. Let's go!" Prynn said leading Tara out of the intersection and into one of the alleys.

Once they were in the safety of some shadows Prynn stopped and crouched low. She pulled out her canteen and drank. Tara grabbed an eca serum vial, loaded the needlegun and injected her arm. She tuned into the electromagnetic signatures around them, in search of any drones or kreepbots. Following Prynn's lead, Tara drank from her canteen until her thirst was quenched. The sun was low in the sky, it wouldn't be long before dark.

"That tunnel was a short cut. Look, we skipped this whole section," Prynn said, gesturing at the map on her wrist device. "Bet we're in lead for the flag! Let's go for it before it gets dark. Com'on this way offers the most cover."

They set off quietly down the alley, with Tara using her eca to scan for any approaching drones and Prynn leading them through the rubble. Tara relished the fresh air after her experience in the maze with Kragen. *What was that about? How was playing Pong entertaining to watch for anyone? He said, 'winner takes all'. All what?* Tara's mind worked through the strange encounter.

They climbed over a large pile of rocks and Prynn held up her hand for Tara to stop. She looked back and whispered, "Another player's coming."

Tara crouched down so she could peer over the pile of rubble but remained hidden. Prynn, who was already at the top of the pile, stayed upright and focused her attention on the player.

"Yow, Angelik!" Prynn called.

"Yow, Prynn! You narbo! How'd you get so far?!" Angelik's taunt carried.

Prynn shot Angelik a snarky smile and said, "I challenge you, Angelik."

Angelik's laugh echoed around the barren landscape. Prynn crossed her arms over her chest and waited.

Tara stayed crouched down and focused her eca to speak to Prynn's mind, 'Wachu doin' Prynn?'

Her question was met with silence from Prynn as Angelik yelled back, "I accept your challenge, Prynn. I'll take all your serums, like I did with Gerrit!"

Angelik challenged Gerrit and took his serums? Tara worried. Prynn moved down the pile of rocks and spoke telepathically to Tara, 'Get gone, Tara. I got this. Don't listen to hir. Ze's full of rot. Go grab that flag and win this!'

Tara hesitated, but when she saw the drone fly over Angelik and Prynn who circled each other, she climbed back down and followed an alternate route. She moved much slower without Prynn and with the sun low in the sky, she was ready to find a spot to hide for the night. Pausing behind a brick wall, Tara opened her jumpsuit and squatted to empty her bladder. Further on were some concrete stairs that led to a platform that had been reduced to gravel. Under the steps was a small opening.

Tara shone her ambitorch inside, it was just big enough for her to squeeze in. *This'll work.* She set it up with her sleeping bag and snacked on a meal bar. As she peeled another pleachee and savoured the sweet juices, she watched the failing light diffused through the shields.

Grateful for the green canister that Prynn had given her that morning, Tara settled in, covering her ears with the muffs and pulled her bag onto her front to crawl feet first into her sleeping bag. She wiggled herself further back into the small opening so she would be hidden from view. The cramped space felt both safe and restrictive. Sleep slowly arrived as Tara focused on her breath. *Inhale, one, two, three, four. Exhale, one, two, three, four.*

32

April 2nd 2640, waxing gibbous moon

Heat radiated from the ambihearth next to the large table in the kitchen, everyone had finished their meal and celebration was in the air. They had to bring extra chairs to squeeze everyone in. Their bellies full and their spirits lifted, there was a renewed drive to keep up their fight against the Federation.

Xain looked at all the happy faces around the table, a pang of guilt consumed his heart that Vi wasn't among them. Brill's rich brown eyes caught his attention. She smiled brightly and leaned across the table.

"How's it Xain? It's good to see you." She said.

"Heya Brill. It's good to have you and your dad back among our ranks." Xain replied.

Her smile spread wider as she turned to her father Tarak and wrapped her arms around him in an embrace. Tarak wraped his arm around his daughter and leaned his head into hers warmly.

"I dreamed this day would come." Tarak said as he stroked Brill's brown hair.

Xain smiled warmly at them and turned his eyes down the table where he saw Alain, Deni, Lyra and Zara sitting together closely. Lyra was showing her parents the new prosthetic arm Ezer built for her. Next to them Akida fed Tobi, who was balanced on Azim's knee. Ezer had an arm around Lino's shoulder as they had a quiet conversation. Sonal was beaming at hir two offspring, Raha and Rohit, who were together for the first time in six years. Ritu was sandwiched between her parents, Asha and Niral. Beside them was Twitch and his mother Pu, she embraced her son tightly after she explained how his father, Haze had died years earlier in a failed attempt to rescue him from the Training compound. Vipin was across from Twitch, his parents were at

Adrshy, the secret encampment in the wild, he was lost in his drink, deep in contemplation. Hami and Hori were in a corner whispering their plan to cross the wedge and hike through the forest to reunite with their mother, who was also at the Adrshy.

Brill reached her long slender brown arm across the table and caught Xain's attention again, "What about Vi and Tara? We don't know what happened. Did Tara get caught? Where is she? We know Vi was thrown in an isolation chamber and never came back." She intently held Xain's attention, set her jaw and asked again, "What happened to them?"

A flutter of butterflies stirred in Xain's stomach at Brill's words and he returned her determined stare.

"It's not good." He replied bleakly, "Vi's been placed under Kragen's net and is one of his agents."

Brill's eyes widened in distress, "An agent? Fek! Wha'bout Tara?"

"Turns out Tara's father is Controller Tristan." Xain explained, "He collected her and she's been positioned as a player. She's been thrown into the Quarter Circuit." Xain glanced over at his father who was next to him.

Zedrik peered back at his son. "We saw Vi lure Tara in the course last night. They're both deeply twisted in the games."

Brill let out a low whistle. Leaning back in her chair and linking arms with her father, she said, "Well, now there are more of us, we can fight to get them out."

Tarak beamed at Brill's determination and nodded his agreement. Brill looked around the group at the table, she made eye contact with each of her friends from the Training compound in turn before focusing on Xain again.

"They split us up and tried to wash us clean of our 'feebler ways'. Program us to be players. Prove to them we had what it takes to play their dank games." There was bitterness in her voice as she mimicked Bridget's words, "To level up, one must demonstrate the necessary qualities to be a player in the Federation games." Brill sighed deeply, "Vi kept us safe, ze'd protect us from the enforcers when possible and kept us hopeful that you'd come back for us. Then you did. Tara shared those songs her mother taught her. Stories of the wild. Do you think they're true? I do. I wanna live there, but there are too many of us still trapped. What are we gonna do?"

"We celebrate tonight. Tomorrow, we get to work." Zedrik said. He turned his eyes tenderly towards Xain and squeezed his son's shoulder. "We've been hidin' for too long. Brill's right, there are too many of us still trapped, and I'm not leavin' until all of them are free of the games, the surveillance and those dank chips. Y'all bein' here is a good omen. Tides are turnin' and together we rise up."

Xain looked around the room as his heart swelled. It had been so long since he'd seen most of these people; to witness their desire to fight gave him a renewed hope. The room settled into a hum as everyone returned to their conversations.

Zedrik caught Brill's attention, "I also believe the stories of the wild are true. In fact, I know they are. Many of us already settled at Adrshy. They'll be in communication with the Cullis from there. While we wait, we fight the only way we know."

"Let me know when I can lend my vocal abilities." She said with a twinkle in her eye.

A grin spread across Zedrik's face. He replied, "Will do."

Xain's attention was drawn to the screen in the corner that showed the Quarter Circuit. Gerrit was in a fight with Reilly, he got the upper hand and flipped Reilly hard onto the ground. After winning the challenge he collected Reilly's eca serums and ran off.

"You missed a lot on the course today." Chester explained as he slipped onto the chair next to Xain.

Xain eyed him with interest, "Oh?"

"While you were busy liberating our people, Tara was playin' so good it's cracked. She's twistin' the perimeters of the game with her eca. It's mad crazy! What Sheena told us about Tara's eca is true. It should be simple enough to send her the encoded message tonight. She'll have that tablet you slipped her." Chester paused to view Xain's response, then said, "Kragen's settin' his talons on her. You missed him enterin' the course to have a virch Pong game with Tara, the first time in history Kragen has entered a Quarter Circuit since he became Main Operator."

"What!?" Xain said in shock. He looked to his father who nodded affirmation. A shadow moved across Xain's face as he asked, "Lemme guess, when they played virch Pong, he won?"

"Yah, he won." Zedrik said.

"Natch he did." Xain said bitterly.

"Yah, natch he did. We're lucky Tristan collected Tara before Kragen did. It gave us time to link up with her. Now when Kragen does collect her. She'll be in the know." Chester said.

"I dunno about lucky. Tristen's wrapped around Kragen's pinky finger!" Xain said, "Ya'll really gonna act like a link up with Tara means she's safe from Kragen, or because Tristan's there? He'll help as much as turdz! As much as he helped Mom!"

Xain composed himself as he looked around the room. Silas moved around the table and leaned on his forearms next to Xain as he looked at the screen. "You know, we got a message from Dillon. He's always been loyal and forthcomin' with useful info." Silas said casually, "He was keen to share how Tristan's kid wanted a map of the fringe territory. Seems Gerrit's posin' as a player. He's been actin' glassy eyed to get by. Dillon met him and Tara at Kijami. Dillon thinks those two are gonna take a hike after the course."

"Gerrit's posin'?" Xain asked skeptically. On the screen, Gerrit was being chased by a Kbot that sounded an alarm to draw players to his location. He was moving steadily but he was nowhere close to Tara. Xain studied him through the screen, "I watched him at that party, he wasn't a creep. He's a good performer though. Do you really think he'd want out?"

"Keep wary until he shows us his intent. For now, the message is for Tara, but if Gerrit proves his resolve in our favour..." Silas let his sentence trail off, shrugging his shoulders.

"You wanna keep an eye on the perimeter and watch it play out live?" Zedrik asked Xain, "You know, watch the ambiwork show."

Xain gave his father a mischievous smirk, "Zang."

33

April 3rd 2640, full moon

Tara's eyes popped open to the dark dusty space she was crammed within. She looked around, confused. After the memory of the day before came back to her, she looked down at her wrist device and saw that she had slept the whole night through. *It doesn't feel like I slept.* She was unable to recall any dreams. Shuffling her way out of the opening, she was relieved to be able to breathe deeper. Quickly, she scanned her surroundings. When she knew it was clear she pulled herself out and shoved her contents back in her bag. The sun was high, some birds soared through the cloud spotted sky. She took a breath and stretched her body, enjoying the relief after being cramped for so long.

She relieved herself behind the broken brick wall and wiped her hands with the sanitowel, pulling open her jumpsuit to inspect where she had been electrocuted. The poultice had dried up and the redness had gone down a little. She removed the meditape and let the used plants fall to the ground. She shoved the balled-up tape into her bag and wiped her hands with the sanitowel again.

She climbed up the rubble to a concrete slab. From her vantage point, she could see most of the city. To her left in the distance was the large tree she had slept in the night before, her heart swelled with gratitude for that time immersed in nature. To her right was the tall obelisk with the red flag mounted on top. She chewed her cheek as she considered her options. *I'm so close to the flag. But where's Gerrit?*

Tara removed her bag, grabbed a serum vial and injected herself. Focusing her eca and scanning the area for any approaching drones or other electromagnetic signatures, it was all clear except for one. Startled, she placed her hand over the pocket that held the two tablets. She could sense a new message on the tablet Xain had given her. Tara bit the tip of her tongue as hope surged in her chest. She opted to read the message with her eca and not reveal she had the tablet. It was a short stream of text that read: *'Feel no way, Tara. This device is a cyph communicator and you can activate the tracker to be on our scope. Use it if needed.'*

Tara's heart swelled and she focused her eyes on the horizon, *It's gonna work. I'm going home.*

She sat down, crossing her shins. She grabbed her canteen and sipped water, then grabbed a meal bar and nibbled. *Do I even need to try and win the flag now? What's the point if Kragen's just gonna twist the game? After playing virch Pong with him, I don't wanna race for the flag. No. I'm not gonna play into his hands. Let someone else get the flag. I don't care. I'm gonna sit here and wait.* Three birds soared through the sky on their way to rest in the branches of the large tree. Tara stretched her legs out over the rubble and tried to relax. Staring up at the clouds floating past the shields, her eyes wandering lazily over the fluffy white shapes, she imagined she was back home in the Sundarvan.

A few minutes later there was the familiar whir of an approaching drone. An annoyance swept over her as she realized Kragen wanted to push her to move. Darting her eyes at the drone and focusing her eca she was struck by an idea. She deactivated the paint balls, tuned into the drone's system and switched off the network. She felt the control of the drone in her mind and used its lens to view the city. With just a thought she steered the drone higher up and carefully started to scan the rubble below.

I wonder how Kragen will react to that? Tara thought snarkily. A satisfied grin spread across her face as she noticed Prynn climb into view from her drone's lens. Tara pulled the drone higher and away from Prynn's sight. *Don't want her destroying my new toy,* she thought and steered the drone down another street in search of Gerrit.

~~~

The windows of the circular tower room were shrouded with thick curtains. Kragen was so absorbed in the course, he hadn't left the room since it started, except to visit the virch room.

Musky stale air settled around him. His dark eyes fixed on the holovid of Tara's relaxed figure as she used her eca to steer his drone through the course.

"Well played, Tara. I'll allow you this sense of freedom, for now." He said and curled the corners of his lips towards his eyes.

Kragen ran his hand under his black silk shirt, gently rubbing his neck and shoulder while drinking her in, *She was super bijou in virch, I bet she'll be a bijou bunny in real life.* He looked at the scores of all the players and smirked as he saw Tara was ahead by 1000 points. *The viewers agree, Tara has this course in the bag.* His eyes darkened as his smile twisted into a vile grin. *Now she's mine. After all, winner takes all. With that rule, I don't need to wait to have her in my collection. I can control her through Tristan. He will be here soon and we can finalize the terms of the arrangements.*

He waved his hand and the course zoomed out to show the whole city with twelve players getting closer to the flag, Tara was the only one resting. He played with his FidgiFlint mindlessly to distract him from his eagerness for what would come after the game was over. A tone signalled someone at the door. Kragen glanced down at his wrist device and thought, *Ah, Tristan, punctual as usual.* He pocketed his FidgiFlint and straightened up.

"Enter." He said.

Tristan entered, followed by a guardian. The guardian set up a tray of fruits, breads and cheeses, within arms' reach of Kragen, then left quietly. Kragen gestured for Tristan to sit across from him.

"Welcome, Controller Tristan." He said.

"Thank you for hosting this viewing party, my liege." Tristan replied with a small bow.

Kragen smiled benevolently. He lazily plucked a grape from the tray and popped it into his mouth, chewing slowly. His eyes wandered back to the course and Tristan followed his gaze.

"Have you enjoyed the course, Controller Tristan?" Kragen asked.

"Yes, my liege. It's a spectacular course." Tristan said.

"Oh good! That pleases me," Kragen smiled brightly. His face morphed into a mock frown as he went on, "Shame about Player Gerrit's performance. String of bad luck with that Kbot on the first day, and again on the second day with all those challenges from the other players."

"Well, for Gerrit's first full-city course, he's keeping up." Tristan said and cleared his throat, "Those Kbots attracted a lot of challenges for him. At least he held his own. You know he's never been a tremendously enthusiastic player. Was that your plan? Give him a chance to level up and gain more viewers?"

Kragen nodded his head solemnly, "Yes, your son has been slow to mature as a player. This course has certainly pushed his limits. It is for his own good."

"He's shown more keenness during training, since Tara's been with us. They seem to have really grown kindred." Tristan added.

Kragen raised his eyebrows with interest and shifted forward eagerly. He waved his hand over the controls and zoomed in on Gerrit. His statistics showed he had six serum vials in reserve and 65% of his current level, he was low in points but had won a few challenges giving him extra viewers. He was still a full day's walk away from the flag.

"He has a ways to go to catch up with Player Tara." Kragen remarked.

With a slight twitch of his nose, Tristan said, "Tara has been playing surprisingly well. Her challenge against Player Yane had an unexpected outcome, as did the way she escaped the penalty box. I'm proud of her and relieved she was unharmed."

Kragen shook his head with disappointment, "Controller Tristan, I would never manipulate the game to harm Player Tara. She is far too important."

Tristan straightened out his platinum suit jacket and replied nervously, "Of course, my liege. I was only surprised."

Kragen plucked another grape and gave Tristan a demeaning look, "You've known me for how long? Have I ever seriously harmed one of my players? No." He softened his expression and went on, "Player Tara has done extremely well on the course. I had no doubt she would. She has the same determination as her mother."

"Yes." Tristan replied stiffly, "Sheena was determined."

Kragen chuckled, "You're still sour she got away from you?"

"No. She got away, but I still was able to win her over. Tara has been my reward." Tristan replied arrogantly.

Without losing his grin Kragen replied, "Tara is a prize. My friend, you most certainly won Sheena over. Unlike Noble Remi. She rejected you and ran to the arms of that terrorist, Zedrik. Had you not failed to identify Remi's family during the festival grounds, she could have been saved all these years of grief. I wonder how my pixie-eyed sister is enjoying the course, watching her offspring in play."

Tristan sucked his cheeks bitterly without reply. Kragen let Tristan stew in his words while he chewed his grapes. They watched as Gerrit climbed over a pile of rubble. Tristan cautiously glanced at Kragen as he ate. He returned his eyes to the holovid and worried about Tara's fate after the course was finished. She lounged while she directed the drone down another street.

"Perhaps what Player Gerrit needs is more incentive." Kragen finally broke the silence by changing the subject, "If he is to bond with my eldest, he needs to level up his game. Let him have a taste of the responsibility of a controller."

"A controller! My liege, that's generous." Tristan said, blinking with surprise.

"He will assist as a controller for the 2nd Quarter Circuit this year." Kragen said.

"Thank you, my liege." Tristan said.

Kragen casually added, "After the course, Operator Stone will test Player Tara's eca personally. She will spend a couple days at the Arcus. Her eca is too unique not to explore further. Think of what we could synthesize from her ability."

Tristan took a slow breath in, "My liege, I implore that

she only stay a short time. She's not acclimatized to her position."

Kragen looked directly at Tristan, "I agree completely. She will remain under your net, naturally. I also will not throw her in the bonding games. Let's not rush her into anything. After the course she needs to stay off view until I grant it, then I want her primarily on private channels. Her trend-z status is powerful and we must harness it for mutual benefits."

"Thank you, my liege." Tristan said, "Seeing as her birthday nears, I would like to arrange a party."

Kragen's eyes lit up, "Birthday party!? Well, that does sound splendid." He frowned dramatically as he went on, "A party would be warranted under normal circumstances. But I'm afraid Operator Stone has already scheduled Player Tara's eca examinations. You understand. Her eca is too important. Besides, she won't know the difference if you miss another one of her birthdays." Tristan shifted uncomfortably in his seat without reply. Kragen pulled a benevolent expression and added, "I will discuss the matter with Operator Stone."

"Thank you, my liege." Tristan responded.

"Now that is settled, I'm sure the viewers would like to see Player Gerrit and Player Tara team up. Let's see if we can't help our two sibling players find each other." Kragen said boisterously. He waved his hand over the controls, a small screen opened up on the holovid and he typed a sequence into the pad. Kragen zoomed out until Gerrit looked like a dot on the map. He eyed Tristan and rubbed his hands together with excitement, "Just watch. Soon your offspring will prove their worthiness as players."

In the next moment a wave began to move through the city. It was made of thousands of nanoKbots that were each a small sphere. As each rolled, together they created a tidal wave that crashed through the streets towards Gerrit. Tristan's eyes widened in shock as the wave crashed into Gerrit and carried him off. The nanoKbots worked together to hold Gerrit in the middle of their spheres as they rolled and spiralled through the streets towards Tara.

34

April 3rd 2640, full moon

Tara was gripped with horror as the wave of nanoKbots crashed into Gerrit. She steered the drone higher, the wave moved through the streets. She jumped to her feet as the wave approached in front of her eyes. Focusing her eca, she saw Gerrit held in the middle of the tiny spheres. She quickly scanned their program and saw the code directed them to deliver Gerrit to her location.

"What?" she gasped in disbelief.

The wave crashed up against the base of the concrete slab without a sound. It paused and spread out into a wall of tiny spheres. A ripple from the outer spheres moved towards its center, out of which Gerrit was forcefully expelled. He landed hard on the concrete slab next to Tara. The nanoKbots slid away moving less turbulently back through the city.

Gerrit groaned and pushed himself up to sit. He was ruffled but unharmed. He looked around and noticed how far he had been carried. Tara startled him as she came to squat at his side.

"Tara? How? What happened?" He asked holding his head. He had not slept the previous night and had been tracked persistently by Kbots that erupted in an alarm each time he found a place to rest. He was exhausted.

Tara shot him an apprehensive look and spoke telepathically, 'Those nanoKbots were programmed to drop you here. I don't know what Kragen's playing at.'

Gerrit furrowed his brow and rubbed his temples with his fingers. He focused his eca and replied, 'Programmed to drop me here? He must want us to team up.' He relaxed and smiled broadly as he added, "Works for me!"

'Yah. Kragen has been enjoying himself.' Tara said telepathically.

Gerrit's smile faltered briefly before he said, "You know, we might enjoy ourselves more now that we can team up. I've had a rough run."

"Oh?" Tara settled in next to him and opened her bag.

"Became a magnet for challengers." He said, "Kbots sounded an alarm so other players could find me. Reilly, then Bronik, Delia, Syrene and even Ziggy came to their alarm."

"Dank. Here, this may help." Tara held out her hand.

Gerrit looked down puzzled by the sight of the sliced pleachee being offered to him.

"Tara, where did you get this?" he asked, but didn't wait for her to answer, he took the fruit and savoured the subtly floral juices. "Not surprised you've aced the course. Fye! We are so close to the flag!"

"I had some help from Prynn." Tara said quietly.

"Prynn? What happened?" Gerrit asked.

"We teamed up." Tara glanced down nervously and finished explaining telepathically, 'Kragen didn't like how I evaded the Kbot and trapped us in a penalty box. After we escaped that we were led down a tunnel. I had to enter a virch maze and play Pong with Kragen. When we climbed out, Angelik showed up and Prynn challenged her. That's when we split up.'

Gerrit eyed her with concern, 'Kragen entered the course and you played Pong with him?'

Tara nodded.

"Well, now that I'm here, we can team up." Pushing himself up to stand and securing his bag again he was bouncing with excitement. He looked at Tara eagerly, "Come on! The sooner we get to the flag the better."

Tara crossed her arms and sulked, *That was Kragen's motive. He dropped Gerrit here so we'd team up and he'd push me to finish the game.* She shot Gerrit a stubborn look and focused her eca to retrieve the drone that she had pirated. As it came into view, Gerrit's attention shot up to it. Tara noticed Gerrit grab a rock, prepared to throw it at the drone.

"Gerrit." she said firmly.

He glanced at her startled. She shook her head. He watched as the drone flew past them and towards the flag. From the lens in the drone, Tara could see several players climbing through the debris of old-era vehicles towards the obelisk in the center of a large public square. Tara noticed that the ground encircling it looked like new-build infrastructure, suggesting a trap was about to be sprung on those players. Gerrit eyed Tara curiously and dropped the rock as he watched the drone fly past. She hovered the drone high in the sky so as not to alarm Reese, Mikhail and Nylah as they approached the flag from three different streets.

"Three players are nearing the flag. No way we can get there faster." She said flatly. Keeping her attention split between the drone and Gerrit she began narrating what the players were doing, "One player has reached the edge the square. They're shooting up. I think that's Mikhail, he's super muscular and bald, has a Copper Rook Division emblem. Reese caught up and has called his attention to Mikhail. They're both stepping into the square towards the obelisk." Tara stopped narrating as she saw the ground lift up under the players creating a circular platform that rose to the height of the flag and started to spin around like a disc.

"Whoa!" Gerrit exclaimed. His eyes wide with shock as the players ran against spinning platform. Each one edging closer to the flag. First Reese was thrown off, followed shortly after by Mikhail. Gerrit lost sight of them as they fell into the safety netting that rolled them into the ejector slides, eliminating them from play. Gerrit let out a chuckle and he squinted towards the flag. He could see the spinning track lowering back to the ground as the obstacle reset.

"Who's the third player?" He asked.

Tara looked through the drone lens and saw a player with long silver hair pulled back in braids. "Nylah's entering the square. You know, I don't want the flag that much."

Gerrit glanced at Tara and flashed one of his wry smiles

as he slung his arm over her shoulder. He pulled her into a hug and said, "Yah, I know."

They stood there watching in the distance as the spinning track rose again, this time with Nylah racing on it.

"Sodz! Nylah's going to get thrown too. We can't do anything from here but watch, Tara." He urged. "Come on. Let's finish this thing together."

Irked by Kragen's manipulation to drive her forward, Tara frowned, *Does it matter? Gerrit's here now. Next step is to get in that transport.* She ducked out from under Gerrit's arm and scooped up her bag.

"Let me shoot up first. How's your eca level? Do you have any serum?" He asked.

Tara glanced at her wrist device which showed her level down to 14%. She rolled her eyes, "I'm fed up with these serums running out."

"How many serum vials do you have?" Gerrit asked.

She glanced in her bag, she had three vials left. Grabbing two she said, "Got these."

She handed Gerrit one. He pressed his lips together in a tight smile, but didn't reply. They both injected themselves and carefully climbed down to the road that led towards the flag.

35
April 3rd 2640, full moon

Vi sat on the thin mattress in hir cell, twisting and rolling one of hir matted locs. Ze was stir-crazy after not knowing what happened to Tara after ze had led her to that intersection. As hir thoughts played back the events from the course, ze was filled with guilt, then a wave of pride interrupted and a quiver rippled across hir shoulders. The gnawing feeling of pride for doing Kragen's bidding kept interrupting hir feelings of animosity towards him. The lingering effects of his eca were leaving deep grooves in Vi's mind.

Vi stared through the small window at the late afternoon sky. Watching clouds float past, ze was immersing hirself in the whispy billows, distracting hirself from the turmoil of hir mind. Vi focused on hir breath the way that Tara had shown hir, *Inhale, one, two, three, four. Exhale, one, two, three, four.*

I'm related to Stone. How did I not know that? He seems just as bitter to learn we're related. He zapped me so many times I'm losing count. Fek! I need to get out of here. This room is making me nutty. It's been one night, no two, since I left the course. Why did I do that to Tara? Because I need to please my leige. Gah! Stop! Focus on breathing.

When the door opened it made Vi jump up. Guardian Rainn entered with a towel, a clean black jumpsuit and a large cup with a lid. She was smiling warmly at Vi.

"Heya Vi. How you holdin' up?" Rainn asked.

Vi exhaled audibly but didn't say anything. Rainn passed Vi the lidded cup and placed the jumpsuit and towel neatly on the mattress. Vi lifted the lid and started to sip the liquid, it was surprisingly good and ze finished it quickly.

"Time to get cleaned up." Rainn said and stepped towards the sink. She waved her hand over the wall, a clicking sound filled the room as a panel opened and a showerhead appeared. She beckoned for Vi to come closer, handing her a washcloth and some soap before stepping to the opposite side of the room to busy herself with some mending from a pocket strapped to her belt.

As Vi finished and dressed in the new jumpsuit, Rainn quickly collected the wet towel, wiped the water from the floor and walls before she gathered the dirty jumpsuit and rolled them into a linen bag she produced from one of her many pockets. She let the bag drop on the ground and gazed at Vi.

"Operator Stone has a task for you tonight." Rainn said.

Vi's face dropped and ze sunk to the floor distraught.

"I know Kragen's twistin' you with his eca." Rainn explained gently, "Feel no way, Vi. No matter what he makes you do, you're loved. Your family is watchin', I relayed your status here in the castle. Tara understands your circumstance as well, she's also bein' entwined. I know it doesn't take it away. I've seen him exploit other players to be his agents. Your family wanted you to know that they successfully liberated a group of your friends en route to the work camps Their numbers are growing again. Hold hope." She took a breath placing her hands on Vi's shoulders, "Sit down, let me help you tidy up your locs."

Vi blinked at Rainn's kind words unsure how to respond. Sitting on the hard floor with Rainn kneeling behind tenderly separating and twisting loose hairs into the locs was a feeling Vi hadn't felt in years. Rainn's presence lifted the mood of the room and Vi let hir eyes close as Rainn gently pulled and rolled hir hair.

When Rainn finished, she placed her hands on Vi's shoulders and squeezed gently. They stayed quiet for a moment and Vi knew the brief reprieve from Kragen's mind games was near an end. Vi lifted one of hir hands to hir shoulder and squeezed Rainn's hand appreciatively.

~~~

The late afternoon sun was hidden behind the clouds as Tara and Gerrit approached the square. Tara focused her eca and used the drone's lens to get a bird's eye view, there were already several players nearby. She gripped Gerrit's arm to hold him back. She spoke into his mind, 'Too many players are there.'

Gerrit crouched behind an old-era vehicle with Tara beside him. Tara's skin crawled as Yane stalk around the edge of the square. She held her breath as he passed by the vehicle they were hiding behind. He was assessing how to approach the obelisk. He crouched low and touched the ground with his hand, nothing happened. As he stood up, he noticed Prynn approaching from the far side of the square. She placed her hands on her hips as she glared at him.

'Prynn's here!' Gerrit spoke into Tara's mind.

Tara focused her eca and spoke to Prynn's mind, 'Don't go for the flag yet, Prynn. Hold off until Yane fails.'

The voice in Prynn's mind startled her and she looked around the square in search of Tara. Yane reached into the shoulder pocket of his jumpsuit under the Gold Knight Division emblem and pulled out a snap sniffer. He held it to his nose inhaling forcefully.

Yane flexed his muscles and yelled across the square, "Don't bother, Prynn. The flag is mine!"

With that Yane sprinted towards the centre of the square, straight for the obelisk. Prynn heeded Tara's words and remained still. The track lifted up in line with the flag and began to spin. Yane was racing towards the flag, straining against the momentum as the track spun underneath him. He managed to stay balanced as he pushed closer to the centre. He gritted his teeth, reaching for the flag. Just as he stretched his fingertips to graze the fabric, suddenly the track stopped and changed direction. Yane was thrown off his feet and off the track into the rebound netting that bounced and rolled him down the ejector slide under the track. The track stopped and lowered back into place, the rebound netting hidden beneath it.

Prynn gaped in shock unable to move as the track reset. Tara and Gerrit stayed crouched behind the car as Bronik entered from another street. He was soaking wet from an encounter with a

Kbot, his red hair sopped on one side of his head.

"Yow Prynn!" Bronik's voice carried across the square, "Did you see what happened to Yane?!"

"Yah!" Prynn called back.

"Round and round and round you go! When you stop, only Kragen knows!" Bronik's husky voice boomed.

"That track is just going to spin players off, again and again. There has to be another way to get that flag." Gerrit whispered, "Can you use your eca to shut it down?"

Tara focused her eca and scanned the square for all the electromagnetic signatures. Oddly there was nothing coming up for the track except for a small reading. She scanned again but still could only pick up on one small electromagnetic signature from the track and it wasn't a switch.

"That's odd." Tara said standing up and heading into the square. Gerrit watched her curiously as they stepped into view.

"Yow! How's it, Gerrit, Tara?" Prynn yelled across the square.

Gerrit gave her a friendly wave. Tara had her eyes down, her eca focused as she walked along the edge of the obstacle. She made her way towards Bronik and crouched down to study the ground. Bronik eyed her with fascination.

When he noticed Gerrit, he goaded, "You're greefing your sibling, Gerrit. Guess you can't handle the game!"

Gerrit glared at him prepared for a challenge, "Do you want a rematch?"

Bronik just laughed playfully and stepped back to give them more space. There was a marble sized hole that Tara was inspecting. Gerrit crouched down beside her to look at it.

"What is it?" He asked.

Swinging her bag from her shoulder she dug through it until she found what she was looking for. She clutched the marble she had won from her time in the virch maze. Throwing her bag back over her shoulders and turning to Gerrit she said, "The track must be pressure activated. I can't deactivate it first. But I have this."

She held out her palm showing Gerrit the small grey marble with a black line around its middle. He eyed it curiously, then his eyes flicked to the ground at the small marble sized hole on the edge of the track, there was a thin black line that crossed the hole. She crouched down holding the marble between her thumb and first finger, twirling it so the black line would align with the one on the ground. Tara took a steadying breath placing the marble in the hole.

The marble sunk in and disappeared. There was a series of clicks and a groove opened along the seam of the track, the marble began to roll along the seam. It came to a stop after travelling one quarter distance of the track. There was another series of clicks and the track erupted in hundreds of dominoes. Gerrit shot Tara a puzzled look as a high-pitched fan noise filled the square. The first domino fell and created a chain reaction that rippled in an intricate design through the entire track. As the last domino fell there was a tremendous shattering as the track broke into a million pieces smashing into a crater beneath. The sides fell way to reveal a bright red funnel slide that dropped to the base of the mountain of rubble that surrounded the obelisk.

Gerrit peered over the edge but before he could say anything, a high-pitched tone erupted in the square and the obelisk sprouted with a series of climbing rungs. Once the tone stopped a series of lasers emerged around the circumference. Swiftly, Gerrit grabbed Tara's hand and jumped into the crater. They hit the slide and spiralled around as they descended. They crashed into a pile at the bottom. Looking up, Tara saw that the lasers were forming cage around the crater. She and Gerrit were the only ones inside.

Gerrit gave her a serious look and said, "Don't use your eca or you might get shocked."

"Yah. Got it." Tara said remembering her experience in the penalty box with Prynn. The obelisk towered high on the top of the mountain of rubble, with the newly appeared rungs it would be feasible to climb to the top and grab the flag. She gawked up at it and said, "That's a high climb."

"At least I'm not going to fight you for it." Gerrit nudged

her with his elbow.

"That's something." Tara muttered.

They each dropped their bags and removed their length of rope. They carefully tied some knots and secured the rope around their waists to create a linked chain. Tara reached for her bag but Gerrit stopped her.

"Let's lighten the load. Dump your gear in my bag." He said and snatched her bag. Tara eyed him suspiciously as he filled his bag and threw it over his back. He gave her a reassuring nod adding, "Trust me, Tara. We'll get through this together."

She took a steadying breath, "Acha. Let's do this."

They trekked through the rubble of the crater and scrambled up the hill of rocks to the base of the obelisk. Gerrit urged Tara to climb ahead of him. She grabbed the first rung and climbed her way straight up.

Tara watched the light fade and the full moon rise as she neared the top of the obelisk. Gerrit glanced down and saw several other players had converged along the perimeter of the crater. After a few more pulls Tara reached the top and stood precariously on the tiny ledge. She clung to the flag pole while Gerrit held onto the rungs below.

"Take it, Tara!" He yelled.

Tara held tight to the pole with one hand and reached up with the other. Stretching on her toes, her fingers caught the fabric, tightening her hand around it. She felt a rush as she tore the flag from the pole. She looked down at Gerrit triumphantly and waved the flag over her head.

In the next instant, the laser cage deactivated and ambiworks erupted around them. Ambilights lit them up from the surrounding rooftops. A loudspeaker erupted with trumpets and an announcer's voice boomed, "Bravo! Player Tara has won!!"

Suddenly, there was a foray of drones approaching. Tara squinted as the ambilights pointed at her. There were butterflies dancing in her stomach anticipating her chance to break free.

Gerrit's eyes glinted with excitement as he yelled over the fanfare, "Hang on, we're almost there!"

36

April 3rd 2640, full moon

"Salut!" Kragen clinked glasses with Tristan. The holovid alight with colourful celebration. Kragen slapped Tristan on his back, "Congratulations!".

The shield shut off and the transport drones flew into the course to pick up players. Each transport had a small cabin, with room enough for two players. As the drone dipped down towards the obelisk a side door opened beside Tara. Gerrit pulled himself up after her and swiftly followed into the transport.

"Thank you, my liege. I enjoyed viewing the course with you. What a treat that my offspring won the 1st Quarter Circuit!" Tristan smiled broadly as he watched it fly off the course.

Kragen grinned at him, "Yes, it pleases me to share it with my old player cohort. A well-deserved win. You know how I enjoy meddling with players. I trust you are satisfied with the score and will disregard my interference. The course is already breaking records with viewership, them teaming up and capturing the flag will payout substantially for both of us."

"Of course, my liege. It has been too many years since I've benefited from your cheat codes. Thank you." Tristan said graciously.

"My pleasure." Kragen waved his hand over the holovid to shut it off. Without its light the room lay shrouded in darkness. He cocked his head to the side arrogantly and said, "You know your responsibilities, Controller Tristan. Taletellers will be eager to hear more about your offspring."

Tristan finished his drink in one swig and bowed towards Kragen before he left the room. Kragen continued to slowly sip his drink deep in thought. When he finished, he stretched his legs and wandered to the window to throw open the heavy curtains, moonlight streamed in. A chime from the communication device on his desk diverted his attention. It was an alert from Stone:

Tara has pirated her transport, as expected. Following from safe distance and will deploy once she lands.

Kragen tapped his acknowledgement. The full moon caught his attention and he glanced out the window into the night sky, "Not so fast, little bijou bunny. We're not done playing."

~~~

Perched on a rocky escarpment, hidden under their cloaking packs, deep in the woods near the perimeter shield, Xain and Zedrik could see the ambiworks in the distance. Zedrik focused his binoculars as the transport drones flew in and carried the players out. All transports flew into the distance, except one which was heading in the opposite direction. Xain felt a gentle buzz from his coat pocket, Tara had activated the tracker on her tablet. A small blue dot appeared on the screen of his device. He sent a ping for Tara to trace. The transport altered course and headed directly towards them.

Zedrik shot a cautious look at Xain, "For this to work she needs to move fast."

"She'll make it." Xain said hopefully.

The transport lowered into a clearing of the woods. Tara and Gerrit swiftly hopped out before it lifted up in the air and flew back from where it came. Tara turned her attention up towards the top of the escarpment, grabbed hold of Gerrit's arm and pointed.

Xain lowered his binoculars and looked at his father pleadingly, "Let me hook up a belay line." Zedrik shook his head sternly and pointed towards the horizon. Xain lifted his binoculars and saw several drones headed their way.

"Fek." He whispered.

"It's too late." Zedrik said, "There wasn't enough time."

"Can we distract them?" Xain offered.

"No." Zedrik said firmly, "Look."

They watched as an anti-eca cannon rushed from one of the drones to where Tara and Gerrit were standing. They were blown over as it drained their eca serum completely. Xain gasped as a small transport flew up. Vi was harnessed to a cable and ze lowered down into the clearing. Xain hardly recognized his sibling; hir locs covered under a silk cap, dressed in an all-black jumpsuit, a pulserod on hir belt, tactical vest with countless devices and recorders strapped to the front and back.

Overcome with excitement for being so close to his sibling, Xain focused his eca and spoke to hir mind, 'Yow Vi! Up here.'

Vi glanced up to them. Zedrik gripped Xain's arm tightly, his brown eyes saddened with remorse for his choice.

"No." He said firmly.

~~~

Tara was stunned as she stared at Vi in the clearing. Hir sudden appearance at the base of the cliff made her freeze. She eyed hir uniform with confusion. Gerrit injected himself with another eca serum his eyes wide as he frantically searched the edge of the clearing.

"Vi? Wachu doin'?" Tara pleaded.

Vi remained silent and just stared at them, hir eyes pained with hir internal struggle.

Gerrit focused his eca to speak telepathically, 'Tara, shoot up! Vi's covered with recorders. Ze's an agent! We don't have anymore time! Look there are drones flying in.'

Struck with the reality of their situation, Tara reached for her bag, but it wasn't there. She remembered Gerrit had consolidated her last vial into his bag. She flushed with anger and yelled, "I don't have any!"

"Here, catch!" He said and tossed her one.

Swiftly, she injected herself with the blue serum. There was a blast and Tara watched in shock as Gerrit flew backwards to the ground after Vi shot him with a neutralizing pulse. Vi aimed at Tara. Tara raised her palms up. They remained still eyeing each other up. Tara's attention was diverted as a drone dropped from the sky and fired an anti-eca cannon at her. She saw it in her mind and was able to dodge the rushing wind by jumping behind a boulder. Her heart raced in her ears as the drone positioned itself above her and fired another anti-eca cannon. Tara curled up into a ball as the wind rushed over her. Drained of her ability, Tara crept out from behind the boulder. Vi was standing in the same spot, panic in hir eyes, the pulserod pointing towards the ground. Gerrit was laying motionless in front of hir. Looking up towards the transport Tara saw several enforcers dropping to the ground from cables.

Her feet felt glued to the spot as she turned back to her friend, "We gotta get outta here! Vi it's time to slip out. Why won't you talk to me!?"

Vi glanced up to the top of the escarpment, hir face screwed up in pain as hir eyes pooled with tears. Hir knuckles were white from gripping the puslerod.

'You know where to go.' Vi managed to speak into Tara's mind before a shock cut through hir. Ze fell to hir hands and knees in pain.

In the next moment, there was a high-pitched sound. Tara looked up in horror as a Kbot flew into the clearing. It fired a flashbomb pulse that rippled down and outwards. Tara grabbed her head as the sound reverberated in her skull. Robbed of her sight and hearing, she reached her hands out and grasped the air.

"Vi!?" She called desperately.

Blinking furiously, Tara was starting to make out shapes of the slender trees in the darkness. As the ringing subsided, she heard enforcers moving in. Filling with panic, she ran. She moved as fast as she could, weaving in and out of the trees. The feeling of being chased consumed her as she pushed forward without knowing which way to go. Between the long shadows in the trees, Tara saw Vi run past. She stopped and looked around frantically.

"Where did ze go?" Tara said to herself. Then called out, "Vi!?"

Panic clutched her stomach as she saw lights behind her. The enforcers were gaining on her. She ran. There was a sudden flash from her left, before she could react, she was pinned to the ground.

Epilogue

Together we fell, scooped from the inside and tossed to the ground. As the tough exterior cracked opened, we settled between concrete slabs and spread out to fill the seam.

For some time there was only darkness. Some rain collected and soaked us thoroughly. Next came the sunlight which warmed us before we continued our journey. We needed to dig.

Resolving to commit to the slow process of sprouting roots, it was only one stage of this experience. From being passed down from our mother through the hands of a human, we will return once more to the earth. Continually cycling through each phase of life. Planted among my kin, we lay ready for the transformation to occur.

The impulse to push down was strong, breaking through the concrete in search of the soil beneath. With each reach and stretch we travel back through the darkness that connects us all.

Trust in the process. The rhythm of us pulsating together taking the earth within our grasp, pulling up to hydrate and feed our core.

With a firm grip the next impulse was to rise up. Slowly pushing up, sprouting from the centre towards the sky above. Our long stems growing taller with tiny leaves.

More roots grow, breaking through the gravel, sandy, earthen soil. Then growing even taller with true leaves that branch outwards. I'm now standing present, like my kin, a beautiful pleachee tree.

Want a sneak peak at book two of A Forest Without Trees before it's released? Simply email: admin@nofi.ca with the subject line answering this question: What fruit tree does Tara find in the Quarter Circuit? I will email you with the first chapter of book two!

About the Author

JP Solanki-Davie is a creative artist with an Honours Bachelor of Arts with Distinction from the University of Toronto.

She built a career as a Registered Massage Therapist and has worked as a Yoga teacher and trainer both locally and internationally.

Born in Canada with roots in India, South Africa and Germany, JP is passionate about celebrating her diverse identity along with those who don't fit the social mould.

Her writing exemplifies her varied knowledge base with an emphasis on nature's healing power.

Glossary

Inspired by the way language evolves over time, I have made up some words of my own imagination along with inspiration from popular culture. The following is my best at offering a glossary with pronunciation guide.

Acha [\ä-chä\] = Hindi word, good, alright, let's go
Ambihearth [\am-bē-hərth\] = fireplace with no flames
Ambilamp / ambilight [\am-bē-lamp\ / \am-bē-līt\] = lamps and other room lights
Ambitorch [\am-bē-tōrch\] = flashlight
Ambiworks [\am-bē-wœrks\]= fireworks
Adrshy [\ä-dri-shē\] = Invisible in Hindi. Name of Seds' encampment in the wild
Bapuji [\bä-pü-jē\] = father in Hindi
Ça va? [\sä-vä\] = Frennch for, How are you? You ok?
Cracked [\krakd\ = Impressive
Dank [\dānk\] = Damn
Deep hole [\dēp\ \hōlə\] = ass hole
Éclat couple [\ek=lat\ kȯp-lə\] = Socially distinct couple
Feebler [fēb=ler\] = an inferior player/one who quits the games
FidgiFlint [fid-ji-flint\] = a toy that spins and is like a lighter
Fek/ Effn [\fek\ / \ef-n\] = Fucking/Fuck
Fegal [\fē-gäl\] = a dirty old man
Flopdoodle [\fläp-düdlə\] = an insignificant / foolish man
Fye [\fī\] = Fire, You're on fire/amazing
Gare [\gär\] = Station in French, reference from Bill & Ted's Bogus Journey.
Gnashgab [\nash-gab\] = someone who always seems to complain
Greefing [\grēf-ing\] = piggy backing on someone else's win
Holo-effect [\hä-lō-ef-ekt\] = hologram used by the Seds for

camouflage

Holotube [\hä-lō-tübə\] = holo- projection from a tablet

Holovid [\hä-lō-vid\] = Holo projection on a surface or room.

Hoverstream [\hä-ver-strēm\] = personal transport vehicle used for crossing rocky terrain.

Kbot [\k-bȯt\] = Stands for: Kreeper Bots, various sizes and uses.

Kip [\kip\] = Bro, reference from Napoleon Dynamite

Locs [lȯks\] = rope-like hair formed by locking or braiding.

Luusid [\lü-sid\] = drug causes user to relax and become passive

Mad crazy [\mad\ \krā-zē\] = Something mind blowing

Natch [\natch\] = naturally

Natty [\natē\] = A Rastafari term for stylish locs formed naturally without cutting, combing or brushing.

Oh Source Fend [\ō\ \sōrsə\ \fend\= OMG!

Pixilated [\pik-sil-ā-ted\]= chronic luusid drug user

Plemp [\plemp\] = Plastic/hemp buidling material

Noble [nō -blə\] = Elite title similar to Lord and Lady

Saps [\saps\] = difficult, hard, upsetting

Snap [\snap\] = drug used to increase strength, an adrenaline rush.

Sodz/Turdz [\sädz\ / \tərdz\] = Shit

Sundarvan [\sün-der-vän\] = Beautiful forest in Hindi. The closest community past the Cullis/Hawk outposts. It's beyond the expanse and river.

TokPuck [\täk-puk\] = A small device to transfer audio messages.

Top player [\täp\ \plāy-ər\] = high scorer

Trend-z [\trend-z\] = Influencer status

QTpi [\q-t-pī\] = a coveted position of player who are runner-ups in the Interlude game.

Yow [\yōw\] = Hey

Zactly [\zak-tlē\]= Exactly

Zang [\zang\] = Cantonese for, excellent. Wayne's World reference.

Character Appendix

Name (age) \pronunciation\ pronouns (in order of appearance)
Tara, \tär-ä\ age 18 She/Her/Hers
Vi (22) \vï\ Ze/Hir/Hirs
Bridget (37) \brid-jet\ She/Her/Hers
Pierce (52) \pirsə\ He/Him/His
Kragen (41) \krāg-en\ He/Him/His
Hami (23) \ha-mē\ She/Her/Hers
Hori (23) \hō-rē\ He/Him/His
Brill (24) \bril\ She/Her/Hers
Desma (24) \des-mä\ She/Her/Hers
Pin (21) \pin\ He/Him/His
Lino (24) \lï-nō\ He/Him/His
Khalil (25) \kha-lēl\ He/Him/His
Raha (19) \rä-hä\ She/Her/Hers
Twitch (22) \twitch\ He/Him/His
Tristan (45) \tris-tan\ He/Him/His
Sheena (39) \shē-nä\ She/Her/Hers
Ada (32) \ā-dä\ She/Her/Hers
Stone (65) \stōnə\ He/Him/His
Zedrik (45) \zed-rik\ He/Him/His
Yoshiro (45) \yō-shēr-ō\ He/Him/His
Remi (44) \re-mē\ She/Her/Hers
Chester (33) \ches-ter\ He/Him/His
Rawlyn (45) \raw-lin\ He/Him/His
Patton (22) \pāt-tȯn\ He/Him/His
Claudia (38) \clȯd-ē-ä\ She/Her/Hers
Gerrit (17) \ger-rit\ He/Him/His
Vishal (53) ? \vish-äl\ He/Him/His
Akshay (60) \äk-shāï\ He/Him/His
Bricker (58) ? \brik-er\ He/Him/His

Jahnu (50) ? \jah-nü\ He/Him/His
Dib (53) ? \dib\ He/Him/His
Duncan (35) \dunk-in\ He/Him/His
Xain (25) \zān\ He/Him/His
Ritu (23) \ri-tü\ She/Her/Hers
Nebba (18) \neb-bä\ She/Her/Hers
Vipin (18) \vi-pin\ He/Him/His
Ito (45) \ē-tō\ She/Her/Hers
Topher (45) \tō-fer\ He/Him/His
Bronik (20) \bròn-ik\ He/Him/His
Slavik (52) \släv-ik\ He/Him/His
Zarya (49) \zär-ēä\ She/Her/Hers
Haru (45) \hä-rü\ She/Her/Hers
Prudence (50) \prüd-ens\ She/Her/Hers
Ga (67) \gä\ She/Her/Hers
Locke (55) \lòk\ He/Him/His
Nylah (18) \nï-lä\ She/Her/Hers
Prynn (17) \prin\ She/Her/Hers
Cari (18) \kò-rē\ She/Her/Hers
Trace (59) \trāsǝ\ He/Him/His
Aria (60) ? \är-ēä\ She/Her/Hers
Vierra (43) \vē-er-rä\ She/Her/Hers
Bhyt (32) \bit\ He/Him/His
Flo (24) \flō\ She/Her/Hers
Berwyn (52) \ber-win\ He/Him/His
Kohl (27) \kōl\ He/Him/His
Mo (18) \mō\ He/Him/His
Lyra (25) \lï-rä \ She/Her/Hers
Zara (21) \za-rä\ She/Her/Hers
Bo (58) \bō\ She/Her/Hers
Nester (13) \nest-er\ He/Him/His
Liss (15) \lis\ She/Her/Hers

Silas (56) \sï-lis\ He/Him/His
Rainn (48) \rān\ She/Her/Hers
Elbion (X 2614) \el-bē-òn\ He/Him/His
Kesia (40) \ke-sē-ä\ She/Her/Hers
Rawlyn (45) \räw-lin\ He/Him/His
Ella (43) \el-lä\ She/Her/Hers
Kharis (X 2591) \ker-is\ He/Him/His
Clifton (X 2591) \clif-tin\ He/Him/His
Max (36) \max\ She/Her/Hers
Isolde (X 2599) \i-zōldə\ She/Her/Hers
Kayn (46) \kāynə\ He/Him/His
Dillon (28) \dil-lin\ He/Him/His
Angelik (19) \an-gel-ik\ Ze/Hir/Hirs
Delia (23) \del-ēä\ She/Her/Hers
Mikhail (23) \mi-kāl\ He/Him/His
Reese (19) \rēsə\ He/Him/His
Reilly (19) \rīl-lē\ Ze/Hir/Hirs
Syrene (20) \sī-rēnə\ She/Her/Hers
Yane (18) \yānə\ He/Him/His
Ziggy(18) \zig-gē\ She/Her/Hers
Stella (21) \stel-lä\ She/Her/Hers
Relt (30) \relt\ He/Him/His
Rabi (27) \rabē\ He/Him/His
Yeva (19) \yā-vä\ She/Her/Hers
Roo (24) \rü\ She/Her/Hers
Daq (20) \dak\ He/Him/His
Dale (26) \dāl\ He/Him/His
Covi (22) \cō-vē\ He/Him/His
Vyn (25) \vin\ Ze/Hir/Hirs
Peach (26) \pēchə\ She/Her/Hers
Brody (30) \brō-dē\ He/Him/His
Sung-Hyun (35) \süng-hyün\ She/Her/Hers

Konnor (34) \kon-ner\ He/Him/His
Knut (32) \nȯt\ Ze/Hir/Hirs
Tommy (12) \tam-mē\ He/Him/His
Eric (29) \er-ic\ He/Him/His
Burke (31) \berk\ He/Him/His
Marri (25) \mär-rē\ She/Her/Hers
Avis (31) \ā-vis\ She/Her/Hers
Ulf (64) \ülf\ He/Him/His
Wolf (42) \wülf\ He/Him/His
Nelli (5) \nel-lē\ She/Her/Hers
Azim (30) \ä-zēm\ He/Him/His
Tobi (18 months) \tō-bi\ He/Him/His
Akida (30) \ä-kē-dä\ She/Her/Hers
Greta (44) \gre-tä\ She/Her/Hers
Sonal (33) \sō-näl\ Ze/Hir/Hirs
Rohit (8) \rō-hit\ He/Him/His
Alain (47) \äl-en\ He/Him/His
Deni (47) \de-nē\ She/Her/Hers
Tarak (45) \tär-äk\ He/Him/His
Ezer (44) \ez-er\ He/Him/His
Zalie (6) \zal-ē\ She/Her/Hers
Freya (64) \fre-yä\ She/Her/Hers
Asha (42) \äsh-ä\ She/Her/Hers
Niral (42) \nē-räl\ He/Him/His
Pu (43) \pü\ She/Her/Hers
Haze (X 2635) \hāzə\ He/Him/His

Manor House
www.manor-house-publishing.com
905-648-4797